Alira's Deadly Sins

Volume 2

Sean Taylor

ALIRA'S DEADLY SINS

A Four-Book Thriller Series

Copyright © 2025 by Sean Taylor

All rights reserved.

Published by Sean Taylor

ISBN: 979-8-9930145-3-1 (Paperback)

First Edition: December 2025

Printed in the United States of America

10 9 8 7 6 5 4 3 2 1

CONTENTS

Book Three – The Third Deception

CONTENTS

Book Four – The Fourth Gambit

Book Three

The Third Deception

SILENTIUM *Silence*

————

"They bought her silence. She sold them false peace."

Prologue

The Weight of Memory

Alira Sinclair sat beside her sister's bed in the afternoon sunlight that streamed through the windows of Riverside Care Facility, reading aloud from a children's book about a brave little mouse who saved her family from danger. Sierra listened with the kind of rapt attention that her damaged mind brought to simple stories, her face showing contentment and peace that had been absent during her brief moments of painful clarity.

At thirty-six years old, Sierra should have been completing groundbreaking research in child psychology, helping traumatized children heal from abuse and neglect, making the kind of difference in the world that her brilliant mind had been designed to achieve. Instead, she sat in a care facility with the cognitive capacity of a seven-year-old, working on paint-by-numbers pictures and listening to stories she'd read herself when she was actually seven.

Dr. Marcus Webb had destroyed all of that ten years ago when he'd sexually assaulted Sierra in his university office, slamming her head against his desk with enough force to cause traumatic brain injury that had permanently erased the person she'd been before that terrible afternoon.

But Dr. Marcus Webb was dead now, his predatory career ended through botanical poisoning that had appeared to be natural heart failure. And Alira carried that death with her like armor against doubt and moral complexity—the first elimination in a mission that had expanded far beyond personal vengeance to become systematic justice for victims that legal frameworks consistently failed to protect.

"That was a good story," Sierra said when Alira finished reading, her voice carrying childlike satisfaction. "The little mouse was very brave. She saved everyone even though she was scared."

"Yes, she was," Alira agreed, setting the book aside. "Sometimes being brave means doing scary things because they're necessary, even when you wish someone else could do them instead."

Sierra's expression shifted subtly, losing some of its childlike vagueness and becoming more focused in ways that always surprised Alira despite years of witnessing these periodic moments of clarity. "You're brave like the mouse. You stop bad men who hurt people. You stopped the bad man who hurt me."

Alira felt her throat tighten with emotion. Sierra's lucid moments were rare and unpredictable, emerging from her damaged consciousness like messages from the brilliant woman she'd been before Webb destroyed her mind. "Yes. I stopped him. He can't hurt anyone else now."

"Good," Sierra said with quiet certainty. "But there are more bad men, aren't there? More men like him who hurt people and don't face consequences because they're too powerful and too protected."

"There are," Alira confirmed, understanding that Sierra deserved honesty even if her damaged mind could only process it in fragments.

"So you have to keep stopping them," Sierra continued, her clarity already beginning to fade back toward confusion. "You have to be the brave mouse for all the people who can't protect themselves. Promise me you'll keep stopping the bad men."

"I promise," Alira said, taking Sierra's hand and feeling the weight of that commitment settle over her once again.

The clarity faded completely, leaving Sierra smiling with vague contentment as she returned her attention to the paint-by-numbers picture she'd been working on before Alira's visit. But the conversation lingered in Alira's mind as she left the care facility that evening, a reminder of why she'd chosen this path and why she would continue walking it regardless of the personal cost.

Sierra's destroyed brilliance. Cassie's murdered potential. And her own transformation from naive art history student into something far more dangerous and purposeful—a systematic hunter of predators who understood that protecting the vulnerable sometimes required working entirely outside the systems designed to deliver justice.

The mission had begun ten years ago in the aftermath of Sierra's assault, when Alira had recognized that Dr. Marcus Webb would escape legal accountability through institutional protection and procedural manipulation. It had crystallized seven years ago when Coach Robert Daniels murdered Cassie to silence her journalistic investigation into his pattern of predatory behavior.

And it would continue for as long as powerful men believed their privilege made them immune to consequences, for as long as legal frameworks consistently failed to hold predators accountable, for as long as vulnerable people needed someone willing to deliver justice that courts refused to provide.

This is the story of how that mission began. Of how a grieving sister transformed herself into a hunter of predators. Of how institutional failures and comprehensive betrayals forged someone capable of eliminating powerful men through methods so sophisticated that their deaths appeared completely natural.

This is the story of Alira Sinclair's education in vengeance, her systematic preparation for a war against predators that would span years and claim multiple lives.

This is the story of the third deception—the origin of a hunter unlike any that law enforcement had encountered before.

Ten years ago, Sierra Sinclair was a brilliant doctoral student with a promising future helping traumatized children. Then Dr. Marcus Webb destroyed her mind and her life through sexual violence that left her with permanent brain damage.

This is what happened next.

UMBRA *Shadow*

———————

"In the shadow of powerful men, monsters hide in plain sight."

Chapter 1

The Making of a Hunter

Ten years earlier

Alira Sinclair stood in the doorway of the hospital room, watching her older sister Sierra sleep fitfully under the harsh fluorescent lights that never truly dimmed, even during the designated nighttime hours when the nursing staff moved through corridors with hushed efficiency. Machines beeped rhythmically, monitoring vital signs that told a story of survival against overwhelming odds—heart rate steady but elevated, blood pressure controlled through medication, oxygen saturation acceptable but requiring supplemental support through the nasal cannula taped to Sierra's bruised face.

Sierra's face was still grotesquely swollen three days after the assault, purple and yellow bruises spreading across her cheekbones and jaw in patterns that suggested repeated blunt force trauma. Her left eye was swollen completely shut, the orbital bone fractured in two places according to the radiology reports that Alira had studied obsessively. Her left arm was encased in a cast from shoulder to wrist, the humerus shattered so severely that surgeons had needed to insert metal plates and screws to stabilize the bone fragments.

But the visible injuries, as horrific as they appeared, were not what terrified Alira most. It was the brain injury—the traumatic damage to Sierra's frontal and temporal lobes that the neurologist had explained with careful clinical detachment—that represented the true catastrophe. The CT scans showed extensive bleeding and swelling, areas of the brain that controlled memory, personality, and executive function damaged in ways that might never fully heal.

Sierra Sinclair had been twenty-six years old, pursuing her doctorate in developmental psychology at one of the country's most prestigious programs, passionate about helping children who had experienced trauma learn to process their pain and rebuild their shattered sense of safety. She was brilliant, driven, and compassionate—the kind of person who'd dedicated her life to healing others' psychological wounds. She was going to change the world, one damaged young mind at a time, using therapeutic techniques she'd developed herself and was refining through her doctoral research.

Now she lay broken in a hospital bed because a man in a position of authority had decided that her brilliance and dedication meant nothing compared to his momentary gratification and his pathological need to dominate and destroy.

"How is she?" whispered Cassandra, Alira's younger sister, as she joined her in the doorway carrying two cups of terrible hospital coffee that had become their sustenance over the past seventy-two hours. At nineteen, Cassie was the baby of the Sinclair family, still soft around the edges where life hadn't yet worn away her faith in justice and fairness and the fundamental goodness of institutional systems.

"The same," Alira replied, her voice hollow with exhaustion and suppressed rage. "The doctors say the physical injuries will heal—the bones will knit, the bruises will fade, the lacerations will close. But the head trauma..." She didn't finish the sentence, couldn't bring herself to articulate the devastating prognosis that the neurologist had delivered with clinical precision that morning.

They both knew that Sierra might never be the same brilliant, vibrant woman who had left for her meeting with Dr. Marcus Webb four days ago, excited about discussing her doctoral thesis and the positive feedback he'd given on her latest research chapter. The Sierra who returned—if she returned at all in any meaningful sense—would be fundamentally different, damaged in ways that no amount of medical intervention or therapeutic support could fully repair.

Sierra Sinclair had been extraordinary. She'd graduated summa cum laude from Stanford at twenty-one with dual degrees in psychology and neuroscience. She'd published three peer-reviewed articles before completing her master's degree. Her doctoral research on trauma-informed therapy for children was groundbreaking, combining cutting-edge neuroscience with compassionate clinical practice in ways that promised to revolutionize how the mental health field approached childhood trauma.

She'd been on track to become one of the leading voices in her field, someone who would train the next generation of therapists, publish transformative research, and directly help hundreds of children heal from experiences that had shattered their sense of safety and trust.

All of that potential, all of that brilliance, all of that compassionate dedication to healing others— destroyed in a single night by a predator who'd seen her talent and passion as nothing more than a challenge to his dominance, a bright flame to be extinguished through violence and violation.

"Did the police arrest him?" Cassie asked, though her tone suggested she already knew the answer, had absorbed enough of the grim reality over the past three days to understand how these situations typically resolved.

Alira's laugh was bitter, sharp-edged with the kind of cynicism that had crystallized in her soul over seventy-two hours of watching institutional systems fail her family with comprehensive efficiency. "Dr. Webb has an alibi. A perfect, unshakeable, witness-verified alibi. He was at a faculty dinner with twelve colleagues when Sierra was attacked—the university president, three department chairs, visiting scholars from Oxford and MIT. All of them prepared to swear under oath that Dr. Marcus Webb was charming and engaged and completely present from six PM until after midnight."

"But Sierra said—" Cassie began, her voice rising with frustrated disbelief.

"Sierra can barely remember her own name right now," Alira interrupted, the words coming out harsher than she'd intended. She softened her tone, reaching out to squeeze her younger sister's hand. "The head injury affected her memory processing. She keeps saying it was Dr. Webb, that she remembers his face, his voice, the things he said to her. But she can't remember any specific details—where exactly the assault occurred, how she got there, what happened before or after. The neurologist says her memories might be fragmented permanently, that the trauma to her temporal lobe has disrupted her ability to form coherent narrative memories."

"And the police think that means she's lying?" Cassie's outrage was palpable, her faith in institutional justice cracking but not yet shattered completely.

"The police think she's confused," Alira corrected, though the distinction felt meaningless. "They believe she experienced a traumatic assault—the physical evidence is irrefutable. But they think her identification of Dr. Webb is the result of trauma-induced confabulation. Her brain filling in gaps with the face of someone familiar, someone she'd been meeting with regularly, rather than accurately remembering her actual attacker."

It was a perfect crime, Alira had come to realize over countless hours of studying the police reports and medical documentation. Webb had drugged Sierra—the toxicology screening had confirmed the presence of rohypnol and ketamine in her bloodstream, a combination that would have rendered her incapacitated but technically conscious. He'd assaulted her brutally and repeatedly, the rape kit evidence showing trauma consistent with violent sexual assault over an extended period. Then he'd beaten her nearly to death and left her in Riverside Park, a location miles from his documented whereabouts, positioned in ways that suggested she'd been attacked by a stranger during a random mugging.

His reputation as a respected psychology professor and his ironclad alibi made him untouchable, while Sierra's trauma-induced memory fragmentation made her an unreliable witness whose accusations could be dismissed as the confused ramblings of someone whose brain had been damaged by her ordeal.

"There has to be something we can do," Cassie said desperately, her hands clenching around her coffee cup hard enough that the cheap paper began to buckle. "We can't just let him get away with this. Sierra deserves justice. She deserves to see the man who destroyed her life face consequences for what he did."

Alira turned to look at her younger sister, seeing the same naive faith in systemic justice that she herself had possessed just a week ago, before Sierra's assault had stripped away every comfortable illusion about how the world actually functioned. Before this nightmare had begun, Alira had believed that evil actions had consequences, that predators were caught and punished, that the system—the police, the courts, the universities, the institutions designed to protect the innocent—actually worked the way they claimed to work.

"The system isn't designed to protect women like Sierra," Alira said quietly, the words emerging from some newly cynical part of her soul that had crystallized during seventy-two hours of watching institutional failure unfold with bureaucratic precision. "It's designed to protect men like Dr. Webb. Respected, powerful, well-connected men whose reputations matter more than the lives they destroy. Men who understand how to exploit every weakness in legal processes, who know exactly which institutional levers to pull to ensure their immunity from consequences."

Cassie's face showed the beginning of the same transformation that Alira had experienced—the painful shattering of comfortable beliefs about justice and fairness, the dawning recognition that the world operated according to rules very different from what they'd been taught to expect.

They stood together in the doorway, watching Sierra's damaged sleep, listening to the mechanical rhythm of machines that kept her stabilized while her broken brain struggled to heal from catastrophic injury. Somewhere in that broken mind, Sierra's brilliant consciousness was trying to reassemble itself from scattered fragments, probably understanding on some level that the person she'd been was gone forever, replaced by someone fundamentally diminished.

That night, after Cassie had finally gone home to shower and rest, Alira remained at the hospital, sitting in the uncomfortable plastic chair beside Sierra's bed. She held her sister's uninjured hand gently, careful not to disturb the IV line, and began conducting research on her laptop.

Dr. Marcus Webb's professional history was impressive and publicly available—Stanford PhD, faculty positions at increasingly prestigious institutions, numerous publications in top-tier psychology journals, awards for teaching excellence and clinical supervision. His research focused on trauma and memory, which Alira found grimly ironic given how he'd weaponized his expertise to ensure his own victim couldn't provide credible testimony about his crimes.

But as Alira dug deeper, moving beyond the official professional narrative into less visible corners of Webb's history, she discovered evidence that Sierra wasn't his first victim. Over the past eight years at his current institution, six female graduate students had left his program unexpectedly—all promising researchers whose academic careers had ended abruptly after working closely with Webb as their dissertation advisor.

The pattern was remarkably consistent across all six cases. Each woman had been an exceptional student, exactly the kind of brilliant, dedicated researcher who would attract Webb's predatory attention. Each had worked closely with him during the early stages of their doctoral program, developing promising research projects under his mentorship. Each had left the program suddenly, usually citing vague personal reasons or family emergencies, abandoning years of invested work and substantial financial investments in their education.

Alira began the difficult process of tracking down these women, using academic networking sites and professional directories to locate them and reach out with carefully worded inquiries. Of the six women, three agreed to speak with her after she explained that her sister had been assaulted and that she was trying to understand Webb's pattern of behavior.

Their stories were remarkably, devastatingly similar.

Jennifer Morrison had been Webb's advisee from 2007 to 2009, working on groundbreaking research about childhood resilience after trauma. During her second year, Webb had begun scheduling increasingly frequent private meetings, ostensibly to discuss her research but actually to establish psychological intimacy that he would later exploit. The meetings had progressed from professional discussions to personal conversations, Webb gradually breaking down appropriate boundaries while positioning himself as a mentor who uniquely understood Jennifer's potential.

The assault had occurred in Webb's home office during what was supposed to be a weekend work session on Jennifer's dissertation proposal. Webb had drugged her wine—Jennifer was certain about this detail though she'd never been able to prove it—and raped her while she was semi-conscious and unable to resist effectively. When she'd threatened to report him, Webb had calmly explained exactly how such a report would destroy her career while leaving his intact: her word against his, her ambiguous decision to drink wine at his home office during a private meeting, her lack of physical evidence given the days that had passed before she'd worked up courage to consider reporting.

Jennifer had left the doctoral program two weeks later, abandoning five years of academic work and substantial student loan debt. She'd never reported the assault because Webb had convinced her—correctly—

that doing so would destroy her professional future while accomplishing nothing.

Rebecca Torres had been Webb's student from 2010 to 2011, recruited to the program specifically because of her innovative research proposals about therapeutic interventions for traumatized adolescents. Her experience had been nearly identical to Jennifer's— gradual boundary erosion, private meetings that became increasingly personal, sexual assault disguised as consensual encounter through drugging and psychological manipulation, followed by explicit threats about the consequences of reporting.

Rebecca had also left the program, also failed to report the assault, also carried the trauma of violation compounded by institutional betrayal.

The third woman Alira contacted, Jasmine Park, had been Webb's most recent victim before Sierra. She'd left the program just eight months ago, and her psychological wounds were still raw and bleeding. Jasmine described Webb's methods with painful clarity—how he'd identified her vulnerabilities and insecurities, exploited her ambition and dedication, created a relationship dynamic where she felt simultaneously valued as a brilliant researcher and worthless as a person who needed his validation to have meaning.

The assault had been brutal and calculated, designed not just to achieve sexual gratification but to destroy Jasmine's sense of agency and self-worth. Webb had photographed parts of the assault—not Jasmine's face, but enough to be recognizable if someone knew what to look for—creating leverage he could use to ensure her silence even if she somehow found courage to report.

Jasmine had gone to the university's Title IX office, thinking perhaps that institutional mechanisms might provide justice where legal systems failed. The investigation had been perfunctory and deliberately inadequate—interviewing Webb, who'd provided plausible alternative explanations for every piece of evidence, speaking with character witnesses who testified to his professional integrity, concluding that Jasmine's accusations were unsubstantiated and possibly motivated by academic disappointment when Webb had provided critical feedback on her research.

"The system protected him," Jasmine told Alira during their phone conversation, her voice thick with tears and rage.

"Every piece of the institution—the department, the university administration, the Title IX office, even some of my fellow students who'd been taught to worship Webb as this brilliant researcher—all of it worked together to ensure he faced no consequences while I was destroyed."

Jasmine had left not just the doctoral program but academia entirely, her dreams of helping traumatized children abandoned because the institution designed to prepare her for that work had instead protected her abuser with comprehensive efficiency.

As Alira sat in the hospital cafeteria at 2 AM, surrounded by research printouts and photographs she'd compiled of Webb's victims—six women whose lives and careers he'd destroyed, plus Sierra who might never recover the brilliant mind he'd damaged through violence—she made a decision that would change the course of her life forever.

The system had failed Sierra comprehensively and with institutional precision. The police had failed Sierra by accepting Webb's alibi and dismissing her testimony as confused rambling. The university had failed Sierra by protecting a predator for eight years while his victims accumulated. The legal system had failed Sierra by creating evidentiary standards and procedural requirements that effectively immunized powerful men from accountability for sexual violence.

But Alira wouldn't fail her sister.

She couldn't bring Sierra's brilliant mind back, couldn't repair the traumatic brain injury that had stolen her sister's potential and future. But she could ensure that Dr. Marcus Webb never destroyed another woman. She could deliver consequences that the system refused to provide. She could demonstrate that some predators, no matter how powerful or protected, would eventually face justice—even if that justice came from outside the institutional frameworks that had so comprehensively failed.

Alira Sinclair, twenty-three-year-old art history graduate student, sat in that hospital cafeteria and felt something fundamental shift in her understanding of how the world worked and what her role in it would be. She'd been raised to believe in rules, in systems, in the idea that civilization was built on laws and institutions that channeled violence into legitimate processes of justice.

But that belief had been a comfortable lie, she now understood. The real rules were simpler and more brutal: power protected power, institutions existed to serve the powerful, and justice for the vulnerable was something they would have to provide for themselves because no one else would provide it for them.

Dr. Marcus Webb would be her first target.

But he wouldn't be her last.

Chapter 2

The First Lesson

Dr. Marcus Webb died three months after Sierra's assault, found in his home office on a Tuesday morning by the housekeeper who arrived at her usual 8 AM appointment to find the esteemed psychology professor slumped over his desk, apparently having suffered a massive heart attack while working late into the previous evening.

The medical examiner attributed his death to acute cardiac arrest resulting from what appeared to be previously undiagnosed coronary artery disease, exacerbated by the stress of his demanding academic schedule and his lifestyle factors—poor diet, insufficient exercise, and the chronic stress that came with managing a prestigious research program and maintaining his reputation as one of the field's leading trauma experts.

The autopsy revealed significant arterial blockage that the ME concluded had been developing for years, a ticking time bomb that had finally detonated during what must have been a particularly stressful evening of work. The toxicology screening showed nothing unusual—just therapeutic levels of the herbal supplements Webb had apparently been taking for general health maintenance, along with trace amounts of various compounds consistent with someone who drank herbal tea regularly.

No one suspected that the "herbal tea" Webb had consumed the previous evening—a carefully prepared blend delivered to his office by a supposed former student expressing gratitude for his mentorship—had been anything other than the health-conscious beverage it appeared to be.

No one knew that the tea had contained precisely measured amounts of foxglove extract and oleander compounds, both cardiac glycosides that would induce the exact kind of fatal arrhythmia that had stopped Webb's heart while leaving virtually no detectable trace in standard toxicological screening.

No one suspected murder because Dr. Marcus Webb had been exactly the kind of stressed, overworked academic whose sudden cardiac death seemed tragic but entirely unremarkable.

Alira had spent those three months between Sierra's assault and Webb's death learning everything she could about natural toxins, studying botanical texts and medical journals and forensic toxicology papers with an intensity that exceeded even her previous academic dedication. She'd discovered that nature provided countless ways to kill that left minimal forensic evidence, especially when the victim had risk factors that made their death seem natural and when the medical examiner had no reason to suspect exotic poisoning rather than common medical emergency.

The foxglove had been particularly elegant in its application. The plant contained cardiac glycosides—specifically digitoxin and digoxin—that affected heart rhythm in ways that were virtually indistinguishable from naturally occurring arrhythmias when administered in the right doses. Medical examiners routinely tested for digitalis in cases of suspected poisoning, but they tested for therapeutic or toxic levels that would indicate intentional overdose. The amounts Alira had used were carefully calculated to remain just below those thresholds, appearing in Webb's system at levels that might be interpreted as background exposure or therapeutic use rather than fatal poisoning.

The oleander had provided complementary effects, its own cardiac glycosides working synergistically with the foxglove compounds to ensure that Webb's heart would fail catastrophically and irreversibly. Oleander was particularly useful because its toxic compounds—oleandrin and neriine—weren't included in standard toxicology panels unless the examiner had specific reason to suspect plant-based poisoning.

Alira had spent weeks perfecting the extraction and preparation process, working in the small laboratory space she'd set up in her apartment using equipment purchased through legitimate scientific supply companies under her student credentials. She'd practiced dosage calculations on plant samples and computer models, ensuring that the final preparation would be lethal but undetectable, fast-acting but appearing natural.

The delivery method had required equal care and planning. Alira had created a false identity—"Emma Richardson," a former student of Webb's who'd gone on to successful clinical practice—and had sent him an elaborate gift basket containing supposedly artisanal herbal teas along with an effusive note about how his mentorship had shaped her career and how she wanted to thank him with organic wellness products she'd discovered during her practice.

Webb's ego and his genuine enjoyment of herbal tea had made him the perfect mark. He'd consumed the poisoned preparation on a Monday evening while working late in his home office, exactly as Alira had anticipated. The cardiac glycosides had begun their work immediately, disrupting his heart's electrical signals and inducing progressive arrhythmia that culminated in complete cardiac arrest approximately forty-five minutes after consumption.

By the time the housekeeper found him the next morning, Webb had been dead for nearly twelve hours, his body already cooling and his heart damage so extensive that even immediate medical intervention couldn't have saved him. The ME's examination revealed exactly what Alira had intended—a stressed academic whose undiagnosed heart disease had finally caught up with him during a late night of intense work.

The university held a memorial service celebrating Webb's contributions to the field of trauma psychology, his innovative research methods, and his dedication to mentoring graduate students. Alira attended, sitting in the back of the auditorium and watching the proceedings with carefully controlled satisfaction as colleagues and administrators delivered eulogies praising a man who'd systematically destroyed at least seven women's lives and careers.

She noticed that none of Webb's former female students attended the memorial. Jennifer, Rebecca, Sarah, and the three others Alira hadn't been able to contact—all were conspicuously absent from the celebration of their predator's life and work. Their absence spoke volumes about Webb's true legacy, even if the assembled mourners were too invested in maintaining comfortable fictions to acknowledge what that absence meant.

Sierra's condition had stabilized in the weeks following Webb's death, though "stabilized" was a relative term that meant her physical injuries were healing while her cognitive damage remained catastrophic and apparently permanent. She'd been transferred from the acute care hospital to a specialized rehabilitation facility that worked with traumatic brain injury survivors, a place where therapists and counselors tried to help patients rebuild whatever fragments of their previous cognitive function might be salvageable.

The prognosis remained devastating. Sierra's IQ, which had tested at 142 before the assault, now measured around 73—borderline intellectual disability that placed her in the range of cognitive function typically associated with children aged seven to nine. Her memory was fragmented and unreliable, her personality had shifted dramatically, and her capacity for abstract reasoning and complex problem-solving had been essentially destroyed.

The brilliant doctoral student who'd been developing groundbreaking therapeutic techniques for traumatized children had been reduced to someone who herself required the kind of patient, simplified care typically provided to children. The neurology team believed this represented her permanent baseline—she would never recover the cognitive capacity Webb's violence had stolen, would never complete her doctorate, would never help the traumatized children she'd dedicated her life to serving.

Alira visited Sierra every Tuesday and Friday evening after her own classes, bringing flowers and children's books that were now appropriate for her sister's diminished cognitive capacity. During one such visit, approximately two weeks after Webb's death, something remarkable happened.

Alira had been reading aloud from a picture book about forest animals—the kind of simple, repetitive story that Sierra could follow and seemed to enjoy—when her sister suddenly reached out and grabbed her hand with surprising strength, her eyes focusing with an intensity and clarity that had been absent since the assault.

"The bad man is gone," Sierra said, her voice clear and certain in ways that were startling given her usual confused, childlike speech patterns. "The bad man who hurt me can't hurt anyone anymore."

The statement was so unexpected, so lucid and purposeful, that Alira initially wondered if she'd imagined it. But Sierra was looking directly at her, her expression showing comprehension and satisfaction that went far beyond her usual intellectual capacity.

"What did you say, Sierra?" Alira asked carefully, setting aside the picture book.

"The bad man is gone," Sierra repeated, squeezing Alira's hand. "Dr. Webb. He hurt me, hurt my brain, made me broken. But now he's gone and he can't hurt anyone else. The angels came and made him go away."

It was the most coherent and complex statement Sierra had made since the assault, demonstrating memory and comprehension that the neurologists had said were probably impossible given the extent of her brain damage. Somehow, buried beneath the cognitive devastation, Sierra retained enough of her former brilliance to understand exactly what had happened—both to her and to Webb.

"Yes," Alira said softly, her throat tightening with emotion. "The bad man is gone. He can never hurt you or anyone else again."

Sierra smiled—a real smile, full of genuine warmth and satisfaction rather than the vacant, confused expressions she usually wore. "Thank you," she whispered, her voice carrying depths of meaning that seemed impossible given her damaged cognitive capacity. "Thank you for making the bad man go away. Cassie and I are safe now because of you."

The recognition was both heartbreaking and validating. Sierra understood, at least in this moment of unexpected clarity, exactly what Alira had done and why. She understood that the legal system had failed to protect her, that institutional mechanisms had prioritized Webb's reputation over her safety, and that justice had required someone to work outside those failed systems.

"I love you, Sierra," Alira said, tears streaming down her face as she held her damaged sister's hand.

"I love you too," Sierra replied, her clarity already beginning to fade back into the childlike confusion that had become her baseline state. "You're a good angel. You make the bad people go away so they can't hurt the good people anymore."

The moment of lucidity passed as quickly as it had arrived, Sierra's attention drifting back to the picture book and the simple story about forest animals that was now appropriate for her intellectual capacity. But Alira carried that moment with her as she left the facility that evening, understanding that somewhere in Sierra's damaged mind, her brilliant sister still existed in fragments, still understood what had been done to her and what Alira had done in response.

The validation was important because Alira had already begun to question her actions, to wonder if killing Webb had been justified or if she'd simply become a murderer operating under the comfortable fiction that she was delivering justice rather than committing premeditated homicide.

But Sierra's lucid recognition suggested that at least one person—the person who mattered most— understood and approved of what Alira had done. Webb's death hadn't restored Sierra's brilliant mind or reversed the catastrophic damage he'd inflicted, but it had ensured he would never destroy another woman the way he'd destroyed her.

That night, Alira sat in her apartment surrounded by the botanical texts and toxicology journals she'd used to plan Webb's murder, and she made a decision that would define the rest of her life. Webb wouldn't be her only target. There were too many predators operating with the same impunity Webb had enjoyed, too many powerful men who used their positions to destroy vulnerable women while institutions protected them from consequences.

The system had demonstrated its fundamental unwillingness or inability to hold these men accountable. Universities prioritized reputation over student safety. Police departments dismissed victims whose testimony was inconvenient or complicated. Courts imposed evidentiary standards that effectively immunized wealthy predators from prosecution. The entire institutional framework was designed to protect powerful men from consequences, regardless of how comprehensively their crimes could be documented.

But Alira had learned that some forms of justice didn't require institutional permission or legal authorization. She'd learned that nature provided weapons that left no trace, that medical examiners could be fooled by deaths that mimicked natural causes, that a sufficiently intelligent and determined person could eliminate predators with methodical precision while leaving no evidence that would trigger investigation.

She would become the justice that the system refused to provide. She would be the consequence that powerful predators thought they could avoid through wealth and institutional protection. She would be the angel that Sierra had recognized—removing bad people so they couldn't hurt good people anymore.

The decision brought clarity and purpose that Alira hadn't felt since before Sierra's assault. Her life had meaning again, direction that went beyond simply processing trauma and grief. She would continue her education, but her real work would be studying the methods and vulnerabilities of predators, learning how to eliminate them with surgical precision while avoiding detection.

Webb had been her first kill, crude but effective. The next ones would be more sophisticated, more carefully planned, more professionally executed. She would learn from each elimination, refining her methods and expanding her capabilities until she became the kind of hunter that predators should fear but never saw coming.

Over the following weeks, Alira began making fundamental changes to her academic and personal life in preparation for her new mission. She would need knowledge, skills, and resources that went far beyond her current art history focus. She would need to become something unprecedented—a scientifically trained, martially skilled hunter of predators who operated entirely outside the legal frameworks that had so comprehensively failed to protect her sister.

The first step was changing her academic trajectory. Alira met with her academic advisor and explained that she'd been reconsidering her educational goals in light of recent family trauma. Art history no longer felt meaningful or purposeful, she explained. She wanted to pursue something more scientific, more grounded in understanding how the world actually worked rather than how humans represented it aesthetically.

Her advisor was sympathetic and accommodating, helping her transition from art history to a dual program in biochemistry and pharmacology. The transition would require additional coursework and extend her undergraduate program by a year, but Alira was willing to make that investment. The knowledge she would gain about chemical compounds, biological systems, and pharmaceutical interactions would be essential for her real work.

She also began taking martial arts classes, starting with basic self-defense instruction and quickly progressing to more sophisticated fighting systems. She studied karate first, learning fundamental striking techniques and body mechanics. Then she added jujitsu, focusing on grappling and submission holds that would allow her to control opponents who were larger and stronger. Finally, she began training in Krav Maga, the Israeli combat system designed for real-world violence rather than sport competition.

Her instructors were impressed by her dedication and rapid progress, though they interpreted her intensity as a trauma survivor's attempt to reclaim agency and physical confidence after experiencing violation. They had no idea that Alira was preparing for offensive operations rather than defensive protection, learning to kill efficiently rather than simply to escape dangerous situations.

Alira also began studying forensic science and criminal investigation procedures, understanding that to successfully commit undetectable murders, she needed to think like the investigators who would examine her work. She learned about evidence collection protocols, autopsy procedures, toxicological screening methods, and the limitations of various forensic techniques.

Most importantly, she began identifying potential targets—powerful men with documented histories of predatory behavior who'd escaped legal consequences through wealth, institutional protection, or procedural manipulation. She created detailed files documenting their patterns, their victims, their methods of operation, and their vulnerabilities.

The work was painstaking and time-consuming, requiring months of research and surveillance before she would be ready to act. But Alira was patient, understanding that hasty action led to mistakes and that mistakes led to exposure and capture.

Three months after Webb's death, Cassie called with devastating news that would accelerate Alira's transformation from grieving sister into systematic hunter of predators.

"It's Sierra," Cassie said, her voice breaking with sobs. "She's been moved to a long-term care facility. The rehabilitation center says she's made as much progress as she's likely to make. This is... this is permanent, Alira. Sierra is never coming back."

The finality of that assessment—the official acknowledgment that Sierra's brilliant mind was gone forever, replaced by someone who would require supervised care for the rest of her life—crystallized Alira's resolve. Webb had stolen Sierra's future, her career, her potential to help traumatized children and contribute to human knowledge about healing psychological wounds.

But Webb had paid for those crimes with his life, and other predators would pay similar prices for their own violations. Alira would make sure of it.

She visited Sierra at the new facility that weekend, finding her sister working on a simple jigsaw puzzle with the concentration and pride that a child might display when completing an age-appropriate task. The puzzle featured cartoon animals in a forest scene—exactly the kind of activity that was now intellectually appropriate for someone whose cognitive capacity had been reduced to that of a seven-year-old.

"Alira!" Sierra exclaimed with unfiltered joy when she spotted her sister entering the common room. "Look at my puzzle! I'm almost done with the squirrel!"

"That's wonderful, Sierra," Alira said, sitting beside her and examining the partially completed puzzle. "You're doing such a good job."

They worked together in comfortable silence for several minutes, Sierra's damaged mind fully occupied by the simple task of matching colors and shapes. Then, without looking up from the puzzle, Sierra spoke with sudden clarity that echoed her previous moment of lucidity.

"You're going to help more people, aren't you?" she asked, her voice losing its childlike quality and becoming more purposeful. "More people like me who got hurt by bad men?"

"Yes," Alira replied honestly, understanding that Sierra deserved truth even if she couldn't fully comprehend its implications. "I'm going to make sure that bad men who hurt vulnerable people face consequences, even when the system won't hold them accountable."

Sierra nodded solemnly, her expression showing comprehension that seemed impossible given her documented cognitive limitations. "Good. That's what I was going to do—help people who got hurt. But I can't anymore because Dr. Webb broke my brain. So you have to do it instead."

"I will," Alira promised, her throat tight with emotion. "I'll do the work you can't do anymore. I'll make sure your suffering has meaning."

Sierra smiled and returned to her puzzle, the moment of clarity passing as quickly as it had arrived. But Alira carried that conversation with her as she left the facility, understanding that Sierra had essentially passed the torch—giving Alira permission and purpose to continue the healing work Sierra could no longer perform, albeit through very different methods than Sierra had intended to employ.

The first lesson was complete. Dr. Marcus Webb had taught Alira that powerful predators could be eliminated through methods that appeared natural, that medical examiners could be fooled by deaths that mimicked common medical emergencies, and that nature provided weapons far more elegant than anything humans had engineered.

But Webb had been a relatively easy target—an older man with genuine health vulnerabilities, operating from a position of academic privilege that made him complacent about personal security. Future targets would be more challenging, requiring more sophisticated methods and more careful planning.

Alira was ready for that challenge. She'd begun her education in the art of invisible justice, and she would continue refining her skills until she became the kind of hunter that predators should fear but never saw coming.

The first sin had been committed, and it would not be the last.

Sierra's broken mind had created a warrior dedicated to ensuring that other women wouldn't suffer the same fate. Dr. Webb's comfortable impunity had cost him his life, and his death would serve as the template for dozens of future eliminations.

The mission had begun, and Alira Sinclair would not stop until either she was caught or the system reformed itself sufficiently that extrajudicial action was no longer necessary to protect the vulnerable from predatory violence.

IUDICIUM *Judgment*

———

"Where courts fail to judge, consequences still find a way."

Chapter 3

The Student Years

After Webb's death, Alira threw herself into her transformed academic program with an intensity that concerned her remaining friends and family members who interpreted her obsessive studying as a trauma response rather than operational preparation. She maintained a perfect GPA across her dual biochemistry and pharmacology curriculum while simultaneously pursuing what appeared to be an exhausting regimen of physical fitness training and martial arts instruction.

Her professors praised her dedication and intellectual rigor, particularly impressed by her focus on natural compounds and their physiological effects. Alira had developed a reputation as a brilliant student with particular expertise in botanical toxins and their mechanisms of action—knowledge she ostensibly pursued for academic interest in developing antidotes and therapeutic applications, but which actually served her far more practical purposes.

During her senior year, Alira completed an independent research project on cardiac glycosides found in various plant species, documenting their effects on human cardiovascular systems with meticulous precision. Her faculty advisor, Dr. Patricia Chen, was enthusiastic about the work's potential applications for developing new treatments for heart failure and arrhythmias.

"This research is genuinely groundbreaking, Alira," Dr. Chen said during one of their weekly supervision meetings. "Your understanding of how these compounds interact with cardiac tissue at the molecular level exceeds what I've seen from most doctoral students. Have you considered pursuing a PhD in pharmacology or toxicology?"

"I've thought about it," Alira replied honestly. "But I'm not sure academic research is the right path for me long-term. I'm more interested in practical applications—understanding how these compounds work in real-world scenarios rather than just documenting their properties in laboratory settings."

The response was carefully calculated to maintain her cover as a serious student while avoiding committing to an academic career that would limit her operational flexibility. A PhD program would consume five to seven years and would subject her to intensive scrutiny from advisors and committee members who might eventually notice inconsistencies between her stated research interests and her actual knowledge applications.

Instead, Alira planned to complete her undergraduate degrees and then establish herself in a position that provided income, flexibility, and social connections while allowing her to continue her real work of hunting predators. She'd already identified several potential cover careers—art gallery management, nonprofit administration, freelance consulting—that would give her the freedom she needed while maintaining a plausible legitimate identity.

Her martial arts training had progressed even more rapidly than her academic work. By the end of her senior year, Alira had earned black belts in three different disciplines and had developed a fighting style that synthesized techniques from multiple systems into something uniquely effective and brutally efficient.

Her Krav Maga instructor, David Rosen, was a former Israeli Defense Forces combat trainer who recognized in Alira something beyond typical student dedication. During a private session in the spring of her senior year, he'd pulled her aside for a conversation that had been both validating and slightly concerning.

"You're not training for self-defense," Rosen observed, his tone matter-of-fact rather than accusatory. "You're training for offense. For combat operations. I've taught hundreds of students over the years, and I can tell the difference between someone learning to protect themselves and someone learning to hurt people very efficiently."

Alira had considered lying, maintaining the fiction that she was a trauma survivor reclaiming physical confidence and agency. But something in Rosen's expression suggested he'd see through easy deceptions, that his decades of combat experience had given him the same ability to read people that Alira had been developing.

"You're right," she admitted carefully. "I'm training for situations that might require offensive capabilities rather than just defensive responses."

Rosen studied her for a long moment, his weathered face showing neither judgment nor approval. "I'm not going to ask why or what you're planning to do with these skills. That's your business. But I will tell you this: the techniques I've taught you are designed for military and law enforcement applications. They're meant to neutralize threats quickly and efficiently, often with lethal force. If you use them outside of legitimate self-defense contexts, you'll be committing serious crimes regardless of your motivations."

"I understand," Alira replied.

"Do you?" Rosen challenged. "Because understanding intellectually and understanding emotionally are very different things. Taking a human life, even if that person deserves it by any reasonable moral standard, changes you fundamentally. I've killed men in combat, men who were actively trying to kill me or my unit. Even those justified killings stay with you, shape how you see the world and yourself."

"My sister was nearly beaten to death by a man who used his position of authority to exploit her trust," Alira said quietly. "He destroyed her brilliant mind, stole her future, and left her with the cognitive capacity of a child. The legal system protected him completely—he had a perfect alibi, institutional support, and the resources to ensure he faced no consequences for what he'd done."

Rosen's expression softened slightly. "And you want to make sure men like him face justice even when the system won't provide it."

"Something like that," Alira confirmed.

"Then let me give you some operational advice from someone who's spent his life studying violence and its applications," Rosen said. "If you're going to go down this path, be smart about it. Don't get angry, don't get emotional, don't let personal feelings cloud your tactical judgment. Plan meticulously, execute precisely, and never assume that you're smarter than the investigators who'll examine your work. Hubris kills more operators than enemy action ever does."

The conversation had ended with an implicit understanding—Rosen wouldn't report his suspicions about Alira's intentions, but he also wouldn't provide additional training once she'd achieved black belt certification. Their student-instructor relationship concluded with mutual respect and carefully maintained professional distance.

Alira's weapons training expanded beyond martial arts to include practical combat skills with knives, improvised weapons, and defensive tools that could be carried legally but deployed lethally when necessary. She studied human anatomy with the precision of a surgeon, learning exactly where to strike or cut to disable or kill an opponent with maximum efficiency and minimum wasted motion.

But despite her growing combat capabilities, Alira remained convinced that physical violence should be her last resort rather than her primary method. Martial arts were important for self-defense and for creating plausible scenarios where predators died during confrontations they'd initiated. But chemical and biological weapons remained far more elegant—they allowed for elimination at distance, created deaths that appeared natural, and minimized the forensic evidence that could connect her to her victims.

During her final semester of undergraduate work, Cassie was accepted to Columbia University's prestigious journalism program on a full scholarship that would cover her tuition and living expenses. At twenty-one, Cassie had maintained the idealism and optimism that Alira had lost after Sierra's assault, still believing that institutional systems could be reformed through exposure and public pressure rather than requiring extrajudicial intervention.

"I'm going to be an investigative journalist," Cassie announced during the family dinner celebrating her acceptance, her voice bright with conviction and purpose. "I want to expose predators like the one who hurt Sierra. Make sure they can't hide behind their reputations and institutional protection anymore. If I can bring their crimes into public light, force institutions to acknowledge what's happening, maybe the system will actually start holding them accountable."

"That's wonderful, Cassie," Alira said, genuinely proud of her younger sister's dedication to justice even if she no longer shared Cassie's faith that exposure would lead to accountability. "The world needs journalists willing to investigate powerful people and tell stories that institutions want to keep hidden."

Sierra, who'd been invited to the family dinner and had been carefully supervised throughout the meal by the care facility staff member who'd accompanied her, clapped her hands with childlike enthusiasm. "Cassie's going to help people! Like the angels help people! She's going to make the bad men face consequences!"

The statement was more insightful than Sierra's damaged cognitive capacity should have allowed, suggesting that somewhere in her broken mind, she retained fragments of comprehension about justice and accountability that transcended her intellectual limitations.

"Yes, sweetheart," their mother said gently, reaching over to pat Sierra's hand. "Cassie is going to help make sure bad people can't hurt others. Just like you wanted to do before... before what happened."

The careful phrasing—"before what happened" rather than "before Dr. Webb destroyed your brain"—was typical of how their family had learned to discuss Sierra's condition. Direct acknowledgment of the violence and its permanent consequences was too painful, so they'd developed a vocabulary of euphemism and careful omission that allowed them to function without constantly confronting the full horror of what had been done to their brilliant sister.

Alira watched the family dinner proceedings with a mixture of love and carefully concealed cynicism. Her mother and father still believed that Sierra had been the victim of a random assault by an unknown attacker— they had no idea that Dr. Webb had been responsible, and Alira had never corrected their misunderstanding. Let them maintain their comfortable fictions about random violence rather than institutional betrayal.

Similarly, her parents had no idea that Alira had killed Webb, that she'd spent three months studying botanical toxins and planning a murder that appeared to be natural cardiac death. They believed their middle daughter was working through trauma by pursuing rigorous academic study and intense physical training, standard responses to feeling powerless in the face of violence.

Only Cassie seemed to suspect that Alira's transformation involved something darker than academic redirection and fitness enthusiasm. During a private conversation after the family dinner, Cassie had pulled Alira aside with an expression of concern mixed with something approaching fear.

"You've changed so much since Sierra was hurt," Cassie said quietly. "You used to be... softer. More willing to believe in people and systems. Now you seem harder, more cynical. Like you've given up on the idea that justice is possible through legitimate channels."

"Maybe I've just learned to see the world more clearly," Alira replied carefully. "The systems we're taught to trust—police, courts, universities, all the institutions that are supposed to protect people and hold wrongdoers accountable—they failed Sierra completely. They prioritized a predator's reputation over her safety, accepted his obviously fabricated alibi, and dismissed her testimony as confused rambling. That kind of comprehensive institutional failure changes how you understand the world."

"But you can't let what happened to Sierra destroy your faith in the possibility of reform," Cassie insisted. "If we give up on institutions, if we decide that working outside the system is the only way to achieve justice, then we're abandoning the very principles that separate civilization from chaos."

Alira studied her younger sister, seeing the idealistic naivety that she herself had possessed before Sierra's assault had stripped away comfortable illusions about how power actually operated in the world. Part of her wanted to protect Cassie's faith in institutional reform, to let her younger sister maintain beliefs that would allow her to pursue journalism with optimistic dedication rather than bitter cynicism.

But another part of her recognized that Cassie's idealism represented a dangerous vulnerability. If Cassie investigated the wrong powerful person, exposed the wrong institutional corruption, she might discover that journalistic exposure didn't protect whistleblowers nearly as effectively as she believed. She might learn, too late, that powerful predators didn't simply accept public accountability—they destroyed anyone who threatened their comfortable impunity.

"Just be careful, Cassie," Alira said finally. "When you start investigating powerful people and their crimes, remember that they didn't achieve or maintain that power by accepting accountability gracefully. They'll fight back with everything they have, and institutions will often protect them rather than you. Don't assume that truth and evidence will shield you from retaliation."

Cassie's expression showed that she'd heard the warning but hadn't fully internalized its implications. "I'll be careful," she promised. "But I can't let fear of retaliation prevent me from pursuing stories that need to be told. If journalists only investigated safe targets, we'd never expose any of the corruption and abuse that institutions work so hard to conceal."

The conversation ended with an embrace and mutual expressions of love and support, both sisters understanding that they were pursuing justice through very different methods but driven by the same commitment to protecting vulnerable people from predatory violence.

Alira graduated summa cum laude with dual degrees in biochemistry and pharmacology in May, delivering a valedictory address about the intersection of natural compounds and medical applications that her professors and classmates interpreted as an inspiring vision for pharmaceutical innovation. None of them understood that her real expertise involved weaponizing those natural compounds to eliminate predators in ways that appeared completely natural and medically unremarkable.

Sierra attended the graduation ceremony with their parents and Cassie, sitting in the audience with the care facility staff member who supervised her during family events. When Alira's name was called and she walked across the stage to receive her diplomas, Sierra stood and applauded with enthusiastic pride that seemed to transcend her cognitive limitations.

"That's my sister!" Sierra called out, her voice carrying across the auditorium with childlike lack of self-consciousness. "She's so smart! She's going to help so many people!"

The statement was more accurate than anyone in attendance understood. Alira would indeed help many people—specifically, the women who would have been victimized by the predators she planned to eliminate over the coming years. She would provide protection and justice that institutional systems consistently failed to deliver, ensuring that powerful men finally faced consequences that wealth and privilege couldn't deflect.

After graduation, Alira enrolled in a master's program in forensic toxicology, explaining to her family that she wanted to pursue work in criminal investigation and evidence analysis. The program would provide advanced training in exactly the methods that investigators would use to examine suspicious deaths, allowing Alira to understand and circumvent detection protocols with professional precision.

She also took a part-time position at a prestigious art gallery in the city, leveraging her original art history background to establish legitimate employment that would provide income and social connections while demanding minimal time commitment. The gallery position was perfect cover—it explained her refined tastes, her knowledge of wealthy collectors, and her ability to move freely in elite social circles where many of her future targets operated.

Her apartment became a sophisticated laboratory and research center, filled with botanical specimens, chemical extraction equipment, and detailed files on potential targets. She'd identified dozens of powerful predators through systematic research—men who'd used their positions to exploit and abuse women while institutional protections ensured they faced no legal consequences.

But Alira was patient, understanding that hasty action created patterns that might eventually be recognized by investigators. She would take her time, choosing targets carefully and spacing eliminations widely enough to avoid creating obvious connections. Each kill would be thoroughly planned and meticulously executed, leaving no forensic evidence that could trigger investigation or create trails that led back to her involvement.

Sierra's condition remained stable in the permanent sense of that word—her physical health was good, her care was adequate, and her cognitive capacity remained frozen at the level of a seven-year-old child. She would never recover the brilliant mind that Webb had destroyed, would never complete her doctorate or help the traumatized children she'd dedicated her life to serving.

But during Alira's regular visits to the care facility—every Tuesday and Friday evening, a schedule she maintained with religious dedication—Sierra occasionally displayed moments of unexpected clarity that suggested her damaged mind retained fragments of her former brilliance.

During one such visit in the fall after Alira's graduation, Sierra had looked up from the picture book they'd been reading together and spoken with sudden lucid intensity.

"The bad men," she said, her voice losing its usual childlike quality. "You're learning how to stop all the bad men, not just the one who hurt me. You're becoming... becoming an angel of justice for people who can't get justice any other way."

"Yes," Alira confirmed, understanding that denying Sierra's insight would be both dishonest and disrespectful to whatever fragments of brilliance remained in her damaged consciousness. "I'm learning methods that will allow me to eliminate predators who use power and privilege to escape accountability for their crimes."

Sierra nodded solemnly. "Good. That's important work. That's the work I was supposed to do—helping people who'd been hurt by bad people. But I can't do it anymore because my brain is broken. So you have to do it for me. You have to be the angel that stops the monsters."

"I will," Alira promised. "I'll make sure your suffering has meaning, that what happened to you leads to other women being protected from similar predators."

"Thank you," Sierra said, her clarity already beginning to fade back into childlike confusion. "Keep stopping the monsters, okay? For all the people who can't stop them themselves."

As Alira drove home that evening, she reflected on how Sierra's damaged mind had given her both permission and purpose for the mission she'd undertaken. Her brilliant sister understood, in the fragmented way that her brain injury allowed, that institutional systems had failed comprehensively and that alternative forms of justice were necessary to protect the vulnerable from predatory violence.

The student years had been about preparation and skill development, transforming herself from a traumatized art history student into a sophisticated hunter of predators. She'd acquired the knowledge to kill with natural compounds that left no forensic trace, the combat skills to defend herself or create plausible self-defense scenarios, and the forensic understanding to avoid detection by investigators examining suspicious deaths.

Now it was time to put that preparation into practice.

Dr. Marcus Webb had been her first kill, crude but effective. The next one would be more sophisticated, more challenging, and more carefully planned. Alira had identified her second target—Coach Robert Daniels, a man whose crimes were even more extensive than Webb's and whose institutional protections were even more comprehensive.

But before she could begin planning Daniels' elimination, Cassie's first year at Columbia would unfold in ways that would accelerate Alira's transformation from careful planner into active hunter.

The nightmare was about to begin again, and this time it would be even more devastating than Sierra's assault.

Chapter 4

The Columbia Nightmare

Cassie's first year at Columbia University went exactly as she'd hoped and planned during the early months. She excelled in her journalism classes, wrote compelling investigative pieces for the university newspaper, and quickly established herself as one of the program's most promising students. Her professors praised her dedication to uncovering truth, her fearlessness in pursuing difficult stories, and her sophisticated understanding of how power operated in institutional settings.

By the spring semester of her freshman year, Cassie had begun investigating what would become her most ambitious story—a comprehensive exposé of sexual harassment and assault within Columbia's athletic department. She'd been contacted by several female athletes who described a systematic pattern of abuse by Coach Robert Daniels, the university's celebrated football coach whose teams had won three conference championships and consistently competed for national rankings.

Daniels was a Columbia institution—fifty-three years old, charismatic and politically connected, beloved by alumni donors who contributed millions to the athletic program. His success on the field had made him effectively untouchable, insulated by layers of administrative protection and the kind of institutional reverence that prevented serious scrutiny of his conduct with female athletes and staff.

But Cassie had spoken with nine women who described remarkably consistent experiences of predatory behavior. Daniels used his authority over athletic scholarships, playing time, and career opportunities to coerce female athletes into sexual relationships. He framed these exploitative arrangements as mentorship and special attention, convincing victims that their athletic success depended on maintaining his favor while keeping the sexual nature of their relationships hidden.

The women Cassie interviewed described sophisticated psychological manipulation combined with explicit threats. Daniels would identify vulnerable athletes— often freshmen or transfer students who were isolated from family support systems and desperate to prove themselves worthy of their scholarships. He'd offer special training sessions, individual coaching, and promises of enhanced playing opportunities that would attract professional scouts.

These "mentorship" relationships would gradually become inappropriate, with Daniels using private training sessions to establish physical intimacy that eventually progressed to sexual assault. When victims resisted or threatened to report his behavior, Daniels would deploy a comprehensive system of retaliation—cutting their playing time, providing negative evaluations to professional scouts, spreading rumors about their athletic commitment and team loyalty, and ultimately forcing them out of the program through orchestrated campaigns of professional destruction.

The most devastating aspect of Daniels' predatory system was how thoroughly it was enabled by institutional complicity. The athletic department administrators knew about the pattern—several women had filed formal complaints over the past decade—but those complaints had been systematically buried through confidential settlements and non-disclosure agreements that prevented victims from speaking publicly about their experiences.

University officials prioritized protecting the football program's reputation and donor relationships over holding Daniels accountable for serial sexual misconduct. They'd created a system where reporting assault meant professional destruction for victims while Daniels faced no consequences beyond occasional quiet settlements funded by the athletic department's discretionary budget.

Cassie had spent months gathering documentation—interviewing victims, reviewing confidential settlement agreements obtained through sympathetic sources within the administration, and building an evidentiary case that would be impossible for the university to dismiss or discredit. Her faculty advisor in the journalism program had praised the work as professional-grade investigative reporting that would likely be picked up by major media outlets once published.

During their weekly phone conversations, Cassie had shared details of her investigation with Alira, her voice carrying the righteous excitement of someone who believed she was about to expose corruption and deliver accountability that institutional systems had failed to provide.

"This is going to be huge," Cassie had said during a call in early March, just three weeks before everything went terribly wrong. "I have nine women willing to go on the record, documentation of settlement payments that prove the university knew about Daniels' pattern, and evidence that administrators actively suppressed previous investigations. Once this story publishes, Daniels will finally face real consequences, and the university will have to implement meaningful reforms."

Alira had listened to her younger sister's enthusiastic optimism with carefully concealed dread, recognizing patterns that Cassie's idealism prevented her from seeing clearly. Powerful predators didn't accept exposure gracefully—they fought back with everything at their disposal, and institutions that had protected them for decades wouldn't suddenly prioritize truth and accountability over reputation management and donor relationships.

"Be careful, Cassie," Alira had warned, not for the first time. "Men like Daniels have extensive networks and resources. If he discovers you're investigating him, he'll do everything possible to prevent publication or discredit your reporting. Don't assume that evidence and truth will protect you from retaliation."

"I'm being careful," Cassie had assured her. "I've kept my investigation confidential, using encrypted communications and secure document storage. Daniels has no idea he's being investigated, and by the time the story publishes, it'll be too late for him to prevent the consequences."

But Cassie had underestimated how thoroughly Daniels had infiltrated Columbia's administrative and security infrastructure. Someone within the journalism program or university administration had been monitoring her investigation and reporting to Daniels about her progress. By mid-March, Daniels knew exactly what Cassie was planning to publish and how damaging the evidence she'd gathered would be to his carefully constructed public image.

The call came on a Thursday night in late March, shattering Alira's world with the same devastating completeness that Sierra's assault had three years earlier.

Alira had been in her graduate laboratory, working late on a research project involving the extraction and concentration of toxic alkaloids from various plant species. Her official research focused on developing antidotes and therapeutic applications, but her actual work involved perfecting methods for creating undetectable poisons that could be delivered through multiple routes and would mimic natural medical emergencies.

Her phone rang at 11:47 PM, the late hour and unknown New York area code immediately triggering alarm. Alira's hands went cold with anticipatory dread as she answered.

"Miss Sinclair? This is Detective Angela Rivera with the New York Police Department. I'm calling about your sister, Cassandra Sinclair."

The world stopped. The test tube Alira had been holding slipped from her nerveless fingers and shattered on the laboratory floor, expensive reagents spreading across the tile in patterns she would later remember with perfect clarity because her brain had been recording every sensory detail of the moment when her life fractured again.

"What happened?" Alira managed to ask, her voice sounding distant and hollow in her own ears.

"I'm very sorry to have to tell you this, but your sister was found deceased in her dormitory room this evening. Based on the preliminary investigation, it appears she took her own life."

Suicide. The word detonated in Alira's consciousness like a bomb, destroying every comfortable assumption about safety and justice and the protection that institutional systems supposedly provided to vulnerable people pursuing truth.

"That's impossible," Alira said, her voice rising with desperate conviction. "Cassie would never commit suicide. She wasn't depressed, she was excited about her work. She was about to publish a major investigative story. She had everything to live for and no reason to—"

"Miss Sinclair, I understand this is extremely difficult to accept," Detective Rivera interrupted with practiced sympathy that failed to conceal bureaucratic impatience. "But your sister left a note expressing feelings of academic overwhelm and emotional distress. These situations are unfortunately more common than you might think among high-achieving students facing pressure to maintain impossible standards."

"What kind of note?" Alira demanded, her analytical mind already identifying the implausibility of the detective's narrative. "Handwritten? Typed? What did it say exactly?"

"The note was typed on your sister's laptop," Rivera replied. "It expressed feelings of inadequacy, anxiety about meeting academic expectations, and a sense that she'd disappointed her family and professors. These are very typical themes in student suicide notes."

"Cassie didn't type personal communications," Alira said, grasping at details that felt significant even through the shock and grief overwhelming her cognitive processes. "She always wrote important things by hand—letters, journal entries, anything emotionally meaningful. She said handwriting made her feel more connected to her thoughts. A typed suicide note doesn't make sense."

"Miss Sinclair, I know you want to find reasons to reject this conclusion," Rivera said with the patronizing gentleness that authority figures deployed when dismissing inconvenient observations from grieving family members. "But denial is a very normal response to sudden loss, especially loss through suicide. It's easier to believe there was some kind of mistake or conspiracy than to accept that someone we loved was suffering in ways we didn't recognize."

Alira understood in that moment that arguing with Detective Rivera was futile. The investigation had already been concluded, the narrative established, the case filed in whatever category New York police used for student suicides. Rivera wasn't interested in evidence that contradicted the official story—she'd already decided what had happened and was simply going through the bureaucratic motions of notifying next of kin.

"I need to see her," Alira said. "I'm driving to New York tonight. Don't let them move her body or disturb the scene until I get there."

"Miss Sinclair, the medical examiner has already transported the body for autopsy, and the dormitory room has been processed by our crime scene unit," Rivera explained. "But I can arrange for you to view your sister's body at the medical examiner's office and review the case file when you arrive. I'll be at the precinct tomorrow morning if you want to discuss the investigation further."

Alira drove to New York that night, her mind racing through everything Cassie had told her about the investigation into Coach Robert Daniels. Her younger sister had been close to publishing a devastating exposé about a powerful predator protected by institutional complicity. Now Cassie was suddenly dead under circumstances that authorities had immediately classified as suicide despite obvious inconsistencies that should have triggered more thorough investigation.

The pattern was sickeningly familiar—a vulnerable woman threatening to expose a powerful predator, followed by sudden death classified as either accident or suicide, followed by institutional acceptance of narratives that protected the predator while discrediting the victim. It was exactly what had happened to Sierra, what had happened to Webb's other victims, what happened whenever justice required challenging men whose power was backed by institutional protection.

But this time was different. This time Alira understood how the system operated, how predators exploited institutional weaknesses, and how deaths could be staged to appear natural or self-inflicted when they were actually carefully orchestrated murders.

Cassie hadn't committed suicide. She'd been murdered because she'd gotten too close to exposing Coach Robert Daniels, and someone—either Daniels himself or someone acting on his behalf—had eliminated her while making her death appear to be the tragic result of academic pressure and mental health crisis.

Alira reached New York at 4:37 AM, too early to contact Detective Rivera but too agitated to simply wait in a hotel room. She drove to Columbia's campus and parked outside Cassie's dormitory building, a modern high-rise structure that housed hundreds of undergraduate students in supposedly secure accommodations.

The building's security was minimal—a card reader at the main entrance that residents could bypass by following other students through the door, security cameras that covered main areas but not individual floors or rooms, and a residential advisor system that depended on students self-reporting emergencies rather than maintaining active supervision.

Anyone with basic social engineering skills could have gained access to Cassie's room, especially someone with university credentials or connections who would appear legitimate to other students. Daniels had both—his athletic department position gave him access to most campus buildings, and his long tenure at Columbia meant he knew security protocols and their vulnerabilities intimately.

As dawn broke over Manhattan, Alira sat in her car watching students emerge from the dormitory for early morning classes or gym sessions, and she made a decision that would define the next phase of her life. She would conduct her own investigation into Cassie's death, using all the forensic knowledge and analytical skills she'd developed. She would prove that her sister had been murdered, identify who was responsible, and ensure they faced consequences that the legal system would never provide.

At 9:15 AM, Alira met with Detective Rivera at the precinct, a functional but depressing building in upper Manhattan that smelled of industrial cleaning products and defeat. Rivera was a woman in her mid-forties, professionally competent but clearly operating under bureaucratic constraints that limited how thoroughly she could investigate student deaths that appeared to be suicides.

"Thank you for seeing me, Detective," Alira said, maintaining careful control over her grief and rage. "I'd like to review the evidence that led you to conclude my sister committed suicide."

Rivera pulled out a thin case file and spread its contents across her desk—crime scene photographs, the alleged suicide note, preliminary autopsy findings, and witness statements from other students who'd seen Cassie in the days before her death.

The photographs showed Cassie's body hanging from a closet rod in her dormitory room, a braided bed sheet serving as the ligature. Her face was swollen and discolored from asphyxiation, her eyes bulging, her tongue protruding. It was a horrific sight that would have devastated Alira if she hadn't been actively analyzing the scene for inconsistencies rather than simply absorbing the emotional impact.

Several details immediately struck her as wrong. Cassie's hands showed defensive wounds—small cuts and abrasions on her knuckles and the backs of her hands that Rivera's report attributed to "self-inflicted injuries during the suicidal episode" but which looked far more consistent with someone who'd fought against an attacker.

The positioning of the body was also suspicious. Cassie's feet were only a few inches off the ground, close enough that she could have easily stood up and relieved the pressure on her neck if she'd changed her mind about committing suicide. In genuine hangings where the victim intended to die, they typically chose heights that made survival impossible once the act was initiated.

Most tellingly, the ligature marks on Cassie's neck showed irregular patterns—areas of deeper bruising mixed with areas of lighter contact—suggesting the sheet had been tightened and loosened multiple times rather than maintaining constant pressure throughout the asphyxiation process. This pattern was far more consistent with someone being strangled by an assailant who periodically adjusted their grip than with a continuous hanging.

"These defensive wounds," Alira said, pointing to the photographs of Cassie's hands. "Your report says they were self-inflicted during the suicide attempt. But they look like fighting injuries—the kind of wounds someone gets when they're trying to defend themselves against an attacker."

"We consulted with a forensic pathologist who confirmed they were consistent with the victim's hands contacting the closet rod and wall during the hanging," Rivera explained with the patient tone of someone who'd addressed this concern before. "When people hang themselves, they often struggle and flail as oxygen deprivation sets in, creating exactly these kinds of injuries."

The explanation was plausible but not convincing to anyone with Alira's understanding of forensic evidence. The cuts on Cassie's knuckles showed directionality and depth consistent with striking a hard surface—like someone's face or body—rather than scraping against a closet rod.

"What about the suicide note?" Alira asked, examining the printout of what was allegedly Cassie's final message. "You mentioned it was typed rather than handwritten."

"Yes, that's correct. Your sister apparently composed it on her laptop shortly before her death."

Alira read through the note, finding language and phrasing that didn't sound anything like Cassie's writing style or emotional expression patterns:

I can't handle the pressure anymore. Everyone expects so much from me, and I keep disappointing them. My professors, my family, my sources who trusted me to tell their stories—I've failed all of them. I'm not strong enough for this work. I'm not brave enough to face what I've uncovered. It's better if I just disappear before I cause more harm.

The note was grammatically correct and emotionally manipulative, but it lacked Cassie's distinctive voice—her tendency toward vivid metaphors, her habit of quoting literary sources, her particular rhythms of self-expression that were as unique as a fingerprint to anyone who knew her writing well.

"This doesn't sound like Cassie," Alira said, though she knew Rivera would dismiss the observation as grief-driven denial. "She wouldn't describe herself as 'not strong enough' or talk about 'disappointing people.' She had incredible confidence in her work and her ability to expose corruption. Three days before her death, she told me she was excited about publishing her investigation and watching the people she'd exposed face consequences."

"Miss Sinclair, people experiencing suicidal ideation often hide their true emotional state from loved ones," Rivera explained with practiced sympathy. "They present a brave face to the world while internally struggling with feelings of inadequacy and despair. The note's content is very consistent with someone who was projecting confidence externally while privately feeling overwhelmed."

Alira recognized that she wouldn't change Rivera's conclusions through verbal argument. The detective had already decided what had happened, supported by institutional pressure to close cases efficiently rather than pursue complicated investigations that might reveal uncomfortable truths about campus security and student welfare.

"Can I see the list of Cassie's belongings that were recovered from her room?" Alira asked, shifting her approach.

Rivera consulted her file and provided an inventory list that included Cassie's laptop, phone, backpack, textbooks, clothing, and personal items. Alira noticed immediately what was missing.

"Where are her investigative files?" she asked. "Cassie was working on a major story about sexual assault in the athletic department. She'd accumulated months of interviews, documents, evidence. Those files aren't listed in the inventory."

"We found her laptop and phone," Rivera replied. "Any digital files would have been on those devices."

"Cassie kept physical files too—printed documents, handwritten notes, source contact information. She always maintained both digital and physical records for important investigations. And her laptop would have shown her recent work—interview transcripts, drafts of her story, correspondence with sources. Did your investigation examine her digital files to see what she was working on?"

Rivera's expression showed discomfort, suggesting she hadn't conducted that level of scrutiny. "Our investigation focused on determining cause of death and whether foul play was involved. We don't typically perform comprehensive reviews of victims' work product in suicide cases."

"So you didn't notice that all of Cassie's investigative materials about Coach Robert Daniels had disappeared from her room and her laptop?" Alira pressed. "You didn't think it was suspicious that a journalism student working on a major exposé of a powerful university figure would suddenly have no physical or digital evidence of that investigation?"

"Miss Sinclair, I understand you're looking for reasons to believe your sister's death wasn't suicide," Rivera said, her patience clearly wearing thin. "But the evidence we have—the body position, the ligature, the suicide note, the absence of forced entry or signs of struggle—all point conclusively to self-inflicted death. I'm very sorry for your loss, but creating conspiracy theories won't bring your sister back or make her death easier to accept."

Alira understood that she'd pushed as far as she could with Rivera without triggering defensive bureaucratic resistance. She thanked the detective for her time and left the precinct with copies of the case file that Rivera had grudgingly provided after Alira explained she'd need them for insurance and legal purposes related to Cassie's estate.

Over the next two weeks, Alira remained in New York, ostensibly making funeral arrangements but actually conducting her own comprehensive investigation into Cassie's death. She used her biochemistry background to review the autopsy findings with forensic precision, her martial arts training to analyze the physical evidence, and her emerging forensic expertise to identify inconsistencies that NYPD had either missed or chosen to ignore.

The autopsy revealed several details that supported Alira's murder theory. Cassie's toxicology screening showed the presence of scopolamine—a drug that caused temporary cognitive impairment and suggestibility while leaving victims technically conscious. The drug was sometimes called "devil's breath" in criminal contexts, known for its use in date rape and robbery scenarios where victims needed to appear cooperative while actually being incapacitated.

The medical examiner's report had noted the scopolamine but attributed it to possible recreational drug use or accidental exposure, despite having no evidence that Cassie had ever used drugs or had any reason to be exposed to such an exotic compound. The presence of the drug should have triggered more thorough investigation into whether Cassie had been drugged to make her compliant during a staged suicide.

Alira also discovered that Cassie's email accounts— both her university account and her personal Gmail— had been accessed from an unknown IP address on the night of her death, approximately two hours before her estimated time of death. Someone had logged into her accounts and systematically deleted messages, files, and documents related to her investigation of Coach Daniels.

The digital forensics were clear and damning, but Alira understood that presenting this evidence to NYPD would accomplish nothing. The department had already closed the case, and reopening it would require acknowledging that their initial investigation had been sloppy and inadequate. Institutional pride would prevent that kind of self-correction, especially when it involved challenging a beloved athletic department figure whose connections extended into law enforcement and university administration.

Alira's investigation expanded beyond the immediate circumstances of Cassie's death to examine Coach Robert Daniels's background and methods more comprehensively. She broke into Cassie's encrypted email backups—accessing servers that the killer hadn't known to target—and recovered the complete investigative files that Cassie had been preparing for publication.

The evidence was devastating and comprehensive. Cassie had interviewed nine women who described consistent patterns of predatory behavior—Daniels using his authority over athletic scholarships and playing opportunities to coerce sexual relationships, deploying psychological manipulation to make victims feel responsible for their own exploitation, and orchestrating professional destruction for anyone who resisted or threatened to expose his conduct.

Most significantly, Cassie had obtained confidential settlement agreements showing that Columbia University had paid at least $2.3 million over the past decade to silence victims and prevent their stories from becoming public. The university's general counsel had drafted language for these agreements that went far beyond standard confidentiality clauses, including provisions that effectively prevented victims from seeking therapy or discussing their experiences even with medical professionals.

The institutional complicity was comprehensive and systematic. University administrators knew about Daniels's predatory pattern, had documented evidence of serial sexual assault, and had deliberately chosen to protect him through confidential settlements rather than hold him accountable through disciplinary processes that would have required public disclosure.

Cassie had been days away from publishing her exposé when she'd been killed. The story would have destroyed Daniels's career, triggered federal investigations into Columbia's Title IX compliance, and potentially resulted in criminal charges despite the difficulties of prosecuting decade-old sexual assaults.

On the day before Cassie's funeral, Alira received an unexpected visit from a young woman named Jessica Martinez, a sophomore track athlete who'd been one of Cassie's sources for the Daniels investigation.

"Your sister was trying to help us," Jessica said, her voice breaking as they sat in a quiet corner of a Manhattan coffee shop. "She was the first person who believed our stories about Coach Daniels without questioning or blaming us. She said she was going to make sure he couldn't hurt anyone else, that she'd expose him in ways that would force the university to actually do something rather than just paying us off and pretending the problem didn't exist."

"What happened to her?" Alira asked, though she already knew the answer with grim certainty.

"She got too close," Jessica replied, tears streaming down her face. "Coach has friends everywhere—police, university administration, athletic department donors, even some journalists who cover Columbia sports. When word got out that Cassie was preparing to publish her story, they couldn't let that happen. He has too much to lose, too many powerful people invested in protecting his reputation."

"Are you saying Coach Daniels killed my sister?"

Jessica's expression showed the complicated mixture of certainty and fear that characterized someone who knew dangerous truth but lacked the power or evidence to prove it. "I can't prove it. None of us can prove it. But we know how he operates, how he silences people who threaten him. Your sister wouldn't have killed herself— she was too committed to exposing him, too excited about finally bringing him down. Someone made her death look like suicide, and Coach Daniels is the only person who had both the motive and the resources to make that happen."

Jessica handed Alira a flash drive, its weight insignificant but its contents potentially explosive. "This is everything Cassie had on Coach Daniels—all the interviews, all the evidence, all the documentation she'd gathered. She gave me a backup copy and told me to keep it somewhere safe in case anything happened to her. I think... I think she knew she was in danger but didn't want to stop pursuing the story."

"Why didn't you give this to the police?" Alira asked, though she already understood the answer.

Jessica's laugh was bitter and defeated. "Because half the police department plays poker with Coach Daniels every Friday night at the university president's house. Because the district attorney's son plays football for Columbia and worships Coach like a god. Because the entire system is designed to protect men like him while silencing women like us. Your sister understood that— it's why she was pursuing journalism rather than trying to work through official channels that consistently fail survivors."

The words echoed what Alira had realized after Sierra's assault, what she'd learned again through her research into institutional failures and predatory behavior. The system wasn't broken—it was working exactly as designed, protecting powerful men while ensuring that challenges to their authority were neutralized through whatever means proved necessary.

"What do you want me to do with this?" Alira asked, hefting the flash drive.

"Whatever you think will actually make a difference," Jessica replied. "Publishing Cassie's story won't work—the university will discredit it as the work of a mentally unstable student who committed suicide before fact-checking could be completed. Going to authorities won't work because they're all compromised by connections to Daniels and the athletic program. Legal action won't work because we've all signed settlement agreements that prevent us from testifying."

Jessica paused, studying Alira with an intensity that suggested she understood more than she was explicitly stating. "But maybe there are other ways to ensure Coach Daniels faces consequences. Maybe there are forms of justice that don't require institutional permission or legal authorization. Maybe someone needs to demonstrate that powerful predators can't escape accountability forever, regardless of how thoroughly they've corrupted the systems that are supposed to hold them responsible."

The implication was clear and devastating. Jessica was essentially asking Alira to do what the legal system wouldn't do—eliminate Coach Robert Daniels through extrajudicial means, ensuring he faced consequences that institutional protections had prevented for over a decade.

"I understand," Alira said quietly, accepting the flash drive and the implicit mission it represented.

Jessica left the coffee shop without further conversation, and Alira sat alone examining the evidence that Cassie had died trying to make public. Her younger sister had believed in institutional reform, in the power of journalistic exposure to force accountability and trigger systemic change. That idealistic faith had gotten her killed by a predator who understood that controlling information and silencing threats was easier than actually reforming his behavior.

But Cassie's death wouldn't be meaningless. The investigation she'd conducted would serve a different purpose than public exposure and institutional reform. It would provide Alira with the comprehensive intelligence she needed to eliminate Coach Robert Daniels with the same methodical precision she'd applied to Dr. Marcus Webb's death.

That evening, alone in her hotel room with Cassie's investigative files spread across the bed, Alira made the decision that would transform her from cautious planner into active hunter. She would kill Coach Robert Daniels not just for what he'd done to his dozens of victims, but specifically for murdering Cassie when her investigation had threatened to expose his crimes and destroy the comfortable impunity he'd enjoyed for over a decade.

The system had failed Sierra by protecting Dr. Webb, and Alira had delivered consequences through careful poisoning that appeared to be natural cardiac death. Now the system had failed Cassie by protecting Coach Daniels and dismissing her murder as suicide, and Alira would deliver even more devastating consequences through methods that would demonstrate her evolving sophistication as a hunter of predators.

Cassie's funeral was held on a gray Saturday morning with rain that seemed appropriate for saying goodbye to someone whose bright idealism had been extinguished by institutional corruption and predatory violence. Their parents were destroyed with grief, unable to comprehend why their youngest daughter—who'd had everything to live for and had seemed so happy and engaged with her work—would have taken her own life.

Alira didn't correct their misunderstanding. Let them believe Cassie had succumbed to academic pressure rather than understanding that their daughter had been murdered for threatening to expose a powerful predator. The truth would be too devastating, and it wouldn't change the fundamental reality that Cassie was gone and would never publish the stories she'd been so passionate about telling.

Sierra attended the funeral with her care facility supervisor, sitting quietly in the family section with tears streaming down her face. Her damaged cognitive capacity couldn't fully comprehend death and loss in adult ways, but she understood on some fundamental level that Cassie was gone and wouldn't be coming back.

After the service, as mourners gathered in the cemetery, Sierra approached Alira with unusual purposefulness. She grabbed her sister's hand and spoke with the kind of clarity that sometimes emerged from her damaged consciousness.

"The bad man killed Cassie," Sierra said, her voice losing its childlike quality and becoming focused and certain. "Like the bad man hurt me. The bad men keep hurting good people, and nobody stops them except you. You have to stop the bad man who killed Cassie. You have to make him go away like you made the bad man who hurt me go away."

It was the most sophisticated and accurate analysis Sierra had managed since her assault, demonstrating that somewhere in her fragmented consciousness, she understood exactly what had happened to Cassie and what Alira's response needed to be.

"I will," Alira promised, squeezing her sister's hand. "The bad man who killed Cassie will face consequences, just like the bad man who hurt you faced consequences. I'm going to make sure he can't hurt anyone else."

Sierra nodded with childlike satisfaction, her clarity already fading but her essential message delivered. "Good. Cassie would want you to stop him. She was trying to stop him with her writing, but he was too strong. So now you have to stop him your way."

As Alira drove back to her apartment that evening, she carried both Cassie's investigative files and Sierra's blessing for what she was about to do. Her sisters' suffering had created her, shaped her into a weapon of justice that could reach predators the law could never touch.

Coach Robert Daniels had destroyed dozens of women's lives and had murdered Cassie when she'd threatened to expose his crimes. Now he would learn what happened when predators encountered someone who understood that some forms of justice required working entirely outside the institutional systems that protected powerful men from accountability.

The second kill was about to be planned and executed, and it would demonstrate Alira's growing sophistication as a hunter of predators who operated with comprehensive impunity until someone decided they deserved to face consequences regardless of how thoroughly they'd corrupted the systems designed to hold them responsible.

Chapter 5

The Sister's Files

Alira spent the two weeks following Cassie's funeral in New York, ostensibly making final arrangements for her sister's estate but actually conducting an intensive investigation into Coach Robert Daniels and the circumstances of Cassie's murder. She'd rented a small studio apartment in Brooklyn under a false name, creating a temporary operational base where she could work without family oversight or institutional scrutiny.

The apartment became a command center filled with Cassie's investigative files, additional research materials Alira had gathered, and the forensic analysis she was conducting into exactly how Cassie's death had been staged to appear like suicide. Every surface was covered with documents, photographs, timelines, and analytical notes as Alira reconstructed both the murder and the broader pattern of Daniels's predatory behavior.

Cassie's files were comprehensive and devastating. Over six months of investigation, her sister had interviewed nine women who'd been victimized by Daniels, obtained confidential settlement agreements that documented Columbia's systematic protection of a serial predator, and gathered evidence that would have destroyed Daniels's career and potentially resulted in criminal prosecution if the story had been published.

Jessica Martinez had been Daniels's most recent victim before he'd begun targeting a sophomore named Amanda Chen. Jessica was a track athlete who'd been recruited to Columbia on a full scholarship, her athletic talent matched by academic excellence that had made her one of the university's most promising students. She'd arrived on campus eager to prove herself worthy of the opportunity, determined to excel both athletically and academically.

Daniels had identified Jessica within weeks of her arrival, recognizing the familiar pattern of vulnerability— a talented athlete from a working-class background, isolated from family support, desperate to maintain the scholarship that represented her only path to higher education. He'd offered special coaching sessions, individual training programs, and promises of connections to professional scouts and Olympic development programs.

The grooming process had been gradual and sophisticated. Daniels had established himself as a mentor figure, someone who uniquely understood Jessica's potential and was invested in helping her achieve greatness. He'd arranged for her to receive academic tutoring, had introduced her to influential alumni donors, had provided equipment and training resources that other athletes didn't receive.

Jessica had been grateful and trusting, interpreting Daniels's attention as evidence that she was special, that her talent justified the extra investment he was making in her development. She hadn't recognized the predatory pattern until it was too late, until Daniels's boundary violations had progressed from inappropriate comments to unwanted physical contact to explicit sexual demands.

The assault had occurred during a supposed training session in Daniels's private office, a space within the athletic complex where he could control access and ensure privacy. He'd drugged Jessica's sports drink—she was certain about this even though she'd never been able to prove it—rendering her cognitively impaired and physically weak while technically conscious.

Daniels had raped her while she was incapacitated, documenting parts of the assault with photographs that he later used as leverage to ensure her silence. The photos showed Jessica in compromising positions but didn't include Daniels himself, creating evidence that could be weaponized to humiliate and discredit her if she ever tried to report what had happened.

When Jessica had threatened to go to authorities, Daniels had calmly explained exactly how such a report would destroy her life while leaving his intact. He'd described the photographic evidence he possessed, the character witnesses who would testify to his professionalism and integrity, the institutional resources he could deploy to paint her as a troubled student seeking attention or revenge for poor athletic performance.

More devastatingly, Daniels had explained that reporting him would result in the loss of her athletic scholarship. Columbia's policies allowed the athletic department to revoke scholarships for students who brought negative attention to the program or created "disruptive conflicts" with coaching staff. Jessica would lose not just her athletic opportunities but her entire education, returning to her working-class family with student loan debt and no degree.

Jessica had remained silent for eight months, enduring continued exploitation while trying to maintain her athletic performance and academic standing. But the psychological toll had become unbearable, and she'd finally approached Cassie after seeing one of her journalism articles about institutional failures in addressing sexual misconduct.

The other eight women Cassie had interviewed described remarkably similar experiences—grooming through mentorship, boundary violations disguised as professional coaching, sexual assault facilitated through drugging or coercion, and systematic threats that prevented victims from reporting to authorities or seeking institutional accountability.

Most devastatingly, Cassie's investigation had revealed that Columbia University administrators had known about Daniels's pattern for over a decade. The confidential settlement agreements she'd obtained—leaked by a sympathetic attorney who worked in the university's general counsel office—showed payments totaling $2.3 million to silence at least eleven victims between 2008 and 2022.

The settlements followed a consistent template. Victims received financial compensation ranging from $75,000 to $350,000, depending on the severity of their assault and their perceived credibility. In exchange, they signed comprehensive non-disclosure agreements that prevented them from discussing Daniels's conduct with anyone—not just media and law enforcement, but also therapists, family members, or future employers who might ask why they'd left Columbia's athletic program.

The NDAs contained provisions that effectively isolated victims from support systems and prevented them from healing through therapeutic processing of their trauma. Some agreements even included clauses requiring victims to deny Daniels's misconduct if directly asked, forcing them to protect their abuser through active lies rather than simply maintaining silence.

Most troubling were the internal university communications Cassie had obtained showing that administrators had deliberately chosen to protect Daniels rather than implement meaningful disciplinary action. Email exchanges between the athletic director, the university president, and general counsel revealed explicit discussions about how settlement payments were cheaper and less reputationally damaging than conducting formal Title IX investigations that might result in Daniels's termination.

One email from the athletic director to the university president had been particularly damning:

Coach Daniels's teams generate approximately $12 million annually in ticket sales, media rights, and donor contributions. His termination would likely result in significant decline in program revenue and alumni engagement. The settlements we've negotiated are a cost-effective approach to managing these situations while preserving the program's competitive and financial performance.

The calculation was explicit and grotesque—victims' lives and wellbeing were worth less than the revenue Daniels generated through successful football teams. Columbia had effectively determined that serial sexual assault was an acceptable cost of maintaining athletic excellence and donor relationships, as long as the victims could be silenced through confidential financial agreements.

Alira spent hours studying these documents, documenting the comprehensive institutional betrayal that had enabled Daniels to operate with impunity for over a decade. The legal system had failed his victims by imposing evidentiary standards that made successful prosecution nearly impossible. The university had failed by prioritizing revenue over student safety. The athletic department had failed by protecting a predator whose success on the field apparently justified any amount of personal misconduct.

But Alira's research extended beyond Cassie's investigative files to examine the specific circumstances of her sister's murder. She used her biochemistry background to analyze the forensic evidence with professional precision, identifying details that NYPD had either missed or deliberately ignored during their cursory investigation.

The scopolamine found in Cassie's toxicology screening was particularly significant. The drug caused temporary cognitive impairment and extreme suggestibility while leaving victims technically conscious and apparently cooperative. It was commonly called "devil's breath" in criminal contexts, used in South America for robbery and sexual assault scenarios where victims needed to appear willing participants while actually being pharmacologically incapable of meaningful resistance.

The presence of scopolamine in Cassie's system was impossible to explain through accidental exposure or recreational use. The drug wasn't available legally in the United States except through very limited medical applications, and it certainly wasn't something a journalism student would have reason to consume voluntarily. Its presence strongly suggested that Cassie had been drugged to make her compliant during a staged suicide.

The dosage calculations were particularly revealing. Based on Cassie's body weight and the concentration found in her blood, Alira estimated she'd been given approximately 3-4 milligrams of scopolamine—enough to produce profound cognitive impairment and suggestibility but not enough to cause complete unconsciousness or obvious physical symptoms that would alert witnesses.

Someone with sophisticated knowledge of pharmacology had calculated the precise dose needed to make Cassie compliant and controllable while maintaining the appearance of normal consciousness. This level of pharmaceutical expertise wasn't something a typical criminal would possess—it suggested either medical training or access to consultants who understood how to weaponize drugs for criminal purposes.

Alira also conducted detailed analysis of the ligature marks on Cassie's neck, using her martial arts knowledge and forensic understanding to interpret the physical evidence. The irregular pattern of bruising— areas of deep tissue damage interspersed with areas of lighter contact—was inconsistent with continuous hanging and strongly suggested manual strangulation with periodic adjustment of grip pressure.

The defensive wounds on Cassie's hands told a similar story. The cuts and abrasions on her knuckles showed directionality and depth consistent with striking hard surfaces—someone's face, chest, or arms during a struggle. These weren't the kind of injuries someone got from flailing against a closet rod during oxygen deprivation. They were fighting injuries, evidence that Cassie had battled her attacker before the scopolamine and physical restraint had overcome her resistance.

Most tellingly, Alira's examination of the crime scene photographs revealed a detail that NYPD had apparently missed or dismissed. The braided bed sheet used as the ligature showed fiber evidence inconsistent with Cassie's bedding. Microscopic analysis of the photographs suggested the sheet had been brought to the scene rather than taken from Cassie's own bed, indicating premeditation and planning rather than spontaneous suicidal impulse.

The cumulative evidence was overwhelming and damning. Cassie had been drugged with scopolamine to make her compliant, manually strangled while she fought against her attacker, and then staged in a hanging position to simulate suicide. The killer had been sophisticated enough to use pharmaceutical agents that wouldn't be detected in routine toxicology screening and had been careful enough to create a crime scene that superficially appeared consistent with self-inflicted death.

But the evidence also revealed the killer's limitations and vulnerabilities. The scopolamine use suggested someone with medical or pharmaceutical knowledge but not necessarily professional training—the dosage was effective but not optimally calculated, leaving higher concentrations in Cassie's blood than would have been ideal for complete concealment. The staging was competent but not perfect, leaving forensic inconsistencies that a more thorough investigation would have revealed.

Alira spent additional weeks researching Coach Robert Daniels's background, connections, and potential access to resources needed for pharmaceutical murder. What she discovered was both predictable and disturbing.

Daniels had extensive connections to Columbia's medical school and athletic medicine program. He regularly consulted with sports medicine physicians about player health and performance optimization, had access to the athletic training facilities where controlled substances were stored, and had cultivated relationships with pharmacology researchers who studied performance-enhancing drugs and their effects.

Most significantly, Daniels had a close personal relationship with Dr. Vincent Cross, a prominent surgeon affiliated with Columbia who specialized in sports medicine and had a documented history of providing athletes with pharmaceutical enhancements that pushed ethical and legal boundaries. Cross had been investigated multiple times for prescribing controlled substances without appropriate medical justification, but his connections within the medical establishment had consistently protected him from serious consequences.

Alira's research suggested that Cross had likely provided Daniels with the scopolamine used to drug Cassie, along with technical consultation about dosage and administration methods. The two men's relationship was well-documented through social media, alumni events, and Columbia athletic department functions where Cross served as team physician and medical advisor.

The connection was significant because it suggested that Cassie's murder hadn't been a spontaneous act of desperation but rather a calculated operation conducted with professional resources and expertise. Daniels had identified the threat Cassie posed, had consulted with Cross about methods for eliminating that threat while minimizing detection risk, and had executed a pharmaceutical murder that would have succeeded in avoiding investigation if not for Alira's forensic knowledge and determination to uncover the truth.

As Alira's investigation progressed, she began receiving threatening messages that confirmed her suspicions about who was responsible for Cassie's death. The messages arrived through various channels— anonymous emails, burner phone texts, notes left on her car windshield—all carrying the same essential warning.

Your sister's investigation died with her. Don't make the same mistake she did. Some people are too powerful to challenge through journalism or amateur detective work. Go home and forget about Columbia athletics.

The messages were unsigned but their origin was obvious. Daniels knew that Alira was investigating Cassie's death and was attempting to intimidate her into abandoning the inquiry before she uncovered evidence that might trigger genuine law enforcement scrutiny. The threats were sophisticated enough to avoid explicit admissions while making the implicit warning unmistakable.

But the messages had the opposite effect from what Daniels intended. Rather than frightening Alira into retreat, they confirmed that she was on the right track and that Daniels was concerned enough about her investigation to attempt intimidation. More importantly, they demonstrated that Daniels believed threats and warnings would be sufficient to neutralize her as a threat—he was applying the same tactics that had worked with previous victims without recognizing that Alira represented something fundamentally different from the young athletes and journalists he'd successfully silenced before.

On her final day in New York before returning home to begin planning Daniels's elimination, Alira met again with Jessica Martinez in a secure location where they could speak without surveillance or monitoring. Jessica had been following Alira's investigation through encrypted communications, providing additional intelligence about Daniels's current activities and vulnerabilities.

"He knows you're investigating him," Jessica said without preamble. "He's told people on the athletic department staff to watch for anyone asking questions about him or about Cassie's death. He's also started being more careful about his movements—varying his routines, checking his car for tracking devices, being paranoid about who he meets with privately."

"Good," Alira replied. "Paranoid predators make mistakes because they're operating outside their comfort zones. Daniels has spent a decade feeling completely secure in his institutional protections. Now he's worried, and worried people do stupid things."

"What are you going to do?" Jessica asked, though her tone suggested she already understood the answer.

"I'm going to ensure Coach Daniels faces consequences that the legal system and Columbia administration refuse to provide," Alira said plainly. "He murdered my sister because she threatened to expose his crimes. He's destroyed dozens of women's lives through systematic sexual exploitation. He operates with complete impunity because institutions value his athletic success more than his victims' wellbeing. That pattern is going to end."

Jessica nodded slowly, her expression showing a mixture of satisfaction, fear, and moral complexity. "I can't officially support extrajudicial action. But I can tell you that if something happened to Coach Daniels— something that made it impossible for him to hurt anyone else—a lot of women would sleep better at night even if they couldn't publicly celebrate his death."

"I understand," Alira said. "And I want you to know that when Daniels faces consequences, it won't be in ways that expose you or the other victims to scrutiny or retaliation. His death will appear completely unconnected to his predatory behavior, just another middle-aged man whose lifestyle finally caught up with him."

"How will you do it?" Jessica asked, genuine curiosity mixing with evident respect for Alira's operational sophistication.

"The same way I eliminated the man who destroyed my older sister's mind," Alira replied. "Through methods that appear entirely natural, that won't trigger investigation or create patterns that might eventually lead investigators back to me. Daniels will die believing it's a random medical emergency, never understanding that he's being punished for crimes that the legal system refused to address."

Jessica reached into her bag and pulled out a thick folder of documents. "These are Coach's medical records from the athletic department health services. I work part-time in the admin office and have access to confidential files. I thought they might be useful for... whatever you're planning."

Alira accepted the folder, immediately recognizing its operational value. Medical records would reveal Daniels's health vulnerabilities, medications, allergies, and any conditions that could be exploited to create deaths that appeared natural. This was exactly the kind of intelligence that would allow her to plan an elimination with professional precision.

"Thank you," Alira said sincerely. "This will help ensure that when Daniels faces consequences, they'll be delivered in ways that don't create collateral damage or expose the women he's victimized to additional scrutiny."

"Your sister would be proud of what you're doing," Jessica said quietly. "Cassie believed in institutional reform and journalistic exposure, but I think if she could see how comprehensively those approaches failed, she'd understand why more direct action is necessary. Some predators are too well-protected to be stopped through conventional means."

As Alira drove back to her apartment that evening, she carried both Cassie's investigative files and the operational intelligence Jessica had provided about Daniels's medical history and current vulnerabilities. The research phase was complete—she understood her target's pattern, his crimes, his institutional protections, and the specific circumstances that had led to Cassie's murder.

Now it was time to plan the execution with the same meticulous precision she'd applied to Dr. Marcus Webb's death, but with significantly more sophisticated methods that reflected her growing expertise as a hunter of protected predators.

Coach Robert Daniels had murdered Cassie because she'd threatened to expose his crimes through journalism and institutional accountability. He would die because Alira had learned that some forms of justice required working entirely outside the systems that protected powerful men from consequences, delivering punishment through methods that appeared natural while actually representing carefully calculated retribution for crimes that legal frameworks consistently failed to address.

The investigation was complete, and the planning for Daniels's elimination was about to begin.

POENA *Punishment*

———

"The mills of God grind slowly, but they grind exceedingly fine." — Henry Wadsworth Longfellow

Chapter 6

The Coach's Last Season

Coach Robert Daniels was a significantly more challenging target than Dr. Marcus Webb had been, requiring Alira to develop methods and approaches that went far beyond the relatively simple poisoned tea delivery that had eliminated her first victim. Daniels was younger—fifty-three compared to Webb's sixty-two— more physically fit from his athletic background, and surrounded by a network of supporters and institutional protections that made him constantly vigilant about potential threats to his carefully constructed public image.

More problematically, Daniels had become paranoid after Cassie's death, apparently recognizing on some level that eliminating a journalist who'd been investigating him might attract unwanted attention from her family members or colleagues. He'd begun varying his routines, checking his office and car for surveillance devices, and being cautious about accepting food or drink from sources he couldn't verify personally.

Alira spent six months planning Daniels's death, studying his routines with the patience of a predator who understood that hasty action created mistakes and that mistakes created patterns that investigators might eventually recognize. She conducted surveillance from multiple positions around Columbia's campus and Daniels's personal residences, documenting his movements with photographic precision and identifying the vulnerabilities in his security protocols.

The research revealed that Daniels was indeed more cautious than he'd been before Cassie's investigation, but his caution followed predictable patterns rather than representing genuine operational security. He varied his routes to and from campus but always within a limited set of options. He checked his office for listening devices but used consumer-grade detection equipment that wouldn't identify sophisticated surveillance. He was careful about accepting drinks from strangers but completely trusting of substances provided by familiar sources within his social and professional networks.

Most importantly, Daniels maintained habits and routines that were deeply ingrained despite his increased vigilance. He arrived at Columbia's athletic complex every morning at 5:15 AM for his personal workout, always alone in the facility before the coaching staff and student athletes arrived for their scheduled training sessions. He prepared his own pre-workout protein shake using supplements and powders he kept in his private office, mixing the concoction in a dedicated blender that he cleaned meticulously after each use.

The morning routine was sacred to Daniels—he'd described it in numerous interviews as his "meditation practice," the private time when he centered himself mentally and physically before engaging with the demands of coaching a Division I football program. He was proud of his discipline and consistency, boasting that he'd maintained the same 5:15 AM workout schedule for over fifteen years regardless of season, travel schedule, or personal circumstances.

That rigid consistency was exactly the vulnerability Alira needed to exploit.

The breakthrough came when Alira discovered Daniels's severe allergy to shellfish—information buried in his medical records that Jessica had provided. The allergy was well-documented, with notes from multiple physicians warning that Daniels had experienced anaphylactic reactions to even trace amounts of shellfish protein. He carried an EpiPen at all times and was meticulous about reading ingredient labels on packaged foods to avoid accidental exposure.

Most people with severe shellfish allergies knew to avoid eating seafood, but few realized that shellfish-derived compounds appeared in numerous non-food products including certain supplements, cosmetics, and pharmaceutical preparations. The glucosamine commonly used in joint health supplements was frequently derived from shellfish chitin, and many protein powders contained shellfish-based ingredients that weren't always clearly labeled or identified.

Alira's pharmaceutical knowledge allowed her to recognize an elegant solution to the Daniels problem. She could create a contaminated supplement that would trigger a fatal allergic reaction while appearing to be nothing more than a tragic accident—a manufacturing defect or labeling error that had inadvertently exposed someone with a known severe allergy to the exact substance that could kill him.

The method would be perfect because it exploited Daniels's own health-conscious behaviors rather than requiring her to gain access to him personally. He prepared his protein shake every morning using supplements he believed were safe, mixing the powder in his private office where no one could tamper with his carefully controlled nutrition regimen. All Alira needed to do was replace his legitimate protein powder with a contaminated version that contained concentrated shellfish extract disguised among the standard amino acid compounds.

Creating the contaminated supplement required sophisticated pharmaceutical knowledge and access to specialized equipment, but Alira had both through her graduate program in forensic toxicology. She used her university laboratory access—ostensibly for her thesis research on detecting contaminants in nutritional supplements—to extract and concentrate shellfish proteins to levels far exceeding what would occur naturally in standard supplement formulations.

The process took several weeks of meticulous work. Alira obtained fresh shellfish from multiple sources, extracted the allergenic proteins using enzymatic digestion and centrifugation, then concentrated the extracts through freeze-drying and chemical stabilization. The resulting powder was odorless, tasteless, and visually indistinguishable from the whey protein and amino acid compounds commonly used in athletic supplements.

Most importantly, the shellfish extract was potent enough that even a single serving of contaminated protein powder would deliver allergenic compounds far exceeding the threshold for triggering anaphylaxis in someone with Daniels's documented sensitivity level. His body would react immediately and catastrophically, his immune system mounting an overwhelming response that would cause airway swelling, blood pressure collapse, and ultimately death unless he received immediate emergency medical intervention.

The challenge was delivering the contaminated supplement in ways that would ensure Daniels actually consumed it while creating plausible deniability about how the contamination had occurred. Alira couldn't simply break into his office and replace his protein powder—that would create obvious evidence of tampering and would trigger investigation into who had access to his private space.

Instead, she needed to exploit Daniels's ego and his susceptibility to products marketed as cutting-edge athletic performance enhancement. Over several months of studying his supplement consumption patterns, Alira had identified that Daniels was constantly experimenting with new products that promised improved recovery, enhanced energy, or optimized body composition. He subscribed to numerous fitness and nutrition industry publications, attended supplement trade shows, and eagerly tried samples from companies claiming to offer revolutionary formulations.

Alira created an entirely fictional sports nutrition company called "Apex Performance Labs," complete with professional-looking website, social media presence, and marketing materials that mimicked legitimate supplement manufacturers. The company claimed to offer "next-generation protein formulations" developed through "proprietary extraction and bioavailability enhancement processes" that provided superior results compared to conventional supplements.

She designed product packaging that looked impressively professional—glossy containers with scientifically sophisticated labeling, ingredient lists that featured impressive-sounding but meaningless compound names, and testimonials from fictional athletes who claimed extraordinary results. Everything about Apex Performance Labs screamed legitimacy and cutting-edge innovation, exactly the kind of brand that would appeal to Daniels's competitive nature and his desire to maintain physical excellence despite his advancing age.

The marketing approach was carefully calculated to overcome Daniels's increased caution about accepting products from unknown sources. Alira sent him an elaborate "VIP sample package" that included not just contaminated protein powder but also legitimate supplements—vitamins, minerals, amino acids—that would test as completely safe and appropriate. The package included a personalized letter explaining that Apex Performance Labs was conducting a limited trial with elite coaches and athletes, offering free products in exchange for feedback and potential endorsement.

The letter emphasized exclusivity and flattery, positioning Daniels as exactly the kind of influential figure whose opinion would be valuable for establishing the brand's credibility within the athletic performance community. It included fake testimonials from other prominent coaches who'd supposedly achieved remarkable results, along with scientific-sounding explanations for why Apex's formulations were superior to conventional supplements.

Most critically, the package included detailed ingredient lists and third-party testing certificates showing that all products were free from banned substances and common allergens. The shellfish extract wasn't listed because it was hidden within a proprietary blend of "bioavailable amino acid complexes"—vague but scientifically plausible language that supplement companies routinely used to obscure their actual formulations.

Daniels' ego and competitiveness made him exactly the kind of target who would be susceptible to this approach. He prided himself on being at the cutting edge of sports science and performance optimization, constantly seeking advantages that would help him maintain the physical prowess that had defined his identity throughout his adult life. The offer to be part of an exclusive trial program for a revolutionary new supplement line would appeal to both his vanity and his genuine interest in athletic performance.

Alira mailed the Apex Performance Labs package to Daniels's home address in early October, timing the delivery to coincide with the middle of football season when Daniels would be particularly focused on maintaining his energy and physical capabilities despite the grueling schedule of coaching a Division I program. She tracked the package through the shipping system, confirming that it had been delivered and signed for by Daniels personally.

Then she waited, maintaining surveillance on Daniels's morning routines to identify when he would begin using the contaminated supplements. The surveillance required patience and discipline—Alira positioned herself in various locations around Columbia's athletic complex during pre-dawn hours, using telephoto photography to observe Daniels through the windows of his private office as he prepared his morning protein shake.

For the first week after the package delivery, Daniels continued using his regular supplements, apparently waiting to finish his current supply before opening the new products. Alira documented each morning's routine with photographic precision, noting exactly which supplement containers he used and how he prepared his pre-workout shake.

On the eighth day after package delivery—a Tuesday morning in mid-October—Alira observed through her telephoto lens as Daniels opened the Apex Performance Labs protein powder container and examined the product with evident interest. He read the label carefully, smelled the powder to assess its quality, then set it aside while he continued his usual morning routine.

The following morning, Daniels prepared his protein shake using the contaminated Apex supplement. Alira watched through her camera lens as he measured out two scoops of the powder, added them to his blender along with water and other ingredients, and mixed everything into the smooth consistency he preferred. He drank the shake while checking his phone and reviewing notes for the day's practice schedule, showing no awareness that he'd just consumed a lethal dose of concentrated shellfish allergen.

The allergic reaction began within minutes. Alira observed as Daniels's expression shifted from routine concentration to confusion and then alarm as he began experiencing the first symptoms of anaphylaxis. His breathing became labored, his face flushing red as his blood pressure spiked in the initial phase of the immune response. He stood up from his desk, one hand going to his throat as his airway began to swell.

Daniels reached for his gym bag where he kept his EpiPen—the emergency epinephrine injector that had saved his life during previous accidental exposures to shellfish. But the concentration of allergen Alira had incorporated into the protein powder was far higher than what would occur through accidental contamination in restaurant food or mislabeled products. The shellfish extract was pharmaceutical-grade and deliberately concentrated to levels that would overwhelm even aggressive emergency intervention.

Alira watched through her camera as Daniels fumbled with his EpiPen, his hands shaking and his coordination deteriorating as anaphylaxis progressed rapidly through his cardiovascular and respiratory systems. He managed to inject himself with the epinephrine, but the dose was insufficient to counter the massive allergic response that was already closing his airway and collapsing his blood pressure.

Daniels staggered toward the door of his office, apparently trying to reach the main athletic complex where early-arriving athletes or staff might be able to call for emergency help. But the anaphylaxis was progressing too quickly, his airway swelling shut faster than the epinephrine could counteract the immune cascade. He collapsed just inside his office doorway, his body convulsing as oxygen deprivation affected his brain and his heart struggled to maintain function despite catastrophically low blood pressure.

By the time the first athletes arrived at the athletic complex at 6:15 AM—exactly one hour after Daniels had consumed the contaminated protein shake—he had been in full anaphylactic shock for approximately forty minutes. They found him unconscious on the floor of his office, his face swollen and cyanotic, his breathing completely absent, his EpiPen lying useless beside his body.

The athletes called 911 immediately, and paramedics arrived within eight minutes. They attempted resuscitation, administering additional epinephrine and providing advanced airway support, but Daniels had been without adequate oxygen for too long. His brain had suffered irreversible damage from prolonged hypoxia, and his heart had sustained injury from the combination of anaphylactic shock and oxygen deprivation.

Daniels was transported to Columbia Presbyterian Hospital where he was placed on life support, but the neurological damage was catastrophic and irreversible. After forty-eight hours of monitoring showing no brain activity and no prospect of meaningful recovery, his family made the decision to withdraw life support. Coach Robert Daniels was pronounced dead at 3:47 PM on Thursday, October 19th, approximately sixty hours after consuming the contaminated protein shake.

The medical examiner's investigation was thorough and professional, exactly as Alira had anticipated. The autopsy revealed all the classic signs of fatal anaphylactic reaction—massive airway edema, pulmonary congestion, cardiovascular collapse. Toxicology screening showed the presence of shellfish proteins in Daniels's stomach contents and bloodstream at concentrations far higher than would be expected from accidental contamination.

The investigation focused on identifying the source of shellfish exposure, given Daniels's well-documented allergy and his usual meticulous attention to avoiding allergenic foods and products. Investigators examined his recent meals, reviewed his supplement regimen, and tested samples from all the nutrition products found in his office.

The Apex Performance Labs protein powder tested positive for shellfish-derived compounds at concentrations approximately fifty times higher than what would be considered safe for someone with severe allergies. The medical examiner concluded that the supplement contained either a manufacturing defect or a deliberate contamination that had exposed Daniels to lethal levels of the allergen he'd spent decades carefully avoiding.

The investigation shifted to examining Apex Performance Labs and how Daniels had come to receive their contaminated product. But the company investigation hit immediate dead ends—the website had been taken down within hours of Daniels's death, the social media accounts had been deleted, and the business address listed on the product packaging led to a commercial mail drop that had been rented under a false identity using forged credentials.

The sample package had been mailed from a postal facility three states away, paid for with cash, and sent through normal commercial shipping that left no useful forensic trail. The product packaging and materials contained no fingerprints or DNA evidence that could identify who had created the contaminated supplement or why they'd targeted Daniels specifically.

Investigators briefly considered the possibility that Daniels had been deliberately murdered through contaminated supplements, but several factors argued against that theory. First, there was no obvious suspect with both motive and the sophisticated pharmaceutical knowledge required to create such a targeted poison. Second, the packaging and marketing materials suggested an elaborate scam operation rather than a murder plot—perhaps a fraudulent supplement company that had used inferior or contaminated ingredients to save money rather than deliberately targeting Daniels for assassination.

Most importantly, Daniels's death appeared to be exactly what it seemed on the surface—a tragic accident where a man with severe allergies had consumed a product that should have been safe but which contained hidden allergens due to either manufacturing defects or unscrupulous business practices. The medical evidence supported accidental death, the investigative trail led nowhere useful, and there was no pattern connecting Daniels's death to other suspicious incidents that might suggest a serial poisoner.

The case was ultimately closed as accidental death caused by anaphylactic reaction to contaminated nutritional supplements, with a recommendation that the FDA investigate supplement industry quality control practices to prevent similar tragedies in the future.

Columbia University held a memorial service celebrating Daniels's twenty-eight years of service to the athletic program, his three conference championships, and his supposed dedication to developing young athletes both on and off the field. University administrators delivered eulogies praising his coaching excellence and his mentorship of student athletes, carefully avoiding any mention of the settlement payments, the silenced victims, or the institutional protections that had enabled his predatory behavior for nearly three decades.

Alira attended the memorial service, sitting in the back of the auditorium and watching the proceedings with carefully controlled satisfaction as administrators and former players celebrated a man whose death had freed dozens of women from ongoing fear and potential future victimization. She noticed that none of Daniels's known victims attended the service—Jessica Martinez and the other athletes Cassie had interviewed were conspicuously absent from the celebration of their predator's life and career.

Their absence spoke volumes about Daniels's true legacy, even if the assembled mourners were too invested in maintaining comfortable fictions to acknowledge what that absence actually meant.

After the service, as attendees gathered outside the auditorium, Alira observed several women who appeared to be former athletes or staff members standing together at a distance from the main crowd. They weren't crying or expressing grief—instead, they spoke quietly among themselves with expressions that suggested relief rather than sorrow, liberation rather than loss.

One of those women was Jessica Martinez, who caught Alira's eye and gave her the slightest nod of acknowledgment and gratitude. The gesture was subtle enough that no one else would notice, but its meaning was unmistakable—Jessica understood that Daniels's death hadn't been an accident, that someone had delivered consequences that the legal system and Columbia administration had consistently refused to provide.

As Alira left the memorial service and drove back to her apartment, she reflected on how the second elimination had demonstrated her growing sophistication as a hunter of protected predators. Webb's death had been relatively crude—a straightforward poisoning that worked because Webb had no reason to be cautious about consuming tea from a supposed grateful former student. But Daniels had required a far more elaborate approach, exploiting his ego and competitive nature through an entirely fabricated supplement company while delivering a poison that would appear to be nothing more than a tragic manufacturing accident.

The method had worked perfectly, creating a death that seemed completely natural and accidental while actually representing carefully calculated punishment for crimes that had destroyed Cassie's life along with the lives of dozens of other women Daniels had victimized throughout his career.

That evening, Alira visited Sierra at her care facility, finding her sister working on a paint-by-numbers picture of a lighthouse overlooking an ocean. Sierra looked up with her characteristic unfiltered joy when Alira entered the common room, but that joy quickly shifted to something more focused and purposeful as she processed her sister's presence.

"You stopped the bad man," Sierra said without preamble, her voice losing its usual childlike quality and becoming clear and certain. "The bad man who hurt Cassie. You made him go away like you made the bad man who hurt me go away."

The insight was remarkable given Sierra's documented cognitive limitations, suggesting that somewhere in her damaged consciousness she maintained fragments of awareness about what Alira was doing and why it mattered.

"Yes," Alira confirmed quietly, understanding that Sierra deserved honesty even if she couldn't fully comprehend all the implications. "The bad man who killed Cassie won't hurt anyone else. He faced consequences for what he did, even though the legal system refused to hold him accountable."

Sierra nodded with childlike satisfaction, then returned her attention to her painting. "Good. Cassie would be happy that the bad man can't hurt people anymore. She was trying to stop him with her writing, but the bad man was too strong and too protected. So you had to stop him your way instead."

"That's exactly right," Alira said, sitting beside her sister and watching her apply careful brushstrokes to the designated areas of the canvas. "Sometimes the only way to protect people from predators is to eliminate the predators completely, especially when all the institutions that are supposed to provide protection have failed."

They sat together in comfortable silence, Sierra focused on her painting while Alira processed the moral weight of what she'd accomplished. Two predators eliminated—Webb and Daniels—and dozens of women freed from ongoing victimization and fear. The legal system had failed comprehensively in both cases, but Alira had delivered consequences through methods that appeared entirely natural while actually representing sophisticated justice for crimes that institutional frameworks consistently refused to address.

The mission was evolving and expanding. Alira had begun as a grieving sister seeking revenge for Sierra's assault, but she'd transformed into something more systematic and purposeful—a hunter of protected predators who would continue eliminating powerful men until either she was caught or institutions reformed themselves sufficiently that extrajudicial action was no longer necessary to protect vulnerable women from predatory violence.

Webb and Daniels were dead, their victims liberated, and their institutional protectors left scrambling to explain how they'd failed to prevent tragedies that were actually carefully orchestrated eliminations. And somewhere in the city, other predators continued operating with similar impunity, unaware that a systematic hunter was studying their patterns and preparing to deliver consequences they believed their power and privilege would always prevent.

The second sin was complete, and Alira Sinclair was ready to continue her work with increasing sophistication and expanding scope.

MEMORIA *Memory*

———

"She remembered every name. Every victim. Every unpunished crime."

Chapter 7

The Education Continues

After Daniels's death, Alira completed her graduate degree in forensic toxicology while simultaneously expanding her operational capabilities in ways that would prepare her for increasingly sophisticated eliminations. The dual-track approach—maintaining her legitimate academic and professional identity while developing expertise in undetectable murder—required extraordinary discipline and compartmentalization, but Alira had become skilled at managing the psychological complexity of living two completely separate lives.

Her master's thesis focused on detecting plant-based toxins in criminal investigations, a project that her faculty advisor praised as groundbreaking work with important applications for forensic laboratories struggling to identify exotic poisons in suspicious death cases. What her advisor didn't understand was that Alira's real expertise lay not in detection but in evasion—she was learning exactly which compounds and delivery methods could circumvent standard screening protocols, which toxins left minimal forensic evidence, and which death presentations would be least likely to trigger comprehensive investigation.

The academic work provided perfect cover for research that would have seemed suspicious in any other context. Alira could order exotic botanical specimens, acquire sophisticated chemical extraction equipment, and conduct experiments with lethal compounds while maintaining the fiction that she was developing improved forensic detection methods rather than perfecting murder techniques.

Her martial arts training continued with equal intensity, though she'd shifted her focus from competition-oriented systems to combat applications that emphasized lethal efficiency over sport performance. She'd earned black belts in three different disciplines—karate, Brazilian jiu-jitsu, and Krav Maga—but her real expertise had developed through private instruction with David Rosen, her Krav Maga teacher who understood that Alira was training for offensive operations rather than defensive protection.

Rosen had continued working with Alira after her black belt certification, providing advanced instruction in techniques that went far beyond what he taught in his regular classes. These private sessions focused on killing methods that left minimal forensic evidence, restraint techniques that could render victims unconscious without visible marks, and tactical approaches for creating scenarios that would appear to be self-defense rather than premeditated assault.

"You're one of the most naturally gifted students I've ever trained," Rosen observed during a session in the spring following Daniels's death. "Your technical execution is nearly flawless, your tactical thinking is sophisticated, and your ability to remain calm under pressure is remarkable. But I worry about what you're planning to do with these skills."

"I've told you before," Alira replied, her voice neutral and controlled. "I'm ensuring that predatory men who use power and institutional protection to escape accountability finally face consequences for their crimes."

"And I've told you that taking human life, even justified life, changes you fundamentally," Rosen countered. "I've killed men in combat, men who were actively trying to kill me or my unit. Those deaths were legally and morally justified by any reasonable standard. But they still stay with you, shape how you see the world and yourself in ways that aren't always healthy or sustainable."

Alira considered this for a moment, then asked the question she'd been contemplating since Webb's death. "How many men did you kill during your military service?"

"Twelve that I know of with certainty," Rosen replied without hesitation. "Probably several more in situations where I couldn't confirm kills definitively. All in combat situations where they were enemy combatants trying to harm Israeli forces or civilians."

"Do you regret any of those kills?"

"No," Rosen said immediately. "They were necessary actions in defense of legitimate targets. But I carry them with me nonetheless—their faces, the moments when life left their eyes, the knowledge that I ended human consciousness through deliberate violence. That weight never fully disappears, even when you're certain the actions were justified."

"I've eliminated two men so far," Alira said quietly. "One who destroyed my sister's brilliant mind through sexual assault and traumatic brain injury. One who murdered my younger sister because she was investigating his pattern of predatory behavior. Neither death troubles my conscience in the way you're describing. I feel satisfaction about their elimination, certainty that the world is objectively better without them, but no guilt or moral doubt."

Rosen studied her with an expression that mixed concern and something approaching professional respect. "That lack of guilt could mean you're genuinely comfortable with the moral calculus of killing predators who escape legal accountability. Or it could mean you're suppressing psychological responses that will eventually surface in unhealthy ways. I've seen both patterns in people who kill outside of combat contexts."

"Which do you think applies to me?"

"I honestly don't know," Rosen admitted. "You're one of the most psychologically controlled people I've ever encountered. Either you've achieved genuine moral certainty about your mission, or you're exceptionally skilled at compartmentalization that will eventually fail in catastrophic ways."

The conversation ended without resolution, but it prompted Alira to engage in deeper self-examination about the psychological sustainability of what she was doing. She began keeping a private journal—encrypted and stored securely—documenting her emotional responses to the eliminations she'd conducted and the planning she was doing for future targets.

The journal entries revealed patterns that Alira found both reassuring and slightly troubling. She felt no guilt about Webb's or Daniels's deaths, no nightmares about their final moments, no intrusive thoughts about whether she'd made correct moral choices. Instead, she experienced satisfaction about protecting future victims, intellectual pride in the sophistication of her methods, and determination to continue expanding her operational capabilities.

But the journal also revealed that Alira was becoming increasingly disconnected from conventional moral frameworks and social relationships. She had few close friends outside of her professional and academic circles, maintained only superficial relationships with family members other than Sierra, and found it increasingly difficult to engage meaningfully with people who believed in institutional justice and legal accountability.

The disconnect was functional for her mission—close relationships created vulnerabilities and complications that could compromise operational security. But it also represented a fundamental transformation in her personality and worldview, a shift from the idealistic art history student she'd been before Sierra's assault to something far more isolated and purpose-driven.

During this period, Alira also expanded her knowledge of criminal investigation procedures and forensic techniques, understanding that successfully evading detection required thinking like the investigators who would examine her work. She took courses in criminal justice and forensic science, attended conferences on death investigation and evidence analysis, and cultivated professional relationships with medical examiners and law enforcement personnel who could provide insights into how suspicious deaths were evaluated.

Most significantly, she began studying the psychology and methods of serial killers—not because she identified with their pathologies, but because understanding how they were caught would help her avoid making similar mistakes. She read extensively about successful and unsuccessful serial murderers, analyzing what patterns had led to their capture and what methods had allowed some to operate undetected for years or decades.

The research revealed several consistent patterns. Serial killers who were caught typically made one or more of several characteristic mistakes: they operated within too-narrow geographic areas, creating clustering that triggered investigative attention; they followed rigid patterns in victim selection or killing methods that allowed profilers to predict their behavior; they kept trophies or documentation that provided physical evidence of their crimes; or they demonstrated escalating risk-taking behavior driven by psychological compulsions they couldn't control.

Alira was determined to avoid all of these pitfalls. She would vary her methods significantly between kills, ensuring that investigators wouldn't recognize connections between apparently unrelated deaths. She would space eliminations widely in both time and geography, preventing the kind of clustering that suggested a single perpetrator. She would keep minimal documentation and no physical trophies that could link her to victims. And most importantly, she would maintain operational discipline rather than allowing psychological drives to push her toward increasingly risky behavior.

The research also reinforced Alira's conviction that her mission was fundamentally different from typical serial killing. She wasn't driven by sexual sadism, power fantasies, or psychological compulsions that characterized most serial murderers. She was executing a carefully planned campaign to eliminate specific targets who met precise criteria—powerful predators who'd escaped legal accountability through institutional protection—rather than killing to satisfy irrational psychological needs.

This distinction was important not just for moral clarity but for operational effectiveness. Serial killers who acted on compulsion eventually made mistakes because their psychological drives overrode rational judgment. But Alira could maintain perfect tactical discipline because she wasn't driven by irrational needs—she was implementing a mission based on carefully considered moral principles and strategic objectives.

Sierra's condition remained stable in the permanent sense that had become the new normal for the Sinclair family. Her cognitive capacity showed no improvement over the years since her assault, remaining frozen at approximately the level of a seven-year-old child despite the sophisticated therapeutic interventions and rehabilitation efforts that her care facility provided. She would never recover the brilliant mind that Webb had destroyed, would never complete her doctorate or help the traumatized children she'd dedicated her life to serving.

But during Alira's regular visits—maintained with religious consistency every Tuesday and Friday evening—Sierra occasionally displayed moments of unexpected clarity that suggested her damaged consciousness retained fragments of awareness far beyond what her cognitive testing would indicate.

During one such visit in the summer following Daniels's death, Sierra had looked up from the coloring book she'd been working on and spoken with sudden lucid intensity that always startled Alira despite her familiarity with these periodic episodes.

"You're learning more ways to stop the bad men," Sierra said, her voice losing its childlike quality and becoming focused and purposeful. "Not just the poison way that stopped the bad man who hurt me, and not just the allergy way that stopped the bad man who killed Cassie. You're learning fighting ways and medicine ways and all different ways to make the bad men go away."

The insight was remarkably accurate given Sierra's documented cognitive limitations, demonstrating comprehension of operational concepts that should have been far beyond her intellectual capacity.

"Yes," Alira confirmed, understanding that Sierra deserved honesty even when her damaged mind couldn't fully process complex information. "I'm developing multiple methods for eliminating predators, ensuring that each death appears natural or accidental in ways that won't create patterns investigators might recognize. Different bad men require different approaches based on their vulnerabilities and the institutional protections surrounding them."

Sierra nodded solemnly, her expression showing the simplified moral clarity that her brain injury had somehow left intact even as it destroyed her capacity for complex reasoning. "That's good. That's smart. The bad men are all different, so you have to be different too. Like... like having different tools for different jobs. Hammers for nails, screwdrivers for screws."

The metaphor was surprisingly sophisticated, suggesting that Sierra's damaged mind retained capacity for abstract reasoning that her cognitive testing didn't reveal. Alira had long suspected that standard intelligence assessments couldn't capture the fragmented brilliance that remained in Sierra's consciousness, couldn't measure the intuitive insights that occasionally emerged from her sister's traumatic brain injury.

"Exactly right," Alira said, squeezing Sierra's hand gently. "Different tools for different jobs. Different methods for different predators. And always making sure that each elimination appears completely natural so that investigators don't recognize what's actually happening."

"The angels have to be smart and careful," Sierra said, her clarity already beginning to fade back toward her usual childlike confusion. "The bad men have lots of protection and lots of friends who help them. So the angels have to be smarter and more careful than the bad men and their friends."

"We are," Alira promised. "We're smarter and more careful than any of the predators we're eliminating. That's why they never see us coming."

Sierra smiled with childlike satisfaction, then returned her attention to her coloring book, the moment of lucidity passing as quickly as it had arrived. But Alira carried the conversation with her as validation and encouragement—somewhere in Sierra's damaged consciousness, her brilliant sister understood and approved of the mission that Alira had undertaken.

As Alira's education and training continued, she also began developing her public identity in ways that would provide operational flexibility while maintaining plausible cover for her actual activities. She accepted a position at a prestigious art gallery in the city, leveraging her original art history background to establish legitimate employment that explained her refined tastes, her knowledge of wealthy collectors, and her ability to move freely in elite social circles where many potential targets operated.

The gallery position was perfect operational cover—it required only twenty to thirty hours per week of actual work, provided a credible explanation for her income and lifestyle, and created natural opportunities to meet wealthy and powerful people who might themselves be predators or who might provide intelligence about other targets worth investigating.

Her apartment became a sophisticated command center that would have seemed shocking to anyone who understood its actual purpose. The visible areas were decorated with tasteful artwork and expensive furniture appropriate for someone working in high-end art sales. But the bedroom had been converted into a laboratory and research facility, filled with botanical specimens, chemical extraction equipment, and detailed files on dozens of potential targets.

Alira had identified over forty men who met her criteria for elimination—powerful individuals with documented histories of predatory behavior who'd escaped legal accountability through wealth, institutional protection, or procedural manipulation. Each had a comprehensive file documenting their pattern of abuse, their victims' experiences, and the specific institutional failures that had enabled their continued predatory behavior.

But Alira was patient, understanding that hasty action created patterns that might eventually be recognized by investigators who specialized in identifying serial criminals. She would take her time, choosing targets carefully and spacing eliminations widely enough to avoid creating obvious connections between seemingly unrelated deaths.

Most importantly, she would vary her methods significantly—not just using different toxins or techniques, but fundamentally changing her approach with each target to ensure that no investigator could recognize a consistent pattern suggesting a single perpetrator. Webb had died from plant-based cardiac glycosides. Daniels had died from allergic reaction to shellfish contamination. Future targets would die through completely different mechanisms that exploited their specific vulnerabilities while appearing entirely natural.

Seven years after Sierra's assault and four years after Cassie's murder, Alira had transformed herself into something unprecedented in the annals of criminal behavior—a scientifically trained, martially skilled, forensically sophisticated hunter of protected predators who operated with methodical precision and complete moral certainty about the necessity and justification of her mission.

She had no illusions about the illegality of what she was doing—murder was murder regardless of how morally justified it might be or how comprehensively the legal system had failed to provide alternative accountability. But she also understood that some forms of justice required working entirely outside the institutional frameworks that had proven incapable of or unwilling to protect vulnerable people from predatory violence.

The education phase was complete. Alira had acquired all the knowledge and skills she would need to continue her mission indefinitely, eliminating predators with increasing sophistication while avoiding the mistakes that had led other serial criminals to capture and prosecution.

Now it was time to return her focus to active operations, identifying and eliminating the next target who deserved consequences that the legal system consistently refused to deliver.

Chapter 8

The Mission Crystallizes

Seven years after Sierra's assault and in the months following Coach Robert Daniels's death, Alira Sinclair completed the transformation that would define the rest of her life. She was no longer the naive art history student who'd believed in institutional justice and legal accountability. She had become something far more dangerous and purposeful—a systematic hunter of predators who understood that protecting vulnerable people sometimes required working entirely outside the frameworks that had so comprehensively failed her family.

The dual elimination of Dr. Marcus Webb and Coach Robert Daniels had taught her essential lessons about operational planning, forensic evasion, and the psychological discipline required to kill without succumbing to guilt or moral doubt. Webb's death through botanical poisoning had demonstrated the elegance of chemical methods that left minimal forensic evidence. Daniels's elimination through contaminated supplements had shown her how to exploit targets' own behaviors and vanity to deliver lethal substances without requiring direct contact or personal presence at the death scene.

But Alira understood that two successful eliminations didn't make her invincible or guarantee future success. Each operation created risk, each kill potentially left traces that investigators might eventually recognize, and maintaining perfect operational security required constant learning and adaptation.

She spent the year following Daniels's death systematically expanding her capabilities in ways that would prepare her for increasingly sophisticated operations. Her apartment became a comprehensive research and training facility, carefully compartmentalized to appear innocuous to casual visitors while actually serving as a command center for operations that would continue for years to come.

The master bedroom had been converted into a laboratory that would have impressed professional toxicologists. Climate-controlled cabinets held botanical specimens collected from around the world— plants whose toxic properties had been documented for centuries but which remained obscure enough that medical examiners wouldn't routinely test for them during standard autopsies.

Alira had organized her collection with scientific precision, each specimen labeled with its Latin name, toxic compounds, physiological effects, and optimal extraction methods. Foxglove (*Digitalis purpurea*) for cardiac glycosides that induced fatal arrhythmias. Oleander (*Nerium oleander*) for compounds that disrupted heart function in ways that mimicked natural cardiac events. Hemlock (*Conium maculatum*) for neurotoxic alkaloids that caused respiratory paralysis. Monkshood (*Aconitum napellus*) for aconitine that stopped hearts while leaving minimal forensic evidence.

But her collection extended far beyond the well-known botanical poisons. She'd acquired rare specimens like *Gelsemium elegans* (heartbreak grass) from China, whose gelsemine alkaloids caused respiratory failure that appeared identical to natural causes. She'd obtained *Abrus precatorius* (rosary pea) seeds, whose abrin content made ricin look crude by comparison. She'd cultivated *Atropa belladonna* (deadly nightshade) for its tropane alkaloids that could be delivered in countless forms.

Each plant represented a different tool for different operational requirements. Some killed quickly and dramatically, useful for situations where rapid death would seem natural given the target's stress levels or physical exertion. Others worked slowly and progressively, allowing for deaths that appeared to result from deteriorating health conditions rather than acute poisoning. Still others created symptoms that mimicked specific diseases, allowing Alira to tailor her methods to targets' documented medical vulnerabilities.

The laboratory equipment she'd assembled would have seemed excessive for someone whose official interest was studying medicinal plants as a hobby. But each piece served essential purposes for Alira's actual work. A rotary evaporator allowed her to concentrate toxic extracts while removing volatile compounds that might be detected during autopsy. A vacuum filtration system enabled purification of alkaloids to pharmaceutical grade. Centrifuges separated plant materials into their constituent compounds with precision that rivaled professional laboratories.

Most importantly, Alira had acquired analytical equipment that allowed her to test her preparations for purity and potency. A basic mass spectrometer—purchased used from a university laboratory upgrading their equipment—let her verify that extracts contained the compounds she intended without contamination that might trigger forensic suspicion. The investment had been substantial, but it was essential for ensuring that her poisons would kill reliably while leaving minimal evidence.

Her martial arts training continued with equal dedication, though her approach had evolved significantly since her early lessons with David Rosen. She'd achieved black belt certification in karate, Brazilian jiu-jitsu, and Krav Maga, mastering the fundamental techniques of each discipline before synthesizing them into a personal fighting style that emphasized lethal efficiency over sport performance.

But Alira had come to understand that physical violence should be her last resort rather than her primary method. Martial skills were important for self-defense and for creating plausible scenarios where predators died during confrontations they'd initiated. But chemical and biological weapons remained far more elegant—they allowed for elimination at distance, created deaths that appeared natural, and minimized the forensic evidence that could connect her to victims.

She'd begun studying anatomy with the precision of a surgeon, learning exactly where to strike or cut to disable or kill opponents with maximum efficiency and minimum wasted motion. But she studied this knowledge primarily to understand how to make deaths appear natural rather than to perfect her killing techniques. A properly placed injection could deliver poison while leaving a mark so small that medical examiners would likely miss it during routine autopsy. Understanding blood flow and tissue density allowed her to predict how quickly various compounds would circulate through victims' bodies.

The psychological dimension of her training was equally sophisticated. Alira had begun studying behavioral analysis and social engineering, learning to read people with the same precision she applied to chemical compounds. She studied the psychology of predators—

how they selected victims, how they justified their behavior, what vulnerabilities made them susceptible to manipulation.

This knowledge was operationally valuable because it allowed Alira to predict targets' behavior and exploit their psychological weaknesses. Predators often shared characteristic traits—narcissism that made them vulnerable to flattery, entitlement that made them careless about security, contempt for their victims that prevented them from recognizing sophisticated threats.

Understanding these patterns allowed Alira to design operations that exploited targets' own psychology against them. Webb had been vulnerable to the ego gratification of receiving gifts from supposedly grateful former students. Daniels had been susceptible to products marketed as cutting-edge performance enhancement. Future targets would have their own psychological vulnerabilities that could be leveraged to deliver poisons or create deadly scenarios.

Alira also expanded her knowledge of forensic investigation procedures, understanding that successfully evading detection required thinking like the investigators who would examine her work. She enrolled in continuing education courses on criminal justice and forensic science, attended professional conferences where medical examiners and law enforcement personnel discussed evidence analysis techniques, and cultivated relationships with people who could provide insights into how suspicious deaths were evaluated.

Most of these contacts had no idea they were providing operational intelligence to someone planning murders. They thought Alira was a graduate student interested in forensic toxicology, someone whose academic curiosity led her to ask detailed questions about autopsy procedures and evidence collection protocols. They were happy to explain their methodologies to an enthusiastic student, never suspecting that she was learning how to circumvent their techniques.

The education was comprehensive and invaluable. Alira learned which toxins were included in standard screening panels and which required specialized testing that would only be ordered if investigators had specific reason to suspect exotic poisoning. She learned how medical examiners distinguished between natural death and homicide, what patterns triggered deeper investigation, and what presentations were most likely to be classified as accidental or medical rather than criminal.

She also studied the psychology and methods of serial killers—not because she identified with their pathologies, but because understanding how they were caught would help her avoid making similar mistakes. She read extensively about successful and unsuccessful serial murderers, analyzing what patterns had led to their capture and what methods had allowed some to operate undetected for years or decades.

The research revealed consistent patterns. Serial killers who were caught typically made one or more of several characteristic mistakes: they operated within too-narrow geographic areas, creating clustering that triggered investigative attention; they followed rigid patterns in victim selection or killing methods that allowed profilers to predict their behavior; they kept trophies or documentation that provided physical evidence; or they demonstrated escalating risk-taking driven by psychological compulsions they couldn't control.

Alira was determined to avoid all of these pitfalls. She would vary her methods significantly between kills, ensuring that investigators wouldn't recognize connections between apparently unrelated deaths. She would space eliminations widely in both time and geography, preventing clustering that suggested a single perpetrator. She would keep minimal documentation and no physical trophies. And most importantly, she would maintain operational discipline rather than allowing psychological drives to push her toward increasingly risky behavior.

The distinction between her mission and typical serial killing was fundamental and important. Serial killers acted on psychological compulsions—sexual sadism, power fantasies, or other irrational drives that eventually overrode tactical judgment and led to mistakes. But Alira was executing a carefully planned campaign based on rational moral principles and strategic objectives. She wasn't killing to satisfy psychological needs; she was eliminating specific targets who met precise criteria.

This meant she could maintain perfect tactical discipline because she wasn't fighting against compulsive drives. She could wait months or years between operations, varying her methods and targets to avoid creating patterns. She could stop completely if operational security required it, resuming only when conditions allowed safe execution.

During this period, Alira also began identifying potential future targets with systematic thoroughness. She created detailed files on dozens of powerful men whose predatory behavior had been documented but who'd escaped legal consequences through wealth, political connections, or institutional protection.

Each file contained comprehensive information: biographical background, career history, documented victims and their experiences, institutional failures that had enabled continued predation, psychological profile, security protocols, daily routines, medical history, known vulnerabilities, and preliminary operational plans for potential elimination.

The files represented months of painstaking research—reviewing news articles, court records, victims' testimonies, and institutional documents. Alira had developed extensive networks of information sources, cultivating relationships with victim advocates, journalists, attorneys, and others who had access to information about powerful predators and the systems that protected them.

Many of these sources had no idea they were providing intelligence that would ultimately be used for murder. They thought Alira was a researcher studying institutional failures in addressing sexual misconduct, or an advocate trying to help victims navigate broken systems. They were happy to share information with someone who seemed genuinely committed to understanding and addressing these problems.

By the time Alira completed her graduate degree in forensic toxicology, she'd identified over forty potential targets who met her criteria. Each represented a powerful predator whose crimes had been extensively documented but who'd escaped accountability through mechanisms that made legal prosecution impossible or unlikely.

But Alira was patient. She understood that hasty action created patterns that might eventually be recognized. She would take her time, choosing targets carefully and spacing eliminations widely enough to avoid triggering the kind of systematic investigation that might reveal connections between seemingly unrelated deaths.

Her selection criteria were rigorous and carefully considered. Targets had to meet multiple requirements: documented history of serial predatory behavior affecting multiple victims; comprehensive failure of legal systems to provide accountability despite credible evidence; ongoing threat to potential future victims; and operational vulnerabilities that would allow elimination through methods appearing natural or accidental.

The last criterion was particularly important. Alira wouldn't target predators whose security was so sophisticated that elimination would require obviously criminal methods. She was hunting powerful men who believed their institutional protections made them invincible, but she would only eliminate those whose vulnerabilities allowed for deaths that wouldn't trigger homicide investigation.

During one of her regular visits to Sierra's care facility in late autumn, approximately eight months after Daniels's death, Alira found her sister working on an elaborate jigsaw puzzle featuring a mountain landscape. Sierra's face lit up with unfiltered joy when she spotted Alira entering the common room.

"Alira! Look how much I finished! The mountains are almost done!" Sierra's enthusiasm was pure and childlike, her damaged mind finding genuine satisfaction in accomplishments that would seem trivial to someone with normal cognitive capacity.

"That's wonderful, Sierra," Alira said warmly, settling into a chair beside her sister to examine the partially completed puzzle. "You're doing such beautiful work."

They worked together in comfortable silence for several minutes, Sierra's concentration fully absorbed by the task of matching colors and shapes. Then, without looking up from the puzzle, Sierra spoke with sudden clarity that always startled Alira despite her familiarity with these periodic episodes.

"You stopped the bad men who hurt me and Cassie," Sierra said, her voice losing its childlike quality and becoming focused and certain. "The bad man who broke my brain, and the bad man who killed Cassie because she was trying to help people. They're gone now, and they can't hurt anyone else."

"Yes," Alira confirmed quietly. "They're gone, and they'll never hurt anyone again."

Sierra nodded solemnly, her expression showing comprehension that seemed impossible given her documented cognitive limitations. "But there are more bad men, aren't there? More men like them who hurt people and don't face consequences because they're too powerful and too protected."

"There are," Alira admitted. "There are many more predators who operate with the same impunity that

Webb and Daniels enjoyed. The systems that are supposed to protect people from them have failed comprehensively."

"So you're going to stop them too," Sierra said, not as a question but as a statement of fact. "You're going to keep being the angel who makes bad men face consequences, even when all the systems and institutions refuse to do it."

"I am," Alira confirmed. "I'm going to continue this work for as long as I can, for as long as predators continue escaping accountability through power and privilege."

Sierra set down the puzzle piece she'd been holding and turned to face Alira directly, her eyes showing unusual focus and intensity. "That's good. That's important. That's the work I wanted to do—helping people who'd been hurt by bad people. But I can't do it anymore because Dr. Webb destroyed my brain. So you have to do it for me. You have to be the protector that all those hurt people need."

She reached out and took Alira's hand with surprising strength. "Promise me you'll keep stopping the bad men. Promise me you won't let the systems that failed me and Cassie keep failing other people. Promise me you'll be the justice that institutions refuse to provide."

"I promise," Alira said, her throat tight with emotion. "I'll keep fighting for people who can't fight for themselves, for victims that systems abandon, for everyone who deserves justice that legal frameworks consistently fail to deliver."

Sierra smiled with childlike satisfaction, then returned her attention to the puzzle, the moment of lucidity passing as quickly as it had arrived. But Alira carried that conversation with her as both validation and obligation—Sierra understood what Alira was doing and why it mattered, even if her damaged mind couldn't fully articulate the moral complexity involved.

As autumn progressed toward winter, Alira finalized her preparations for relocating to begin the next phase of her mission. She'd accepted a position at the Whitmore Gallery, a prestigious art establishment that would provide steady income and social cover while demanding minimal time commitment. The gallery job was perfect—it explained her refined tastes, her knowledge of wealthy collectors, and her ability to move freely in elite social circles where many potential targets operated.

The position also provided flexibility for operational work. Gallery hours were predictable but not demanding, leaving Alira with substantial time for surveillance, planning, and execution of eliminations. The work brought her into contact with wealthy and powerful people who might themselves be predators or who might provide intelligence about other targets worth investigating.

She rented an apartment in a gentrified neighborhood that offered the right balance of accessibility and anonymity. The building had sufficient security to deter casual criminals but not so much that her movements would be constantly monitored. Her neighbors were young professionals who kept to themselves, creating an environment where Alira could operate without attracting unwanted attention or curiosity.

The apartment itself was carefully designed to serve her dual purposes. The public areas—living room, dining area, kitchen—were decorated with museum-quality artwork and expensive furniture appropriate for someone working in high-end art sales. Visitors would see nothing unusual or suspicious, just refined taste and modest affluence.

But the master bedroom became her operational center, locked and off-limits to any guests. Behind that closed door, Alira maintained her laboratory, her research files, her weapons and equipment—everything she would need to continue her mission for years to come.

On her final visit to Sierra before relocating, Alira found her sister unusually contemplative. They'd finished reading a children's book together, and Sierra was staring out the window at the care facility's small garden with an expression of profound sadness that seemed to transcend her cognitive limitations.

"I miss being smart," Sierra said suddenly, tears streaming down her face. "I miss being able to help people like I was supposed to help people. I miss Cassie and all the things we were going to do together. I miss the person I used to be before the bad man destroyed my brain."

Alira felt her own tears beginning, moved by the rare moment when Sierra's awareness of her own condition broke through the merciful cognitive fog that usually protected her from understanding what she'd lost.

"I know, sweetheart," Alira said softly, pulling her sister into an embrace. "I know how much you've lost, and I know how unfair and terrible it is that Dr. Webb could destroy your brilliant mind and face no consequences until I made sure he couldn't hurt anyone else."

"Promise me something," Sierra said, her voice muffled against Alira's shoulder. "Promise me that my brain getting broken and Cassie dying will mean something. Promise me that you'll use what happened to us to protect other people from the same kind of bad men. Promise me that our suffering won't be for nothing."

"I promise," Alira said firmly. "Your destroyed brilliance and Cassie's murdered potential have given me purpose and direction. I'm going to spend the rest of my life ensuring that predators like Webb and Daniels face consequences, that vulnerable people have protection that institutions refuse to provide, and that your suffering leads to other women being safe from the men who would destroy them."

Sierra pulled back and looked at Alira with sudden clarity, her damaged mind producing one of its occasional flashes of profound insight. "You're going to save so many people. You're going to be the angel that stops the monsters when nobody else will. And someday, when you've stopped all the monsters you can stop, you'll be able to rest knowing that me and Cassie would be so proud of what you've done."

As Alira left the care facility that evening, she carried Sierra's blessing like armor against doubt and moral complexity. Her sisters' suffering had created her mission, their destroyed lives had given her purpose, and their implicit approval validated the path she'd chosen.

The education was complete. The preparation was finished. The mission had crystallized into something clear and purposeful that would define the rest of Alira's life.

She would hunt predators with scientific precision and tactical sophistication, eliminating powerful men whose institutional protections made them immune to legal accountability. She would vary her methods to avoid pattern recognition, space her operations to prevent investigative clustering, and maintain operational discipline that would allow her to continue her work for years or decades.

Dr. Marcus Webb and Coach Robert Daniels were dead, their victims liberated, and their institutional protectors left scrambling to explain tragedies that were actually carefully orchestrated eliminations.

And somewhere in the city where Alira was relocating, other predators operated with similar impunity, unaware that a systematic hunter was beginning her work in earnest—someone who understood that protecting the vulnerable sometimes required working entirely outside the legal frameworks that had failed so comprehensively and repeatedly.

The mission would continue until either Alira was caught or the institutional failures that necessitated her work were reformed sufficiently that extrajudicial action was no longer necessary.

Alira Sinclair had become an angel of justice for people who couldn't get justice any other way. And she was ready to demonstrate, again and again, why powerful predators should fear consequences even when every institution designed to deliver accountability had failed.

The backstory was complete. The vigilante had been forged in the fires of her sisters' destruction. And the hunt was about to begin in earnest.

The Hunter Emerges

Present Day - Seven Years Later

Detective Marcus Hale sat at his desk on a cold Monday afternoon in early December, working through case files with the methodical attention that had defined his fifteen-year career in law enforcement. Outside his window, the city was preparing for the holidays—lights strung across storefronts, shoppers bundling against the winter cold, the annual transformation into something almost magical despite the underlying reality of crime and suffering that defined Hale's professional world.

But Hale's attention wasn't on the festivities. He was reviewing three case files that had been nagging at him for months, creating cognitive dissonance he couldn't quite articulate or resolve.

Richard Blackwood, dead from cardiac arrest during an attempted sexual assault. The investigation had been straightforward—Blackwood had attacked a woman named Alira Sinclair, she'd defended herself, and Blackwood's pre-existing heart condition had made him vulnerable to fatal cardiac event when subjected to the stress of physical confrontation. Case closed as justified self-defense, no criminal charges filed.

Senator William Hayes, dead from massive stroke three months later. The investigation had revealed no suspicious circumstances—Hayes had cardiovascular disease, chronic stress, and lifestyle factors that made stroke entirely plausible. The medical examiner had found nothing unusual, toxicology screening showed only therapeutic levels of his prescribed medications, and the death had been classified as natural causes.

Both investigations had been thorough and professional. Both conclusions had been supported by comprehensive forensic evidence. Both deaths appeared to be exactly what they seemed—one justified self-defense, one natural medical emergency.

So why did Hale keep returning to these files, reviewing details that should have been unremarkable?

The connection was obvious once he'd noticed it: both men had well-documented histories of sexual misconduct, and both had died shortly after encounters with Alira Sinclair. Blackwood during a confrontation where Sinclair had been present. Hayes after Sinclair had apparently discussed cardiovascular health supplements with his staff members.

Individually, the deaths were unremarkable. Collectively, they suggested a pattern that Hale's detective instincts couldn't ignore.

He'd begun researching Sinclair's background more thoroughly, discovering details that added complexity to what should have been a simple narrative of trauma survivor turned advocate for other victims. Sinclair had two sisters—Sierra, who lived in a specialized care facility after suffering traumatic brain injury during a sexual assault ten years ago, and Cassandra, who'd died seven years ago in New York under circumstances officially ruled suicide.

The assault on Sierra had never been solved, the case remaining officially open but practically abandoned due to the victim's memory loss and lack of physical evidence. But Hale's research had revealed that Sierra had been a doctoral student working with Dr. Marcus Webb, a psychology professor who'd died of apparent heart failure shortly after accusations against him had been quietly dismissed by his university.

Cassandra's death had occurred while she was investigating Coach Robert Daniels, a Columbia University athletic director accused of serial sexual assault. Daniels himself had died years later from anaphylactic reaction to contaminated supplements— a death that had been ruled accidental despite occurring shortly after Cassandra's "suicide."

Four powerful men with predatory histories. Four deaths that appeared natural or justified. And all four deaths connected, however distantly, to the Sinclair family.

The pattern was circumstantial and wouldn't support criminal charges. But the pattern was also compelling enough that Hale couldn't simply dismiss it as coincidence.

He opened a new file on his computer and labeled it "Pattern Analysis—Sinclair." He began documenting everything he'd discovered about Alira Sinclair's background, her sisters' tragedies, and the suspicious deaths of men who'd either harmed her family or had been targeted by family members' investigations.

The exercise was speculative and probably futile—drawing connections between unrelated deaths based on nothing more than shared victim history and tangential connections to a woman who appeared to be an innocent trauma survivor. But Hale had learned over fifteen years of detective work to trust his instincts even when evidence didn't support them.

And his instincts were screaming that Alira Sinclair was not what she appeared to be.

If his theory was correct—if Sinclair really was systematically eliminating predatory men through methods sophisticated enough to appear completely natural—then she represented something unprecedented in criminal behavior. Not a serial killer driven by psychological compulsion, but a hunter executing a calculated mission to eliminate specific targets who met precise criteria.

She would be intelligent, disciplined, patient enough to space eliminations widely and vary methods sufficiently to avoid creating obvious patterns. She would understand forensic investigation well enough to circumvent standard detection protocols. And she would be nearly impossible to catch using conventional investigative techniques.

Hale spent the rest of the afternoon developing a preliminary profile based on what he knew about Sinclair. Highly educated with advanced degrees in biochemistry and forensic toxicology. Skilled in martial arts based on how efficiently she'd neutralized Blackwood despite significant size disadvantages. Psychologically controlled enough to maintain normal professional and social relationships while potentially planning murders. And driven by a mission to protect vulnerable people from predators that the legal system consistently failed to hold accountable.

The profile was both fascinating and troubling. If Sinclair was what Hale suspected, she was operating from moral certainty that would make her extremely difficult to deter or catch. She wasn't killing for pleasure or to satisfy psychological compulsions—she was eliminating predators she believed deserved death, acting as judge, jury, and executioner for men whose institutional protections made them immune to legal accountability.

As Hale saved his preliminary analysis and prepared to leave the office for the evening, his phone rang with a call that would transform his theoretical investigation into something far more urgent and personal.

"Detective Hale? This is Dr. Jennifer Rogers from Student Health Services at the university. I'm calling about an incident involving your daughter, Emily. She came to our office this afternoon reporting... well, I think you should come down here as soon as possible."

Hale's blood ran cold. "What happened? Is Emily okay?"

"Physically, she's unharmed. But she's reporting an incident with Marcus Sterling, the fitness trainer at Apex Fitness. Detective Hale, I think your daughter has been sexually assaulted."

The world stopped. Emily—his twenty-one-year-old daughter, brilliant and ambitious and trusting—had been victimized by exactly the kind of predator that Hale spent his professional life investigating.

"I'll be there in ten minutes," Hale managed to say, his voice hollow with shock and rage.

As he drove to the university health center, Hale's mind was already racing through the implications. Marcus Sterling was a prominent fitness trainer with wealthy clients and powerful connections. He'd been accused of misconduct before, but those accusations had been quietly settled through confidential agreements that prevented victims from speaking publicly.

If Sterling had assaulted Emily, the legal system would likely fail to provide justice just as it had failed countless other victims. Sterling had resources, legal representation, and institutional connections that would make successful prosecution difficult or impossible.

But Alira Sinclair—if she was what Hale suspected— had demonstrated that some predators faced consequences even when the legal system failed to deliver them.

For the first time in his career, Detective Marcus Hale understood why someone might choose to work outside the legal frameworks he'd spent his life defending. And for the first time, he found himself hoping that a suspected killer was exactly what he thought she was— because his daughter deserved justice, and if the system couldn't provide it, perhaps someone else would.

The pattern analysis file would remain open on his computer, but Hale's investigation had just become far more complicated than academic curiosity about suspicious deaths.

The hunter and the detective were about to enter into an uneasy dance, neither yet understanding how their confrontation would ultimately conclude.

CULPA *Guilt*

————

"The guilty sleep soundly because they believe themselves untouchable."

Book Four

The Fourth Gambit

IMPUNITAS *Impunity*

———

"Impunity is not innocence—it is merely delayed accountability."

Prologue

The Convergence

The morning after Marcus Sterling's name first crossed Detective Hale's desk, he sat in his unmarked sedan outside Apex Fitness, watching the steady stream of well-dressed women entering and leaving through the building's gleaming glass doors. The gym occupied three floors of converted warehouse space in the city's most exclusive district, its floor-to-ceiling windows and minimalist design projecting exactly the kind of sophisticated affluence that attracted wealthy clients seeking transformation.

Hale had been researching Sterling for two weeks, ever since his pattern analysis of the Blackwood and Hayes deaths had led him to investigate other powerful men with documented histories of sexual misconduct who might fit the profile of potential targets. Sterling's name had appeared on three different victim advocacy databases—a fitness trainer whose clients had filed complaints that were invariably settled through confidential agreements that silenced accusers while allowing him to continue operating with impunity.

The pattern was sickeningly familiar. Sterling used the same institutional protections that had shielded Blackwood and Hayes—wealth, professional reputation, legal intimidation, and the systematic destruction of anyone who dared challenge him publicly. Eight women had reportedly been victimized over five years, their accusations buried under non-disclosure agreements and aggressive legal tactics that made continued resistance financially and psychologically impossible.

If Hale's theory about Alira Sinclair was correct—if she really was systematically eliminating predators who had escaped legal accountability—then Marcus Sterling seemed like exactly the kind of target she might select next.

But proving that theory required catching Sinclair in the act, and Hale had spent months failing to find any concrete evidence connecting her to the deaths of Blackwood and Hayes. Both investigations had been textbook examples of thorough police work, and both had concluded exactly as Sinclair had apparently intended—one justified self-defense, one natural medical emergency.

Hale took a sip of cold coffee and continued his surveillance, watching Sterling emerge from the building's main entrance to greet a new client with the kind of charming attentiveness that photographed well and masked predatory intent. The woman was young, attractive, and visibly nervous—exactly the profile Sterling preferred, according to the victim reports Hale had compiled.

Somewhere in the city, Alira Sinclair was likely conducting her own surveillance, studying the same patterns and vulnerabilities that Hale had documented, planning an elimination with the same methodical precision she'd apparently applied to removing Blackwood and Hayes from positions where they could continue exploiting vulnerable women.

The question that haunted Hale was whether he should try to stop her—or whether some part of him was secretly hoping she would succeed where legal systems consistently failed.

His daughter Emily had started attending Apex Fitness three weeks ago, drawn by the gym's reputation for exclusive clientele and transformative training programs. Hale had tried to discourage her choice without explaining his concerns about Sterling, but Emily was twenty-one years old and determined to make her own decisions about where she worked out.

The convergence of his investigation, his daughter's proximity to a suspected predator, and his theoretical hunter of predators felt like the kind of coincidence that wasn't coincidental at all—like pieces of a puzzle clicking into place in ways that would force Hale to confront questions about justice, accountability, and the limits of legal frameworks that he'd spent his career avoiding.

As he pulled away from his surveillance position that morning, Hale felt the weight of something inevitable settling over him. Events were converging toward a confrontation he couldn't predict or control, and the outcome would likely force him to choose between his professional obligations and his personal convictions about what predators like Sterling actually deserved.

The fourth gambit was about to begin, and Detective Marcus Hale would find himself at its center in ways he couldn't yet imagine.

Chapter 1

Entering the Lion's Den

Apex Fitness occupied three floors of a converted warehouse in the city's most exclusive district, its floor-to-ceiling windows and minimalist design screaming expensive sophistication to anyone passing by on the tree-lined street below. The building's industrial architecture had been transformed into something sleek and modern—exposed brick painted pristine white, polished concrete floors, chrome fixtures that reflected the abundant natural light streaming through massive windows.

Alira studied the building from across the street, sitting in a small café with a clear view of the gym's main entrance. She'd been conducting surveillance for two weeks, documenting the steady stream of well-dressed women who entered and left throughout the day, noting the security cameras positioned at key access points, observing the patterns of staff arrivals and departures.

Marcus Sterling had built his empire on the intersection of vanity and insecurity, creating a temple to physical perfection that attracted wealthy women desperate to transform their bodies and, by extension, their lives. His client list read like a society page directory—socialites, executives, trophy wives, young professionals with disposable income and deep anxieties about aging, weight, and physical desirability.

It was exactly the kind of environment where a sophisticated predator could operate with impunity, using the vulnerable psychology of women seeking transformation to establish relationships that would gradually become exploitative and abusive.

Alira had spent three months researching Sterling before beginning her operational planning. At thirty-five, he was younger than Senator Hayes had been and significantly more physically dangerous than any of her previous targets. Dr. Webb had been an aging academic whose predatory behavior relied on institutional authority and psychological manipulation. Coach Daniels had been athletic but complacent, his decades of institutional protection making him careless about personal security. Richard Blackwood had depended on wealth and legal intimidation to control his victims. Senator Hayes had used political power and congressional connections.

But Sterling was different. He combined sophisticated psychological tactics with genuine physical prowess that made direct confrontation extremely risky. His athletic background as a collegiate wrestler meant he had real combat training, not just the casual fitness of someone who worked out regularly. At thirty-five, he was in his physical prime—strong, fast, and experienced in controlling opponents through technique rather than just brute force.

This would require different operational planning than Alira had employed with her previous four eliminations. Webb had been vulnerable to botanical poisoning delivered through seemingly innocent gifts. Daniels had been susceptible to contaminated supplements that exploited his allergies and ego. Blackwood had died during a confrontation that Alira had engineered to appear like justified self-defense. Hayes had been eliminated through gradual poisoning that mimicked natural stroke.

Sterling would require something new—a method that acknowledged his physical advantages while exploiting psychological vulnerabilities that his success and ego had created.

Sterling's background was telling. He'd been a collegiate wrestler at a Division II school, achieving moderate success but never reaching the elite level that would have earned him national recognition or professional opportunities. After graduation, he'd drifted through various personal training positions at commercial gyms before recognizing that his real talent wasn't athletic achievement but rather exploiting the psychological vulnerabilities of women seeking physical transformation.

He'd founded Apex Fitness seven years ago with financing from wealthy investors whose wives and daughters would become his first clients and, in several cases, his first victims. The business model was brilliant in its cynicism—charge premium prices for "holistic transformation" that promised not just physical fitness but complete lifestyle optimization, then use the intimate relationships developed through intensive personal training to break down clients' boundaries and psychological defenses.

Alira's research had identified at least twelve women who'd been victimized by Sterling over the past five years, though she suspected the actual number was significantly higher. Most victims had been too ashamed to report his behavior, convinced through Sterling's psychological manipulation that they'd somehow invited or deserved his sexual exploitation. The few who had filed complaints had been discredited through Sterling's connections in the fitness industry and his carefully crafted public image as a champion of women's empowerment.

The pattern was sickeningly familiar—the same institutional protection that had shielded Webb, Daniels, Blackwood, and Hayes now insulated Sterling from consequences. Universities protected professors, athletic departments protected coaches, wealth protected businessmen, political connections protected senators, and the fitness industry protected its celebrity trainers. Different institutions, same fundamental failure to hold powerful predators accountable for systematic abuse.

Sterling would identify clients who were vulnerable—often women going through divorces, recovering from relationship trauma, or struggling with body image issues that made them desperate for validation. He'd position himself as a mentor and guide, someone who uniquely understood their potential and was invested in helping them achieve not just physical transformation but complete personal empowerment.

The grooming process was gradual and sophisticated, refined over years of successful predation. Initial training sessions would focus on legitimate fitness instruction, establishing Sterling's expertise and building trust. Then the sessions would become increasingly personal—discussions about relationships, sexuality, self-worth, intimate details that created psychological intimacy while breaking down appropriate professional boundaries.

Sterling framed this boundary erosion as therapeutic and empowering, convincing clients that true transformation required addressing psychological barriers that manifested as physical limitations. He used language borrowed from therapy and personal development—talking about "emotional blocks," "surrendering to the process," "trusting the journey toward authentic self."

Once sufficient psychological intimacy had been established, Sterling would begin introducing physical contact that was ostensibly related to training but which was actually designed to normalize his hands on clients' bodies and test their comfort levels with increasingly inappropriate touch. Adjusting form during exercises, providing "manual resistance" during strength training, offering massage therapy as part of recovery protocols.

The sexual exploitation would follow naturally from this foundation of psychological manipulation and normalized physical contact. Sterling would frame sexual encounters as part of the transformative process, suggesting that sexual confidence and physical fitness were inseparable, that clients who resisted his advances were actually resisting their own growth and empowerment.

Women who objected or threatened to report his behavior would face a comprehensive intimidation strategy. Sterling would deploy his considerable charm to convince them they'd misunderstood his intentions, that their discomfort reflected their own psychological limitations rather than his misconduct. If charm failed, he'd shift to explicit threats—he had photographs and videos from training sessions that could be selectively edited to suggest the relationship had been consensual or even initiated by the client, connections within the fitness industry who would blacklist them from other gyms, attorneys who specialized in defamation suits against women who made "false accusations."

The system was sophisticated and effective. Sterling had been operating with complete impunity for years, accumulating victims while building a public reputation as an innovative trainer who empowered women to achieve their full potential.

But Sterling's success had made him careless in ways that created operational opportunities for someone with Alira's capabilities and experience. She'd learned from each of her previous eliminations—Webb had taught her the elegance of botanical poisons, Daniels had demonstrated how to exploit targets' vanity and health anxieties, Blackwood had shown her the importance of creating plausible self-defense scenarios, and Hayes had refined her understanding of gradual poisoning that mimicked natural medical decline.

Sterling's ego and his pattern of targeting vulnerable women meant he would be susceptible to exactly the kind of infiltration Alira was planning—a seemingly vulnerable client who would appeal to all his predatory instincts while actually being far more dangerous than he could possibly recognize.

Alira had created a new identity for this operation: Lauren Mitchell, a hedge fund manager going through a difficult separation from her husband of eight years. The backstory was comprehensive and plausible—she'd prepared financial records showing substantial income from investment management, created social media presence documenting a high-powered career and deteriorating marriage, and developed a psychological profile that would appeal to Sterling's preference for wealthy, vulnerable, isolated women.

The Lauren Mitchell persona was designed to trigger all of Sterling's predatory instincts. A woman with money who could afford premium training fees. A woman experiencing emotional trauma that would make her dependent on external validation. A woman whose professional success would make her feel inadequate about her physical appearance and personal life. A woman isolated from supportive relationships who would be seeking masculine guidance and approval.

Perfect bait for a predator who couldn't resist the combination of wealth, vulnerability, and psychological neediness.

At 2 PM on a Tuesday afternoon in early June, Alira entered Apex Fitness for her introductory consultation appointment. She'd scheduled the meeting during mid-afternoon hours when the gym would be relatively quiet, allowing for extended conversation without the distraction of peak training periods.

The receptionist who greeted her was a perfectly sculpted young woman in her early twenties—Jessica

Rodriguez according to her name tag—who looked like she'd stepped directly from a fitness magazine cover. Her body was lean and muscular, her posture perfect, her smile professionally enthusiastic in ways that suggested extensive training in customer service.

"Ms. Mitchell! Welcome to Apex Fitness," Jessica said warmly, her voice carrying the practiced enthusiasm of someone trained to make every client feel special and important. "I'm so excited you're beginning your transformation journey with us. Marcus has been looking forward to meeting you."

The fact that Sterling had been "looking forward" to meeting Alira suggested he'd already reviewed her intake forms and identified her as exactly the kind of target he preferred. The forms had been masterpieces of calculated vulnerability—detailing Lauren Mitchell's deteriorating marriage, her struggles with self-worth, her desperate desire to become the kind of woman who deserved love and respect.

Every answer had been designed to trigger Sterling's predatory interest while establishing the psychological profile he found irresistible—a successful woman who felt like a failure, someone whose professional accomplishments couldn't compensate for perceived inadequacies in her personal life and physical appearance.

"Thank you," Alira replied, allowing nervous energy to color her voice in ways that suggested genuine anxiety about beginning this process. "I have to admit, I'm a little intimidated. It's been a long time since I've been in a gym, and I've let myself go pretty badly since my separation."

"Don't worry about that at all," Jessica assured her with practiced sympathy. "Marcus specializes in helping women rebuild their confidence along with their bodies. He has an amazing gift for seeing the potential in everyone, for understanding exactly what each client needs to achieve true transformation."

The language was telling—"seeing the potential," "understanding what each client needs"—framing Sterling's predatory assessment of vulnerability as some kind of empathetic insight rather than the calculated evaluation it actually represented.

Jessica led Alira on a tour of the facility, beginning on the main floor—a vast space filled with state-of-the-art equipment arranged with aesthetic precision. Massive windows flooded the area with natural light that reflected off mirrored walls, creating an environment that was simultaneously inspiring and intimidating. The equipment was top-of-the-line, the kind of specialized machines that cost tens of thousands of dollars and were designed for serious athletes rather than casual fitness enthusiasts.

Alira noted the layout carefully as Jessica explained the various training zones. Multiple exits provided escape routes if needed. Security cameras covered main areas but there were blind spots—corners and transitional spaces where the camera coverage didn't overlap effectively. Sterling's private office overlooked the main workout area from a mezzanine level, positioned to allow him to observe the entire floor while maintaining physical separation that emphasized his authority.

"Our philosophy here is holistic transformation," Jessica explained as they walked toward the stairs leading to the second floor. "Marcus believes that true fitness comes from addressing not just physical conditioning, but emotional and psychological barriers as well. He uses an integrated approach that combines cutting-edge training protocols with psychological coaching designed to help clients overcome the mental obstacles that prevent them from achieving their full potential."

Perfect predator-speak, Alira thought. Framing psychological manipulation as therapeutic intervention, creating language that would make boundary violations seem like breakthroughs rather than abuse. She'd heard variations of this rhetoric from all her previous targets— Webb's therapeutic language about "breakthrough sessions," Daniels's talk about "holistic athlete development," Blackwood's presentation of his assaults as "passionate encounters," Hayes's framing of exploitation as "mentorship relationships."

They climbed to the second floor, which housed specialized training rooms and what Jessica called "recovery suites"—private spaces where clients could receive massage therapy, nutritional counseling, and "psychological coaching" from Sterling himself. The rooms were soundproofed and equipped with treatment tables that could serve multiple purposes, creating environments where Sterling could isolate clients while maintaining the fiction that everything happening was professionally appropriate.

"Marcus personally handles all our VIP clients," Jessica said, her voice taking on an almost reverent tone that suggested Sterling had cultivated loyalty through charm, manipulation, or possibly his own exploitation of staff members. "He has waiting lists months long, but he agreed to take you on personally after reviewing your intake forms. He said your situation resonated with him deeply and that he believes he can help you achieve the transformation you're seeking."

The statement confirmed what Alira had suspected—Sterling had identified her as a high-value target based on the vulnerability and wealth signals in her intake materials. He was clearing space in his schedule specifically to accommodate someone he viewed as ideal for his predatory pattern.

"When will I meet him?" Alira asked, maintaining the nervous-but-eager tone that would reinforce Sterling's assessment of her as vulnerable and malleable.

"He's finishing a session now, but he wanted to introduce himself before you left today," Jessica replied. "He's very hands-on with his approach to client relationships. He believes that personal connection is essential for the kind of deep transformation that Apex provides."

As if summoned by her words, Marcus Sterling emerged from one of the private training rooms on the second floor, followed by a visibly shaken young woman who looked like she'd been crying. The woman—blonde, early twenties, athletic build—hurried past them without making eye contact, clutching her gym bag like a shield against further contact.

Alira noted the woman's body language with clinical precision—shoulders hunched defensively, gaze averted, movements quick and furtive as though trying to escape without triggering additional attention. Classic trauma response, suggesting she'd just experienced something that had violated her boundaries and left her psychologically destabilized. The same body language Alira had observed in Webb's victims leaving his office, in the athletes who'd worked with Daniels, in the women Blackwood had assaulted, in Hayes's former staff members.

Different predators, different environments, but the psychological damage was universally recognizable.

Sterling himself was exactly as Alira had expected from her research—tall and muscular with the kind of aggressive good looks that photographed well and intimidated effectively. At thirty-five, he moved with fluid confidence born from years of athletic training and absolute certainty that he was the most important person in any room. His fitted athletic wear showed off his physique in ways that were obviously intentional, designed to establish physical dominance while maintaining professional appearance.

"Ms. Mitchell," he said, his voice carrying warm authority as he approached with hand extended for greeting. "Welcome to Apex. I've been looking forward to meeting you."

His handshake was firm without being crushing, lasting just long enough to establish physical contact while maintaining plausible professionalism. But Alira caught the way his eyes assessed her body with practiced efficiency, cataloging assets and vulnerabilities the same way a predator evaluated potential prey—noting physical appearance, psychological presentation, economic status, all the factors that determined whether someone was worth the investment of his grooming process.

The assessment was identical to what Alira had experienced during her first encounters with all her previous targets. They all had that same calculating gaze, that same evaluation of vulnerability and exploitability. Sterling wasn't unique—he was just the latest iteration of a pattern Alira had studied extensively.

"Thank you for agreeing to work with me personally," Alira replied, allowing bashfulness to creep into her voice while she studied Sterling's micro-expressions and body language. "I know you must be incredibly busy with your other clients."

"Never too busy for someone genuinely committed to transformation," Sterling said smoothly, deploying the kind of flattering attention that made clients feel special and valued. "I read your intake forms, and I have to say, your story resonated with me deeply. Separation can be devastating to a woman's sense of self-worth, but it can also be an opportunity for rebirth—a chance to become the person you were always meant to be rather than the person your marriage required you to become."

The psychological hooks were already being set, Alira noted. Framing her fictional separation as opportunity rather than failure, positioning himself as someone who understood her pain and could guide her toward something better. The language was carefully calculated to appeal to someone experiencing genuine emotional trauma and seeking external validation.

"I just want to feel strong again," Alira said, delivering the line she'd prepared specifically to encourage Sterling's savior complex. "I want to look in the mirror and see someone worthy of respect, someone who deserves to be valued for who she is rather than being discarded when she stops meeting someone else's needs."

"That's exactly what we're going to accomplish together," Sterling assured her, his hand settling on her shoulder in a gesture that would seem supportive to observers but carried undertones of possession and dominance that Alira recognized immediately. "True strength comes from understanding and accepting your nature as a woman, then building on that foundation. Too many women try to compete with men on masculine terms, denying their essential femininity in pursuit of some androgynous ideal of power. Real empowerment comes from embracing what makes you uniquely female and developing strength that enhances rather than suppresses those qualities."

The statement was pure manipulation disguised as empowerment philosophy—establishing a framework where Sterling would define "feminine strength" in ways that served his predatory interests, where resistance to his advances could be framed as resistance to authentic womanhood, where submission to his authority would be positioned as embracing rather than denying personal power.

"When can we start?" Alira asked with apparent eagerness.

"Tomorrow morning, six AM," Sterling replied without hesitation. "I like to work with my special clients before the gym gets busy—more privacy, more focus, more opportunity for the kind of breakthrough moments that lead to genuine transformation. Early morning sessions also create accountability—if you can commit to being here at six AM consistently, it demonstrates you're serious about change rather than just playing at self-improvement."

Perfect, Alira thought. Early morning sessions in private spaces, exactly the scenario she needed for what she had planned. Sterling was establishing patterns that would serve her operational requirements while believing he was creating conditions that would facilitate his own predatory exploitation.

"I'll be here," she promised.

As Alira left the gym that afternoon, she felt the familiar anticipation that came with beginning a new hunt. Sterling was following his predictable pattern, escalating gradually toward the moment when he would overplay his hand and give her the opening she needed.

But this operation would be her most challenging yet. Webb had been vulnerable through age and complacency. Daniels had been susceptible to ego-driven carelessness about health products. Blackwood had been reckless in his assault attempts. Hayes had been medically vulnerable and dependent on routines that could be exploited. Sterling was younger, more physically capable, more paranoid about potential threats, and operating in an environment where his security measures and staff loyalty created complications that hadn't existed with her previous targets.

She would need to be more careful, more patient, more willing to endure Sterling's boundary violations while waiting for the perfect moment to strike. Most importantly, she would need to maintain her cover as vulnerable Lauren Mitchell even as Sterling's predatory behavior escalated toward assault. The performance would be psychologically demanding—allowing Sterling to believe he was successfully manipulating her while actually studying his methods and planning his elimination.

But Alira had learned from four successful eliminations that patience and discipline were more important than speed. She would let Sterling get close, would allow him to believe his grooming was working, would endure whatever violations were necessary to create the perfect killing ground.

And when the moment came, Marcus Sterling would discover that some prey were far more dangerous than they appeared—that the vulnerable woman he'd been exploiting was actually a hunter who'd been studying his every move and planning his death with the same methodical precision she'd applied to eliminating Webb, Daniels, Blackwood, and Hayes.

Tomorrow morning, the operation would begin in earnest.

The fifth elimination was underway.

NEMESIS *Divine Retribution*

————

"Those whom the gods would destroy, they first make arrogant."

Chapter 2

The Detective's Daughter

Detective Marcus Hale sat in his unmarked sedan across the street from the university medical center, watching students stream in and out of the main entrance with the kind of youthful invincibility that came from not yet understanding how fragile life actually was. At forty-six, Hale had spent enough years investigating violent crimes to know that safety was an illusion and that vulnerability could strike anyone regardless of precautions or good judgment.

But knowing these truths intellectually didn't prepare him for the phone call he'd received three hours ago from his daughter Emily's roommate, her voice shaking with panic as she explained that Emily hadn't come home last night and wasn't answering her phone. The roommate had checked with Emily's boyfriend, her study group, the library where she usually worked late— no one had seen her since yesterday afternoon when she'd mentioned going to the gym for a training session.

Hale had immediately called Emily's cell phone, getting only voicemail. He'd texted, getting no response. He'd used his police credentials to ping her phone's location, discovering it was turned off or dead. And then, with growing dread, he'd begun calling hospitals.

The university medical center had admitted an unidentified young woman matching Emily's description at 11:47 PM the previous night. She'd been brought in by ambulance after being found unconscious in the parking lot of a commercial building in the city's business district. No identification, no phone, just a gym bag with workout clothes and a water bottle.

Hale had arrived at the hospital within twenty minutes of that call, his detective's training warring with a father's panic as he navigated the bureaucratic maze of emergency room protocols and patient privacy policies. When they finally allowed him into the ICU to identify the patient, his worst fears had been confirmed.

Emily lay in the hospital bed, her face swollen and bruised, her left arm in a cast, her breathing supported by a ventilator. Machines beeped rhythmically around her, monitoring vital signs that told a story of survival against terrible odds. But the neurologist's preliminary assessment had been devastating—severe traumatic brain injury, extensive intracranial bleeding, uncertain prognosis for meaningful recovery.

The doctor had explained the injuries with clinical precision that barely masked his own concern. Emily had sustained blunt force trauma to the back of her head, likely from being thrown or pushed into a hard surface with significant force. The impact had caused her skull to fracture in two places, driving bone fragments into brain tissue and triggering massive hemorrhaging. She'd also suffered injuries consistent with sexual assault—vaginal tearing, bruising on her inner thighs, defensive wounds on her hands where she'd apparently tried to fight off her attacker.

Emergency surgery had relieved the pressure on Emily's brain and stabilized her condition enough to survive transport to ICU. But the neurological damage was extensive and potentially permanent. The surgeon had been careful not to offer false hope—Emily might wake up in hours, days, weeks, or never. And if she did wake up, there was no way to predict what cognitive capacity she would retain.

Hale had spent the past three hours sitting beside his daughter's bed, holding her hand and trying to process the incomprehensible reality that Emily—brilliant, ambitious, twenty-one-year-old Emily who was supposed to be invincible—might never wake up, might never finish her pre-med degree, might never become the doctor she'd dreamed of being since childhood.

His ex-wife Patricia was on a flight from Seattle, having dropped everything when Hale called with the news. They'd been divorced for eight years, the marriage a casualty of Hale's obsessive dedication to his work and Patricia's inability to live with the emotional distance that created. But their love for Emily had remained constant and unwavering, the one thing they'd both gotten absolutely right even when everything else in their relationship had fallen apart.

A nurse entered the ICU room, checking Emily's vital signs and making notes on the computerized chart. She was young—probably not much older than Emily—with the kind of practiced composure that came from working in an environment where life and death were constantly in balance.

"Any changes?" Hale asked, though he already knew the answer from the unchanged pattern of beeps and digital readouts.

"No changes," the nurse confirmed gently. "Her vitals are stable, which is good. The neurologist will be making rounds in about an hour and can give you a more comprehensive update then."

After the nurse left, Hale forced himself to shift from devastated father to functioning detective. Emily had been attacked, assaulted, and left for dead. Someone had done this to his daughter, and that person would face consequences regardless of how long it took or what Hale had to do to ensure accountability.

He'd already contacted his partner, Detective Sarah Martinez, and requested that she take lead on investigating Emily's assault. Hale couldn't be the primary investigator on a case involving his own daughter—departmental policy and basic investigative ethics prevented that kind of conflict of interest—but Martinez would keep him informed and would pursue the case with the same intensity Hale would have brought to it himself.

Martinez had arrived at the hospital within an hour of Hale's call, bringing the preliminary information she'd gathered from the patrol officers who'd responded to the initial 911 call. The building where Emily had been found was a mixed-use commercial property that housed several businesses including a high-end fitness center called Apex Fitness on the first three floors.

Apex Fitness. Hale's memory immediately flagged the name as familiar, though he couldn't immediately place why. He pulled out his phone and searched his email, finding what he'd been looking for—a message from Emily three weeks ago, enthusiastically telling him about a new gym she'd joined and her "amazing trainer" who was helping her get in better shape for the upcoming pre-med program challenges.

"I think I know where to start," Hale told Martinez, showing her Emily's email. "She'd been training at Apex Fitness. That's probably where she was yesterday afternoon before the assault."

Martinez made notes, her expression carefully neutral in ways that suggested she was already thinking like a detective rather than reacting emotionally to the situation. "I'll get security footage from the gym and the surrounding area. Interview the staff and any members who might have seen Emily yesterday. Find out who this trainer is and whether he has any history of inappropriate behavior with clients."

"Her gym bag was with her when she was found," Hale added, his detective's mind cataloging details even through the fog of shock and grief. "But no phone, no wallet, no identification. Either the attacker took those items, or Emily left them somewhere before the assault occurred."

"Could be robbery," Martinez suggested, though her tone indicated she didn't believe that explanation. "But the sexual assault component suggests this was more personal than opportunistic theft."

They both knew the statistics. The vast majority of sexual assaults were committed by someone the victim knew—acquaintances, friends, colleagues, romantic partners. Stranger assaults existed but were statistically rare compared to assaults by known perpetrators who'd used familiarity and trust to create opportunities for violence.

Emily's trainer at Apex Fitness would be the obvious first interview subject, particularly given that she'd apparently been at the gym shortly before the assault occurred.

Martinez left to begin the investigation, promising to keep Hale updated on every development. Hale remained at Emily's bedside, his mind cycling between grief and rage and desperate hope that his daughter would wake up and be able to tell him exactly who had done this to her.

But even as he held Emily's hand and willed her to open her eyes, Hale's detective instincts were already working through the implications of her injuries and the circumstances of her discovery. The traumatic brain injury was severe enough that even if Emily woke up, she might not remember the assault. The neurologist had explained that trauma-induced amnesia was common in cases of significant head injury—the brain essentially erased memories formed immediately before and during the traumatic event as a protective mechanism.

Which meant Hale might be facing the same devastating situation that had destroyed Alira Sinclair's family years ago—a victim who couldn't testify about her assault because brain injury had stolen her memories, leaving investigators with physical evidence but no way to definitively identify the perpetrator or prove what had actually occurred.

The parallel was uncomfortable and immediately apparent. Hale had spent months studying the Sinclair family's history as part of his investigation into the suspicious pattern of deaths he'd been tracking. He knew that Sierra Sinclair had been sexually assaulted, suffering traumatic brain injury that left her unable to provide coherent testimony about her attack. He knew that her alleged attacker had escaped prosecution because Sierra's memory loss made her an unreliable witness.

And he knew that the alleged attacker—Dr. Marcus Webb—had died three months after Sierra's assault, killed by what appeared to be natural heart failure but which Hale suspected might have been botanical poisoning administered by Alira Sinclair.

Hale had no proof of Alira's involvement in Webb's death or in any of the other suspicious deaths he'd been tracking. All he had were patterns—predatory men with documented histories of sexual misconduct, dying under circumstances that appeared natural but which occurred at moments when they were vulnerable to exposure or facing potential consequences. And all those deaths had tangential connections to Alira Sinclair or her family's tragedies.

The connections were circumstantial. They wouldn't support criminal charges or even justify official investigation into Alira as a suspect. But they were compelling enough that Hale had opened a personal file labeled "Pattern Analysis—Sinclair" and had been quietly documenting what he believed might be a series of vigilante eliminations disguised as natural deaths.

Now Hale's own daughter was lying in an ICU bed with catastrophic brain injury following a sexual assault, potentially facing the same memory loss that had prevented Sierra from identifying her attacker. The system that Hale had spent his career defending—the legal framework of evidence and testimony and due process—might fail Emily just as comprehensively as it had apparently failed Sierra Sinclair.

And if Hale's suspicions about Alira were correct—if she really had taken justice into her own hands after the legal system failed her family—then for the first time in his career, Marcus Hale was beginning to understand why someone might make that choice.

Six hours later, Detective Martinez returned to the hospital with preliminary findings from her investigation. She found Hale still sitting beside Emily's bed, his hand holding his daughter's as though physical contact could somehow will her back to consciousness.

"Can we talk outside?" Martinez asked quietly, her expression suggesting she had information that Hale needed to hear but wouldn't want to discuss in Emily's presence.

They moved to a small consultation room down the hall from the ICU, a sterile space designed for delivering bad news to families of critical patients. Martinez laid out several photographs and documents on the table between them.

"Emily was definitely at Apex Fitness yesterday afternoon," Martinez began without preamble. "Security footage shows her arriving at 4:15 PM and meeting with her personal trainer, Marcus Sterling. They went to a private training room on the second floor at 4:23 PM."

She pulled out a photograph of Sterling—a publicity shot from the gym's website showing a muscular man in his mid-thirties with the kind of aggressive good looks that would appeal to women seeking physical transformation.

"Sterling has been Emily's trainer for the past three weeks," Martinez continued. "According to the receptionist I interviewed, Emily was enthusiastic about the training and mentioned several times that Sterling was helping her build confidence along with physical strength."

"When did she leave the gym?" Hale asked, his voice carefully controlled despite the rage building in his chest.

"That's where things get problematic," Martinez said, her expression grave. "Security footage shows Emily entering Sterling's private training room at 4:23 PM, but there's no footage of her leaving. The cameras don't cover the private rooms—Sterling apparently insisted on that for 'client privacy' when the gym was built. And the emergency exit from the second floor leads to a back alley that isn't covered by the building's security system."

"So Sterling could have assaulted her in that private room, then taken her out through the emergency exit without being recorded," Hale said, the investigative implications immediately clear.

"That's one possibility," Martinez confirmed. "But Sterling claims Emily left through the main entrance around 6 PM, after their session ended. He says she seemed fine, maybe a little tired from the intense workout but otherwise normal. He has no explanation for why the security footage doesn't show her leaving."

"Did you interview him directly?"

"Briefly, at the gym. He was cooperative, expressed shock and concern about Emily's assault. Said he had no idea anything bad had happened to her until I showed up with questions. He offered to provide any assistance the investigation needed."

"Did he consent to providing DNA samples?" Hale asked, knowing that DNA evidence from the rape kit would be crucial for identifying Emily's attacker.

"He refused," Martinez said bluntly. "Said he'd be happy to cooperate with the investigation but that he wanted to consult with an attorney before providing any biological samples. Which is his legal right, but obviously it looks suspicious given the circumstances."

Hale felt his hands clenching into fists, forcing himself to breathe deeply and maintain the professional detachment that years of detective work had trained into him. Sterling had refused DNA testing, which meant he either had something to hide or was being cautious based on legal advice. Either way, it created a significant obstacle for the investigation.

"What about his alibi for the time after Emily allegedly left the gym?" Hale asked.

"That's where things get more complicated," Martinez replied, pulling out additional documents. "Sterling claims he had dinner with a client at an upscale restaurant from 7 PM to 9:30 PM. The client—Victoria Ashford, wife of a prominent venture capitalist—confirms his alibi. Restaurant staff remember them being there. Credit card receipts and security footage support the timeline."

"So if Emily was assaulted between 6 PM and 11 PM when she was found, Sterling has a documented alibi for a significant portion of that window," Hale said, recognizing how the timeline would complicate prosecution even if they eventually obtained evidence connecting Sterling to the assault.

"There's more," Martinez said grimly. "I did some background research on Sterling and Apex Fitness. He's been accused of sexual misconduct by at least four former clients over the past five years. All four cases were settled through confidential agreements that included substantial payments and non-disclosure clauses. The settlements were handled by a law firm that specializes in defending wealthy individuals against sexual assault allegations."

"So Sterling has a documented pattern of predatory behavior, access to Emily during the timeframe when the assault likely occurred, and no alibi for the critical period between the end of their training session and his dinner appointment," Hale summarized.

"Correct. But he also has expensive legal representation, a documented alibi for part of the relevant timeframe, and the fact that we can't definitively prove Emily was still at the gym when the assault occurred. Without her testimony or DNA evidence connecting Sterling to the assault, we're going to have a very difficult time building a prosecutable case."

Hale understood exactly what Martinez wasn't saying directly—the legal system that was supposed to deliver justice for victims like Emily was already showing signs of the same failure that had allowed Sterling to assault at least four other women without facing criminal consequences.

"What's the next step?" Hale asked, though he already knew the answer would be frustratingly inadequate.

"We continue gathering evidence," Martinez said. "Interview other Apex Fitness clients and staff members, see if anyone witnessed anything suspicious or can provide information about Sterling's behavior with Emily. Analyze the DNA evidence from the rape kit and hope for a match in the criminal database. And wait for Emily to wake up so she can tell us what actually happened."

"And if Emily doesn't wake up? Or if she wakes up with no memory of the assault?" Hale asked, the questions carrying the weight of his own family's current nightmare.

Martinez's expression showed sympathetic understanding mixed with professional realism. "Then we work with whatever physical evidence we have and hope it's enough to overcome Sterling's legal defenses. But honestly, Marcus... cases like this are incredibly difficult to prosecute even under the best circumstances. Without the victim's testimony, we're facing significant obstacles."

After Martinez left to continue her investigation, Hale returned to Emily's ICU room and resumed his vigil beside her bed. His daughter lay motionless except for the mechanical rise and fall of her chest driven by the ventilator, her face peaceful in ways that concealed the catastrophic damage occurring inside her brain.

Hale's phone buzzed with a text message from Martinez: "Just interviewed another former Apex client who claims Sterling assaulted her two years ago. She signed an NDA and received $150K settlement. Says there are at least six other women with similar stories. Sterling's attorney is already blocking our attempts to interview additional victims, citing confidentiality agreements."

The pattern was sickeningly familiar. Sterling was protected by the same institutional mechanisms that had apparently shielded the predators in the cases Hale had been investigating—men with resources, legal representation, and systems designed to silence victims rather than hold perpetrators accountable.

For months, Hale had been developing a theory that Alira Sinclair might be eliminating predatory men through methods sophisticated enough to appear completely natural. He'd documented patterns, identified connections, and developed profiles that suggested—though couldn't prove—that Sinclair might be operating as a systematic hunter of powerful predators who'd escaped legal accountability.

He'd believed that even if his suspicions were correct, even if Sinclair's targets deserved punishment, vigilante justice was wrong. That working outside legal frameworks created more problems than it solved. That personal vengeance couldn't substitute for institutional justice no matter how comprehensively those institutions had failed.

But now his own daughter was lying in a hospital bed with catastrophic brain injury following an assault by a predator who would almost certainly escape legal consequences. And Hale found himself understanding—really understanding for the first time—the desperation that might drive someone to work outside systems that consistently failed to protect vulnerable people from predatory violence.

If his suspicions about Alira Sinclair were correct—if she really had eliminated the men connected to her family's tragedies—he was beginning to comprehend why. Not just intellectually as a detective analyzing criminal behavior, but viscerally as a father watching his daughter fight for survival while her attacker hid behind expensive lawyers and institutional protections.

He sat beside Emily's bed through the long night, holding her hand and wrestling with questions that had no good answers. Questions about justice and vengeance, about legal systems and moral certainty, about what a father was supposed to do when the institution he'd spent his career defending failed to protect his own daughter from a predator who'd been assaulting women with complete impunity for years.

By dawn, Marcus Hale had made a decision that would have seemed impossible just twenty-four hours earlier.

If the legal system failed Emily the way it had apparently failed Sterling's other victims, if the investigation couldn't build a prosecutable case despite overwhelming circumstantial evidence, if Sterling continued operating with impunity while Emily lay comatose or brain-damaged...

Then Hale would find another way to ensure Marcus Sterling faced consequences for what he'd done.

Even if that meant allowing—or actively enabling—someone else to deliver the justice that legal frameworks consistently refused to provide.

And if Alira Sinclair was what Hale suspected she might be, if she was already hunting Sterling for her own reasons...

Then perhaps it was time for the detective and the vigilante to have a very different kind of conversation.

UMBRA MORTIS *Shadow of Death*

_____

"He never saw her coming. They never do."

Chapter 3

Escalation

Alira arrived at Apex Fitness at 5:45 AM the following morning, dressed in expensive workout clothes that struck the right balance between athletic functionality and the kind of carefully curated appearance that would appeal to Sterling's assessment of wealth and status. The gym was nearly empty at this hour—just Sterling and two other trainers working with early-morning clients in the main area, their voices echoing in the vast space designed to accommodate dozens of people during peak hours.

Sterling met her at the entrance with the kind of energetic enthusiasm that seemed impossible for the early hour, his physical presence even more imposing in person than it had been during their brief introduction the previous afternoon. He moved with the fluid confidence of someone completely comfortable in his body, wearing fitted athletic wear that showcased his physique while maintaining the professional appearance necessary for his role as fitness authority.

"Good morning, Lauren," he said, using her first name with immediate familiarity that was calculated to establish intimacy while breaking down the formal boundaries that "Ms. Mitchell" would have maintained. "I'm impressed—most new clients struggle with the 6

AM commitment for at least the first few weeks. The fact that you're here on time tells me you're serious about transformation rather than just playing at self-improvement."

"I'm committed," Alira replied, allowing nervous energy to color her voice. "I know change won't happen unless I'm willing to do the work, even when it's uncomfortable or inconvenient."

"That's exactly the mindset we need," Sterling said approvingly, his hand settling on her shoulder in a gesture that would seem supportive to observers but which Alira recognized as the beginning of his boundary-testing process. "Real transformation requires pushing past comfort zones, accepting guidance even when your instincts resist, trusting the process when your mind tries to sabotage your progress."

He led her to a private training room on the second floor—a mirrored space equipped with specialized equipment and, most importantly, no security cameras. Alira had confirmed this during her reconnaissance, noting that Sterling deliberately chose spaces where his "breakthrough sessions" couldn't be recorded or monitored.

"Before we begin the physical work," Sterling said, closing the door behind them and positioning himself to block her direct access to the exit, "I like to establish a baseline understanding of my clients' relationship with their bodies. Physical fitness is impossible without psychological honesty about what's preventing you from achieving your potential."

He gestured for her to sit on a bench while he positioned himself in a chair directly across from her—close enough to establish intimacy, positioned to maintain control of the space and her movements within it.

"Tell me about your marriage," he said, his voice taking on the practiced cadence of a therapist conducting an intake session. "What happened to make you feel so disconnected from your own power and self-worth?"

For the next twenty minutes, Alira spun an elaborate tale of emotional neglect and psychological manipulation by her fictional husband, painting herself as a woman whose confidence had been systematically destroyed through years of subtle undermining and explicit criticism. Every detail was designed to present her as isolated, vulnerable, and desperately in need of male validation—exactly the psychological profile that Sterling found most appealing in potential victims.

Sterling listened with intense focus, asking probing questions about her self-image, her relationships, her sexuality, and her deepest insecurities. His questions grew increasingly personal as the session progressed, framed as necessary for developing her fitness program but actually serving to establish psychological dominance and normalize invasive inquiry into intimate details of her life.

"Physical transformation requires vulnerability," Sterling explained when Alira expressed mild discomfort with some of his questions. "You can't rebuild strength without first acknowledging weakness in all its forms—physical, emotional, sexual. I need to understand every aspect of your relationship with your body and your sense of self as a woman."

The session continued with Sterling putting her through basic exercises, using each movement as an opportunity for physical contact—adjusting her posture, guiding her form, establishing the normalization of his hands on her body. His touch was professional enough to maintain plausibility but lingering in ways that tested her boundaries while creating the foundation for future escalation.

"You have excellent natural flexibility," Sterling observed, his hands on her hips as he guided her through a stretching routine, his body positioned close enough that she could feel his breath on her neck. "That suggests you'll respond well to the more advanced techniques I have in mind for your program. Flexibility is both physical and psychological—the ability to surrender to guidance, to accept intensity even when it feels overwhelming."

Alira noted how Sterling's breathing had changed subtly, how his pupils had dilated slightly despite the bright lighting. He was becoming aroused by the power dynamic, by her apparent submission to his authority, by the psychological and physical control he believed he was establishing.

"What kind of advanced techniques?" she asked, allowing nervousness to creep into her voice.

"Techniques that require complete trust between trainer and client," Sterling replied, his hands moving from her hips to her shoulders, his touch becoming more possessive. "Some women find them uncomfortable at first because they challenge deeply held beliefs about appropriate boundaries and the nature of empowerment. But that discomfort is usually just resistance to growth—your mind protecting outdated ideas about femininity and strength that actually limit your potential."

Perfect predator logic, Alira thought. Framing boundary violations as therapeutic breakthroughs, making resistance seem neurotic rather than rational, positioning submission as empowerment rather than exploitation.

The first session ended with Sterling announcing that he wanted to see her progress with "specialized resistance training" during their next meeting. As Alira gathered her things, she caught him watching her with the satisfied expression of a hunter who believed his trap was working perfectly.

"Same time tomorrow?" he asked.

"Of course," Alira replied, maintaining her cover as the eager, vulnerable client. "I'm already feeling stronger, more capable. Thank you for pushing me past my comfort zones."

Over the following two weeks, Sterling's sessions with Alira followed a predictable pattern of escalation that demonstrated both his systematic approach to grooming and his growing confidence that she was successfully being manipulated. Each morning session began with increasingly invasive psychological probing—questions about her sexuality, her fantasies, her relationship with pleasure and pain, her willingness to surrender control to someone who "understood her needs better than she understood them herself."

The physical component of the training became progressively more intimate. Sterling had Alira perform exercises that required her to be in vulnerable positions while he provided "guidance" and "correction" that involved extensive touching. His hands roamed more freely with each session, ostensibly adjusting her form but actually mapping her body with increasing boldness.

"Strength training is fundamentally about learning to accept intensity," Sterling explained during their fifth session, his body pressed against hers from behind as he supposedly helped her maintain proper alignment during a modified plank exercise. "Most women resist intensity because they've been taught to fear their own capacity for power. Real empowerment comes from surrendering to someone who can guide you through that intensity toward genuine strength."

By the second week, Sterling had begun scheduling what he called "recovery sessions" in addition to their regular training—private appointments in one of the soundproofed "recovery suites" where he provided massage therapy that was becoming increasingly sexual in nature. His touches lingered in areas that had nothing to do with muscle recovery, his comments about her body became more explicitly sexual, and his expectations for physical intimacy grew more obvious with each encounter.

"Your body is responding beautifully to the training," Sterling said during one such session, his hands on her inner thighs under the guise of addressing muscle tension. "But I'm noticing some residual holding patterns—places where you're still protecting yourself, maintaining barriers that prevent full integration of physical and emotional strength. True transformation requires releasing those protective mechanisms completely."

When Alira tensed at his increasingly inappropriate touching, Sterling used her discomfort as a teaching moment—exactly as he'd done with countless victims before her.

"There it is," he said, his voice taking on an excited edge that suggested he found her resistance arousing rather than off-putting. "That protective instinct, that fear of surrendering control. That's exactly what we need to work through if you're going to achieve genuine empowerment rather than just surface-level fitness improvements."

But while Sterling believed he was successfully grooming another victim, Alira was methodically documenting his pattern and planning his elimination. She noted the progression of his boundary violations, catalogued his psychological manipulation tactics, and identified the specific vulnerabilities in his security and routine that would allow for operational execution.

Most importantly, she began observing Sterling's interactions with other clients, recognizing that she wasn't his only current target. There was a young blonde woman—early twenties, athletic build—who'd been training with Sterling for several weeks and who showed the classic signs of someone being groomed through the same systematic process Alira was experiencing.

The woman's name was Emily, according to conversations Alira overheard at the gym's reception desk. She was a pre-med student, enthusiastic about fitness, grateful for Sterling's "special attention" and his willingness to provide intensive personal coaching that went beyond standard training sessions.

Alira watched Emily's interactions with Sterling during the times when their gym schedules overlapped, noting how Sterling deployed the same psychological tactics with her that he was using with Alira—the invasive personal questions, the normalization of inappropriate touching, the framing of boundary violations as therapeutic breakthroughs.

Emily was several weeks ahead of Alira in Sterling's grooming timeline, which meant she was closer to the moment when Sterling would escalate from psychological manipulation and inappropriate touching to actual sexual assault. The recognition created operational urgency—Alira needed to eliminate Sterling before he destroyed Emily's life the way he'd destroyed at least twelve other women over the past five years.

But Alira also understood that hasty action created mistakes, and mistakes created patterns that investigators might recognize. She needed to be patient, to allow Sterling to continue his escalation with her while ensuring that Emily remained safe until the operation could be executed properly.

During their tenth training session, Sterling's behavior shifted in ways that suggested he was preparing to escalate beyond the psychological manipulation and boundary testing that had characterized their previous encounters. The session was scheduled for 6 AM as usual, but Sterling had sent a text message the previous evening suggesting they meet at 5:30 AM instead "for a special intensive session that requires extra time and privacy."

Alira arrived at the designated time, finding the gym completely empty except for Sterling. Even the other early-morning trainers who usually arrived around 5:45 AM hadn't yet appeared, leaving Sterling and Alira alone in the vast facility.

"I'm glad you could come early," Sterling said as he met her at the entrance, his demeanor more intense than she'd seen during previous sessions. "We're going to work on breaking through some of the psychological barriers that have been limiting your progress. This requires complete privacy and your full commitment to trusting the process even when it feels uncomfortable."

He led her not to their usual training room but to one of the soundproofed recovery suites on the third floor—a space Alira had identified during her reconnaissance as Sterling's preferred location for assaults. The room was equipped with a massage table, dim lighting that could be adjusted to create intimate atmosphere, and most importantly, a door that locked from the inside with no external override.

"Today we're going to work on your relationship with surrender," Sterling explained, his voice taking on the commanding edge that indicated he was shifting from grooming phase to actual assault. "True strength comes from understanding when to yield to superior guidance, when to accept that someone else knows what you need better than you know yourself."

His hands settled on her shoulders with more force than usual, turning her to face the massage table. "I want you to remove your outer layer and lie face-down on the table. The techniques I'm going to use require direct skin contact for proper effect—clothing creates barriers that prevent the kind of deep transformation we're working toward."

It was the moment Alira had been waiting for—Sterling dropping the pretense of professional training and making explicit sexual demands that would constitute assault if she complied under the coercion he'd been building through weeks of psychological manipulation.

"I don't think I'm comfortable with that," Alira said, backing away slightly while maintaining her cover as someone who was confused and uncertain rather than deliberately baiting a predator.

Sterling's expression hardened in ways that revealed the anger lurking beneath his charming façade. "Lauren, we've talked about this resistance pattern. You came here because you need transformation, because your life isn't working, because you need someone who can guide you past the psychological limitations that have been holding you back. But transformation requires discomfort. It requires trusting me completely, even when—especially when—your instincts tell you to protect yourself."

He moved toward her with deliberate purpose, his body language shifting from seductive to threatening. "You don't get to pick and choose which parts of the process you're willing to engage with. Either you're committed to genuine change, or you're just wasting both of our time pretending you want something you're not brave enough to actually pursue."

Alira allowed fear to show in her expression while her mind catalogued Sterling's tactical positioning and calculated optimal responses to his escalating aggression. He was blocking her access to the door, using his size and physical presence to intimidate her into compliance, deploying the same combination of psychological pressure and physical threat that he'd used to assault at least twelve women over the past five years.

"I need to leave," Alira said, moving toward the door with apparent panic.

Sterling grabbed her arm, his grip firm enough to prevent her movement without being so forceful that it would leave obvious bruises. "You're not leaving. We haven't finished your session, and you need to understand that running away from discomfort is exactly the pattern that's kept you weak and powerless. Today you're going to learn what it means to surrender completely, to accept guidance even when every instinct tells you to resist."

His other hand reached for the door lock, engaging the mechanism that would prevent external entry while trapping them both inside the soundproofed room where his previous assaults had occurred.

But Sterling had made a critical miscalculation. He'd assessed Alira as another vulnerable victim whose weeks of grooming had prepared her to submit when confronted with explicit demands. He had no idea that the woman he was attempting to assault was actually a highly trained fighter who'd been studying his every move and planning his death with methodical precision.

The kata began with a simple wrist break—a basic aikido technique that Sterling never saw coming. One moment his hand was on her arm in a controlling grip, the next his wrist was bent at an unnatural angle and Alira had spun away from his grasp with movements so fluid they seemed choreographed rather than defensive.

"What the fuck—" Sterling began, but Alira was already moving into a follow-up strike.

She targeted his solar plexus with a precise palm strike that disrupted his breathing and created the disorientation necessary for follow-up techniques. Sterling staggered backward, his expression shifting from shock to rage as he recognized that his supposed victim was actually someone with sophisticated combat training.

"You little bitch," he snarled, launching himself at her with the aggressive forward charge that wrestlers defaulted to when surprised by resistance.

Alira sidestepped his attack with minimal movement, using his momentum against him to execute a hip throw that sent him crashing into the massage table. The table shattered under his weight, expensive equipment scattering across the floor as Sterling struggled to regain his footing.

"Stay down," Alira said, her voice no longer soft and vulnerable but clear and commanding, carrying the authority of someone completely in control of the confrontation. "This doesn't have to get worse for you."

But Sterling was already scrambling to his feet, his ego and his rage overriding any tactical assessment of whether he was actually capable of overpowering someone with Alira's evident training. He charged again, this time managing to close distance and drive her backward against the wall.

They grappled briefly, Sterling trying to use his superior size and wrestling experience to pin her while Alira worked to break free and create the distance necessary for her striking techniques to be most effective. His hands closed around her throat—not yet applying lethal pressure but demonstrating his intent to harm rather than just restrain.

Alira drove her thumbs into the pressure points behind Sterling's ears, a technique that caused immediate disorientation and disrupted his grip. As he recoiled from the pain, she brought her knee up into his groin with sufficient force to drop him to the floor, gasping and temporarily incapacitated.

She could have finished him then—could have applied a blood choke that would render him unconscious in seconds, could have struck pressure points that would cause permanent damage or death. But Alira understood that this first physical confrontation served a different operational purpose than immediate elimination.

She needed Sterling alive and frightened, needed him to understand that the woman he'd been grooming was actually someone far more dangerous than he'd recognized. Most importantly, she needed to create a scenario where Sterling's own actions and choices would eventually lead to his death in ways that couldn't be traced back to her involvement.

As Sterling lay on the floor clutching his groin and fighting for breath, Alira collected her gym bag and moved toward the door.

"This is your warning," she said, her voice cold and controlled. "Stop targeting vulnerable women. Stop using your position to exploit people who trust you. Because if you don't, you'll eventually encounter someone who won't stop at a warning."

She unlocked the door and left Sterling in the destroyed recovery suite, walking calmly through the empty gym and out into the early morning darkness.

The first strike had been delivered. Sterling now knew that she wasn't the vulnerable victim he'd believed her to be, which would make him more cautious about future attempts to assault her specifically. But it would also make him paranoid and angry, emotional states that would cloud his judgment and make him careless about security measures that might otherwise protect him.

More importantly, the confrontation had established a plausible self-defense scenario that Alira could reference if Sterling turned up dead under circumstances that required explanation. She'd fought back against an attempted assault, demonstrating her willingness to defend herself physically when necessary.

When Sterling died—and he would die, soon—investigators would find evidence of a violent struggle in the recovery suite, documentation of his attempted assault, and a clear pattern suggesting he'd victimized the wrong woman and paid the ultimate price for his predatory behavior.

But first, Alira needed to ensure that Emily remained safe while the operational planning reached its final stages. She'd observed enough of Sterling's pattern to recognize that Emily was in immediate danger, potentially just days away from experiencing the same assault that Sterling had attempted with Alira.

As she drove away from Apex Fitness, Alira was already calculating how to accelerate Sterling's elimination while creating circumstances that would make his death appear to be a tragic accident or justified consequence of his own violent behavior.

The hunt was entering its critical phase, and Marcus Sterling's days of predatory impunity were rapidly coming to an end.

CUSTOS *Guardian*

_____

"When no one else would protect them, she became their shield."

Chapter 4

The Assault

Emily Hale arrived at Apex Fitness at 4:15 PM on a Tuesday afternoon in early June, her mind preoccupied with the upcoming anatomy exam she'd been studying for all week. The pre-med program at the university was demanding, and Emily prided herself on maintaining perfect grades while also taking care of her physical health through regular training sessions with Marcus Sterling.

Sterling had been an amazing discovery three weeks ago when Emily had joined Apex Fitness on the recommendation of a sorority sister. He was intense but encouraging, pushing her past limits she hadn't known she was capable of exceeding, helping her develop not just physical strength but the kind of mental toughness that would serve her well in medical school.

"Emily!" Jessica called from the reception desk as Emily signed in. "Marcus wanted me to let you know he's adjusted your session time today. He has a scheduling conflict later, so he'd like to get started a bit early if possible—maybe 4:30 instead of 5:00?"

"That works perfectly," Emily replied, grateful for the earlier start time that would give her more evening hours for studying. "I'll just change and head up."

In the locker room, Emily changed into her workout clothes while reviewing anatomy flashcards—her typical routine of maximizing every available minute for productive activity. She'd always been driven, always been focused on achievement, qualities that her father Marcus Hale both admired and worried about. He'd expressed concern about her joining an expensive gym, suggesting she could maintain fitness through the university's athletic facilities, but Emily had explained that the specialized training was worth the investment.

Sterling met her at the entrance to the second-floor training area, his usual energetic enthusiasm seeming slightly more intense than normal. "Thanks for being flexible about the time change," he said, his hand settling on her shoulder in the familiar gesture that had become standard during their sessions. "I want to work on some advanced resistance techniques today, which require extra focus and privacy."

He led her not to their usual training room but to one of the recovery suites on the third floor—a space Emily had seen but never used before. "I thought we'd change up the environment," Sterling explained when she expressed mild surprise. "These rooms are designed for intensive one-on-one work without the distraction of other gym members. Plus, the equipment here is specialized for the techniques I want to teach you."

The suite was smaller than the regular training rooms, equipped with a massage table, various resistance bands and specialized equipment, and lighting that could be dimmed for what Sterling called "mindfulness integration exercises." He closed the door behind them and engaged the lock—something he'd never done during their previous sessions.

"For these advanced techniques to be effective, we need absolute privacy," Sterling explained, noting Emily's glance at the locked door. "The whole point is creating an environment where you can focus completely on pushing past your psychological barriers without worrying about external observation or judgment."

Emily felt a flutter of unease but dismissed it as nervousness about trying something new and challenging. Sterling had been nothing but professional during their three weeks of training, and she trusted his judgment about what she needed to advance toward her fitness goals.

"Before we begin the physical work," Sterling said, positioning himself between Emily and the door in ways that seemed casual but which actually controlled her movement options, "I want to talk about something I've noticed during our sessions. You're incredibly disciplined and focused, which is admirable. But I think you're also protecting yourself psychologically— maintaining control in ways that prevent you from accessing your full potential."

"I'm not sure I understand," Emily replied, confused about how psychological analysis related to fitness training.

"Strength isn't just physical," Sterling said, moving closer with the kind of intense focus that made Emily feel simultaneously valued and uncomfortable. "True power comes from understanding when to surrender control, when to trust someone else's guidance completely even when your instincts tell you to maintain protective barriers. That's what separates good athletes from great ones—the willingness to be vulnerable in pursuit of excellence."

His hand settled on her shoulder again, but this time the touch felt different—more possessive than supportive, lingering longer than professional contact would justify. "Today I want you to try something that might feel uncomfortable at first. I want you to practice surrendering to guidance completely, accepting intensity even when it triggers your protective instincts."

"What kind of intensity?" Emily asked, the unease growing stronger despite her efforts to dismiss it as irrational anxiety.

"Physical and psychological," Sterling replied, his other hand moving to her other shoulder so that he was facing her directly, his body positioned close enough that she had to look up to maintain eye contact. "Trust exercises that require you to overcome your natural tendency to maintain control. It's similar to what therapists do with EMDR therapy—creating controlled discomfort to process and overcome psychological limitations."

He reached for the bottle of enhanced sports drink he'd prepared—something he'd told Emily contained specialized electrolytes and amino acids designed to optimize her performance during intensive training. "Start by drinking this. It's formulated to help with the advanced work we're doing today—keeps your blood sugar stable and your mind focused even when exercises push you into uncomfortable territory."

Emily accepted the bottle and took several long drinks, trusting Sterling's expertise about nutrition and supplementation. The drink tasted slightly different from the regular sports drinks she was used to—more bitter, with an aftertaste that lingered unpleasantly. But Sterling had explained that high-quality supplements often tasted worse than commercial products because they contained active ingredients at therapeutic levels rather than being designed primarily for palatability.

"Good," Sterling said, watching her drink with unusual intensity. "Now I want you to do some breathing exercises while the supplements take effect. Close your eyes, focus on your breath, and practice surrendering conscious control—just allowing your body to relax completely while trusting that I'm guiding the process."

Emily complied, closing her eyes and attempting the mindfulness breathing that Sterling had taught her during previous sessions. But within minutes, she began feeling strange—dizzy and disoriented in ways that seemed disproportionate to simple breathing exercises. Her thoughts became fuzzy and disconnected, her body feeling heavy and uncoordinated.

"I feel weird," she said, opening her eyes with effort. The room seemed to tilt slightly, and Sterling's face appeared somehow distorted—his features too sharp, his expression predatory in ways that her increasingly impaired cognition struggled to process.

"That's normal," Sterling assured her, his voice seeming to come from very far away despite his physical proximity. "The breathing exercises combined with the supplements create an altered state that helps bypass your conscious resistance. Just relax into it. Trust the process. Let me guide you."

His hands were on her again, but now the touching was unmistakably sexual rather than professional—sliding from her shoulders down her arms, moving to her waist, beginning to pull at her clothing with intent that even Emily's drugged consciousness recognized as wrong and dangerous.

"Stop," Emily said, trying to push his hands away. But her body wasn't responding properly—her movements were slow and uncoordinated, her strength seeming to have evaporated. "I don't want... this isn't..."

"Yes it is," Sterling said, his voice taking on a commanding edge that carried none of the supportive warmth she'd associated with him during previous sessions. "This is exactly what you need, what you've been working toward whether you consciously recognized it or not. Surrender, Emily. Stop fighting the process and accept what's happening."

Emily tried to stand, tried to move toward the door, but her legs wouldn't support her weight properly. She stumbled and Sterling caught her, his arms around her waist in a grip that was restraining rather than supportive. His hands were pulling at her workout clothes, removing barriers while Emily's drugged consciousness struggled to comprehend what was happening and mount effective resistance.

"No," she managed to say, her voice weak and slurred. "Please... I need to leave... this isn't right..."

"You're not leaving," Sterling said, lifting her toward the massage table with strength that her impaired state couldn't effectively counter. "You're going to learn what real transformation feels like, what it means to surrender completely to someone who understands your needs better than you understand them yourself."

Emily tried to fight—tried to push him away, tried to scream, tried to do anything that might stop what was clearly about to happen. But the drug he'd given her had stolen her coordination and strength, leaving her technically conscious but functionally helpless as Sterling positioned her on the massage table and continued removing her clothing.

The assault itself would remain fragmented and nightmarish in Emily's memory—disconnected sensory impressions of violation and pain, Sterling's weight on her body, his hands holding her down when she tried to resist, his voice telling her to "relax" and "accept" what was happening as though her resistance was psychological dysfunction rather than entirely appropriate response to being raped.

At some point during the assault, Emily's impaired consciousness registered that Sterling had stopped— not because he'd changed his mind or experienced moral awakening, but because something had interrupted him. There were voices, sounds of other people in the gym, some distraction that pulled his attention away from completing the rape he'd clearly intended.

"Fuck," Sterling muttered, pulling away from Emily and hastily adjusting his clothing. "Stay here. Don't move. Don't say anything to anyone or you'll regret it in ways you can't imagine."

He left the room, locking it from the outside to prevent Emily from escaping while he dealt with whatever interruption had occurred. Emily lay on the massage table, her drugged mind trying to process what had happened and what was still happening, trying to formulate some plan for escape or rescue despite the cognitive impairment that made coherent thought nearly impossible.

She managed to roll off the table, her body hitting the floor with a impact that sent pain shooting through her shoulder. She needed to get to the door, needed to find help, needed to escape before Sterling returned to complete the assault he'd begun.

Using the wall for support, Emily pulled herself upright and stumbled toward the door, her hands fumbling with the lock mechanism that Sterling had engaged. Her fingers weren't working properly—the fine motor control necessary to operate the lock seemed beyond her current capabilities—but desperation drove her to keep trying despite repeated failures.

She could hear Sterling's voice outside, talking to someone with the false warmth and professional competence that had fooled her into trusting him. He would be back soon, would return to finish what he'd started, unless Emily could somehow get the door open and escape.

The lock finally yielded to her clumsy efforts, the door swinging open to reveal the empty third-floor hallway. Emily lurched forward, her drugged body barely capable of maintaining balance as she moved toward the stairs that would lead to the main floor and hopefully to other people who could help her.

But her coordination was deteriorating rapidly as the drug continued affecting her system. She made it to the top of the stairs and began descending, but her legs gave out halfway down the flight. She tumbled forward, her body unable to catch itself or control the fall, her head striking the concrete edge of the bottom stair with devastating force.

Emily's last conscious thought before darkness claimed her was that she needed to tell someone what Sterling had done, needed to warn other women, needed to ensure he faced consequences. But then consciousness fled completely, her body lying motionless at the bottom of the stairwell while blood pooled beneath her fractured skull.

Jessica Rodriguez discovered Emily's body at 5:47 PM when she came upstairs to check on why the third-floor lights were still on after business hours. She found the young woman lying unconscious at the bottom of the stairwell, her face swollen and beginning to bruise, blood matting her hair where her head had struck the concrete.

Jessica screamed and immediately called 911, her training as a first responder kicking in as she checked

Emily's vital signs and positioned her carefully to prevent additional injury. Emily was breathing but unresponsive, her pulse weak and thready, her pupils unequal in size—all signs suggesting serious head trauma.

The paramedics arrived within eight minutes, their assessment confirming Jessica's worst fears. Emily had sustained severe traumatic brain injury and needed immediate emergency intervention. They loaded her onto a stretcher with careful attention to cervical spine protection and rushed her to the university medical center's trauma unit.

Marcus Sterling appeared in the stairwell as the paramedics were preparing Emily for transport, his expression showing exactly the right amount of shock and concern that an innocent trainer would display when discovering that a client had been seriously injured.

"Oh my God, what happened?" he asked, his voice carrying genuine-seeming distress. "Emily and I finished our training session maybe forty-five minutes ago. She said she was going to shower and then head home to study. I have no idea how she ended up on the third floor or why she was using these stairs."

"Did she seem okay when your session ended?" one of the paramedics asked while continuing to work on stabilizing Emily for transport.

"She seemed fine," Sterling replied smoothly, deploying the false narrative he'd already constructed. "Maybe a little tired from the workout—we did some intensive resistance training—but otherwise completely normal. Certainly nothing that would suggest she was in danger of falling or having some kind of medical emergency."

Jessica looked at Sterling with an expression that suggested she wasn't entirely convinced by his account, but she said nothing in front of the paramedics. She'd worked at Apex Fitness for two years, had seen Sterling with countless female clients, had noticed patterns that troubled her but which she'd never felt empowered to question or report.

After the ambulance departed with Emily, Sterling turned to Jessica with an intensity that felt threatening despite the careful neutrality of his words. "This is obviously a tragic accident—Emily must have gotten disoriented or dizzy after our intensive session and fallen while trying to navigate the stairs. But I need you to understand that any speculation or gossip about what happened could create serious liability issues for the gym. If police or attorneys start asking questions, you should refer them to our legal team rather than offering your own theories."

The implicit threat was clear—Jessica's job security and potentially her professional future depended on maintaining the narrative that Emily's injuries resulted from a simple accident rather than anything more sinister occurring at Apex Fitness.

"Of course," Jessica said carefully, understanding that challenging Sterling would accomplish nothing except endangering her own employment. "I'll let legal handle any official inquiries."

Sterling returned to his office and immediately called his attorney—the same legal representative who'd handled his previous settlement negotiations with assault victims. The attorney listened to Sterling's account of Emily's "accidental fall" and provided explicit instructions about how to handle potential police investigation.

"Do not speak to police without me present," the attorney said firmly. "Do not provide any samples or evidence without a warrant. Do not make any statements that could be interpreted as admitting liability or responsibility. If they want to interview you, invoke your right to have legal counsel present and then call me immediately."

"What about security footage?" Sterling asked, knowing that the cameras would show Emily entering his private training room but not exiting—a gap that might raise questions about what had occurred during their session.

"The footage shows a client attending a scheduled training session, nothing more," the attorney replied.

"Any injuries she sustained after leaving your session are not your responsibility unless there's evidence you directly caused them. And since you were nowhere near the stairwell when she fell, there's no way to establish that connection."

Sterling ended the call feeling reasonably confident that his legal protections would hold. He'd assaulted women before and escaped consequences through exactly this combination of legal maneuvering and institutional protection. Emily's case would be no different—tragic accident, unfortunate outcome, but nothing that could be definitively connected to Sterling's actions in ways that would support criminal prosecution.

What Sterling didn't know was that Emily's father was a detective with fifteen years of experience investigating violent crimes, or that Detective Marcus Hale would bring the full force of his professional expertise and personal rage to bear on ensuring Sterling faced consequences regardless of how sophisticated his legal defenses might be.

And Sterling certainly didn't know that Alira Sinclair— the woman he'd attempted to assault just days earlier— was already planning his elimination with the same methodical precision she'd applied to killing four previous predators who'd believed themselves untouchable.

The assault on Emily Hale had set in motion a chain of events that would culminate in Sterling's death, though the exact mechanism and timing remained to be determined by variables that were still unfolding.

But one thing was certain: Marcus Sterling's days of predatory impunity were numbered, and the countdown had already begun.

TENEBRAE *Darkness*

———

"She did not fear the darkness. She had become it."

Chapter 5

The Coma

Emily Hale remained in a medically induced coma for the first seventy-two hours following her admission to the university medical center's intensive care unit. The neurosurgical team had performed emergency craniotomy to relieve the massive intracranial pressure caused by bleeding and swelling in her brain, removing a section of her skull to allow the damaged tissue room to expand without causing additional catastrophic injury.

The surgery had been technically successful—they'd stopped the bleeding, evacuated the accumulated blood, and stabilized Emily's condition enough that she was no longer in immediate danger of death. But the prognosis remained uncertain and troubling. The traumatic brain injury was extensive, affecting multiple areas of her brain including regions responsible for memory formation, executive function, and possibly consciousness itself.

Detective Marcus Hale had maintained constant vigil at his daughter's bedside since her admission, leaving only for brief periods when hospital staff insisted he needed rest or when Detective Martinez required his input on the investigation. His ex-wife Patricia had arrived from Seattle within hours of his initial call, and they'd established an uneasy partnership in their shared terror—taking turns sitting with Emily, talking to her unconscious form, willing her to wake up and be the brilliant, driven young woman she'd been before Marcus Sterling had destroyed her life.

The neurologist, Dr. Lee Han, provided daily updates that were carefully worded to avoid offering false hope while also not completely crushing the desperate optimism that kept Hale and Patricia functioning through the nightmare.

"Emily's brain activity shows some encouraging signs," Dr. Han explained during one such update on the fourth day of her hospitalization. "She's not brain-dead— there's definite neural function occurring. But the pattern of activity suggests she's in a state of minimal consciousness rather than true awareness. She may be processing some sensory input at a subconscious level, but there's no indication she's able to integrate that information into coherent thought or purposeful response."

"When will you bring her out of the medically induced coma?" Hale asked, his voice rough from days of minimal sleep and constant stress.

"We've actually already begun reducing the sedation," Dr. Han replied. "Over the next twenty-four to forty-eight hours, the medications will clear her system and we'll see what level of consciousness she can achieve on her own. That will give us a much clearer picture of the extent of her injuries and her potential for recovery."

"And if she doesn't wake up?" Patricia asked, the question they'd both been avoiding voicing explicitly.

Dr. Han's expression showed compassionate honesty. "Then we'll be facing difficult decisions about long-term care options and quality of life considerations. But let's not get ahead of ourselves. Many traumatic brain injury patients surprise us with their resilience. Emily is young, previously healthy, receiving excellent medical care. Those factors all work in her favor."

After Dr. Han left, Hale and Patricia sat in silence on opposite sides of Emily's bed, each holding one of their daughter's hands as machines beeped rhythmically around them.

"This is my fault," Hale said finally, the guilt he'd been carrying since Emily's injury finding voice. "I should have been more involved in her life, should have known she'd joined this gym, should have checked out this trainer before she started working with him. If I'd done my job as a father instead of being so focused on my cases—"

"Don't," Patricia interrupted firmly. "This isn't your fault, Marcus. Emily is twenty-one years old, an adult making her own decisions about where to train and who to trust. You couldn't have prevented this any more than I could have. The only person responsible for what happened to our daughter is the man who assaulted her."

"Marcus Sterling," Hale said, the name carrying all the rage and helplessness he'd been feeling since identifying Sterling as the primary suspect. "Who's going to walk away from this without facing any consequences unless we can build a case that his expensive attorneys can't dismantle."

"What's the status of the investigation?" Patricia asked, though she already knew that Hale had been receiving constant updates from Detective Martinez despite technically being removed from the case due to his personal involvement.

"Martinez is doing everything possible," Hale replied. "But we're facing the same obstacles that allow predators like Sterling to operate with impunity for years. No security footage of what actually happened in that private training room. Sterling claiming Emily left his session in good health and that her injuries must have occurred sometime later. His attorney blocking every attempt to obtain DNA samples or conduct more thorough interviews. And most critically, Emily can't testify about what he did to her."

He gestured toward their unconscious daughter, his voice breaking. "Even if Emily wakes up, she probably won't remember the assault. The neurologist says trauma-induced amnesia is almost inevitable with this level of head injury—her brain will have erased the memories formed immediately before and during the traumatic event as a protective mechanism. Which means the bastard who did this will get away with it because the legal system requires victim testimony to prosecute sexual assault cases effectively."

Patricia's expression showed the same impotent rage that Hale felt. "So Sterling just... continues operating? Continues assaulting women? Faces no consequences despite destroying our daughter's life and God knows how many others?"

"Unless we find evidence compelling enough to overcome his legal defenses," Hale confirmed. "Martinez has identified at least six other women who've been assaulted by Sterling over the past five years. All of them settled through confidential agreements that included substantial payments and non-disclosure clauses. All of them too frightened or too legally constrained to testify publicly about what he did to them."

"Can't those settlement agreements be challenged? Shouldn't there be some legal mechanism that prevents predators from using money to silence their victims indefinitely?"

"There should be," Hale agreed bitterly. "But the legal system values contract enforcement and confidentiality agreements more than it values holding powerful men accountable for sexual violence. Sterling's attorneys drafted those settlements specifically to make them legally bulletproof—violation of the NDAs would result in massive financial penalties that the victims can't afford, plus additional legal action that would publicly destroy them."

They sat in heavy silence, both understanding that the system Hale had spent his career defending was failing their daughter just as comprehensively as it had failed Sterling's previous victims.

On the sixth day of Emily's hospitalization, the sedation had been fully withdrawn and medical staff were waiting to see what level of consciousness she would achieve on her own. Hale and Patricia maintained their vigil, watching for any sign that Emily was emerging from the coma that had protected her brain during the critical early healing period.

Dr. Han conducted regular neurological assessments, testing Emily's reflexes and responses to various stimuli—pain, light, sound, verbal commands. The results were mixed and frustrating. Emily showed some basic reflexive responses to painful stimuli, suggesting her brain stem was functioning adequately. Her eyes would occasionally open, though they didn't track movement or focus on objects in ways that indicated conscious visual processing.

"She's in what we call a vegetative state," Dr. Han explained during his afternoon rounds. "Her brain is managing basic autonomic functions—breathing, heart rate, sleep-wake cycles—but there's no evidence of conscious awareness or purposeful interaction with her environment. This could be temporary as her brain continues healing, or it could represent a more permanent state depending on the extent of the damage."

"How long before we know which it is?" Hale asked, the question emerging more harshly than he'd intended.

"Weeks to months," Dr. Han replied honestly. "Traumatic brain injury recovery doesn't follow predictable timelines. Some patients emerge from vegetative states days after we expect them to remain unconscious. Others take months or years to show improvement. And some, unfortunately, never regain meaningful consciousness despite our best interventions."

After Dr. Han left, Hale remained at Emily's bedside, holding her hand and talking to her even though he had no way to know if she could hear or process anything he said.

"Emmy, I need you to fight," he said quietly, using the childhood nickname that had fallen away as she'd grown into the serious, driven young woman lying motionless in the hospital bed. "I know you're in there somewhere, and I know your brain is doing everything it can to heal. But you have to keep fighting, have to keep trying to come back to us. Your mom and I need you. The world needs you—all those patients you were going to help as a doctor, all the lives you were going to save."

He paused, his voice breaking. "And I need you to wake up so you can tell me what happened, so we can make sure the man who did this to you faces consequences. Because right now, he's going to walk away. He's going to continue assaulting other women unless we can build a case strong enough to overcome his legal protections. And the only way we can do that is if you can testify about what he did to you."

There was no response, no flicker of awareness, no sign that Emily had heard or understood anything he'd said. Just the steady beep of monitors and the mechanical rhythm of the ventilator that continued supporting her breathing.

While Hale maintained his bedside vigil, Detective Martinez was methodically building the strongest case possible given the evidentiary limitations she faced. She'd interviewed Jessica Rodriguez extensively, documenting the receptionist's account of Emily's arrival at the gym, Sterling's request for an earlier session time, and the discovery of Emily's body at the bottom of the third-floor stairwell.

Jessica had been cooperative but clearly frightened about potential professional consequences of speaking too openly about her suspicions regarding Sterling's behavior. She'd worked at Apex Fitness for two years and had observed patterns that troubled her—the way Sterling isolated certain clients in private training rooms, the number of young women who'd left the gym abruptly after working with him, the whispered conversations among female members about Sterling being "intense" or "crossing boundaries."

But Jessica had never reported these observations to management or authorities because Sterling was the gym's primary revenue generator and because challenging him would have meant losing her job. She was a single mother with two young children, dependent on her Apex Fitness salary and health insurance, unable to afford the economic consequences of becoming a whistleblower.

"I knew something was wrong," Jessica told Martinez during one particularly emotional interview. "I could see it in how some of the women looked after their sessions with Sterling—that shaken, confused expression of someone who's experienced something traumatic but isn't sure if they're allowed to call it that. I should have said something, should have done something to warn them or protect them. But I was too afraid of losing my job to act on what I knew was happening."

"You're not responsible for Sterling's actions," Martinez assured her, though she understood the guilt Jessica was carrying. "The person accountable for Emily's assault is Sterling himself, not the people who were too economically vulnerable to challenge him."

Martinez had also obtained the security footage from Apex Fitness, confirming that Emily had entered Sterling's private training room at 4:28 PM and that no footage existed of her leaving. The cameras covering the third-floor stairwell showed Emily stumbling down the stairs alone at 5:43 PM—nearly seventy-five minutes after entering Sterling's room—her movements clearly impaired and uncoordinated in ways consistent with either severe intoxication or drug-induced cognitive dysfunction.

The footage was suggestive but not definitive. It showed that something had happened during the seventy-five minute gap, something that had left Emily so impaired she couldn't navigate stairs safely. But it didn't prove Sterling had assaulted her or administered drugs without her consent, and his attorneys would argue that Emily might have taken something voluntarily or experienced some kind of spontaneous medical event.

Most frustratingly, Sterling had refused all requests to provide DNA samples or submit to interviews without his attorney present. When Martinez had finally conducted a formal interview with Sterling's attorney in attendance, Sterling had deployed a carefully crafted narrative that was almost impossible to refute without Emily's testimony.

"My client conducted a routine training session with Ms. Hale from approximately 4:30 PM to 5:15 PM," the attorney stated for the record. "The session involved intensive resistance training in one of our private recovery suites. Ms. Hale appeared tired but otherwise normal when the session concluded. She mentioned wanting to shower before heading home to study. My client left the facility shortly after 5:30 PM for a dinner appointment that is documented through restaurant receipts and witness testimony. He had no knowledge of Ms. Hale's injuries until he was contacted by police the following day."

"Why did the session occur in a private recovery suite rather than in the regular training rooms where security cameras document sessions?" Martinez asked, knowing the answer but wanting it on record.

"The advanced techniques my client was teaching required specialized equipment available only in the recovery suites," the attorney replied smoothly. "Additionally, many clients prefer privacy for intensive sessions where they may need to make mistakes and struggle without concern about being observed by other gym members."

"Why is there no security footage showing Ms. Hale leaving the recovery suite if the session ended at 5:15 PM but she didn't fall on the stairs until 5:43 PM?"

"The recovery suites are equipped with private showers and changing facilities. My client assumed Ms. Hale was using those facilities before leaving, which would explain the time gap. He has no way to know what Ms. Hale did during those twenty-eight minutes because he'd already left the building."

The narrative was plausible enough to create reasonable doubt, which was all Sterling needed. Without Emily's testimony or DNA evidence definitively linking Sterling to the assault, Martinez was facing an uphill battle to build a prosecutable case.

The DNA evidence from the rape kit was both helpful and limited. It confirmed that Emily had been sexually assaulted—there was clear evidence of vaginal trauma and the presence of seminal fluid. But without Sterling's DNA for comparison, investigators couldn't definitively prove he was the perpetrator. The DNA profile could be entered into criminal databases to check for matches with known offenders, but if Sterling had never been arrested and forced to provide samples, his profile wouldn't be in the system.

Martinez had also obtained a warrant to search the recovery suite where Emily's session had occurred, finding evidence that supported the narrative of violent assault but which didn't definitively prove Sterling's involvement. The massage table had been damaged—one of its legs partially broken in ways consistent with it being used during a struggle. There were bloodstains on the floor that DNA testing confirmed belonged to Emily, likely from injuries sustained during the assault or the subsequent fall.

Most significantly, toxicology analysis of Emily's blood drawn during her emergency room admission showed the presence of scopolamine—a drug that caused temporary cognitive impairment and extreme suggestibility while leaving victims technically conscious and apparently cooperative.

"The scopolamine is huge," Martinez told Hale during one of their updates. "Emily couldn't have taken that drug voluntarily—it's not recreationally available and has no legitimate therapeutic use in the context of fitness training. Someone administered it to her with intent to incapacitate her cognitive function while maintaining enough consciousness that she could appear to be participating voluntarily."

"Can we prove Sterling gave it to her?" Hale asked, though he already knew the answer.

"Not definitively," Martinez admitted. "He could claim she ingested it elsewhere before their session, or that someone else gave it to her after she left his room. Without her testimony about him providing her with a doctored sports drink or supplement, we can't establish the chain of administration in ways that would survive legal challenge."

The investigation continued over the following two weeks, Martinez documenting every possible piece of evidence while understanding that the case was fundamentally hobbled by Emily's inability to testify. The medical examiner had classified Emily's injuries as consistent with sexual assault and traumatic fall, but couldn't definitively rule on whether the fall was accidental or the result of drug-induced impairment administered by her assailant.

The district attorney's office reviewed Martinez's case file and delivered the verdict that Hale had been dreading: insufficient evidence to prosecute. Without victim testimony, without DNA comparison proving Sterling's involvement, without definitive proof that he'd administered the scopolamine, the case couldn't meet the evidentiary standards required for criminal charges.

"We could potentially pursue assault charges based on the physical evidence and the scopolamine," the assistant district attorney explained during a meeting with Martinez and Hale. "But Sterling's attorneys would argue that Emily's injuries occurred after she left his session, that the scopolamine could have come from another source, and that no evidence directly links their client to any criminal act. A jury would have reasonable doubt, which means we'd lose at trial and Sterling would walk away completely exonerated."

"So we do nothing?" Hale asked, his voice dangerously quiet. "We just let Sterling continue operating his gym, continue assaulting women, continue destroying lives because the legal system requires a level of proof that's impossible to obtain when victims are too drugged or brain-damaged to testify?"

"We don't have sufficient evidence to prosecute at this time," the ADA said carefully. "If Emily wakes up and can provide testimony about what occurred, or if we obtain DNA evidence linking Sterling to the assault, we can revisit the charging decision. But based on current evidence, proceeding to trial would likely result in acquittal and would prevent us from re-filing charges even if better evidence emerges later."

After the meeting, Hale sat in his car in the parking garage, his hands gripping the steering wheel hard enough to make his knuckles white. The system had failed Emily just as comprehensively as it had failed every other victim of powerful predators who understood how to exploit legal procedures and evidentiary requirements to escape accountability.

His phone buzzed with a text from Patricia: "Dr. Han says Emily is showing some increased brain activity. They're cautiously optimistic she might emerge from the vegetative state soon. Please come back to the hospital."

Hale drove back to the medical center, his mind cycling between desperate hope that Emily would wake up and provide the testimony needed to prosecute Sterling, and terrible certainty that even if she woke up, her brain injury would have erased the memories that could ensure justice.

When he arrived at Emily's ICU room, he found Patricia sitting beside their daughter's bed with an expression of fragile hope.

"She opened her eyes," Patricia said, her voice breaking with emotion. "Not just reflexive blinking—actual eye opening that seemed purposeful. And when I spoke to her, I think... I think she tried to focus on my voice. Dr. Han says it's still too early to know if this represents genuine consciousness or just improved reflexive responses. But it's something, Marcus. It's more than we've seen in two weeks."

Hale moved to Emily's bedside and took her hand, studying her face for any sign of awareness. As he watched, Emily's eyes opened again, her gaze seeming to wander across the room without focusing on anything specific.

"Emmy," Hale said quietly. "Can you hear me? If you can hear me, try to squeeze my hand."

There was no response, no squeeze, no indication that Emily had processed his words or could comply with the simple command.

"She's fighting," Patricia said, more to herself than to Hale. "She's trying to come back to us. We just have to give her time and keep believing she'll make it."

But as Hale sat with his unconscious daughter, he understood with terrible clarity that even if Emily woke up, even if she regained consciousness and cognitive function, she would likely never remember what Marcus Sterling had done to her. The traumatic brain injury had almost certainly erased those memories permanently, leaving Emily without the ability to testify and leaving the legal system without the evidence needed to hold Sterling accountable.

Which meant Marcus Sterling would continue operating Apex Fitness, would continue assaulting vulnerable women, would continue exploiting the same legal protections and institutional failures that had allowed him to victimize at least seven women over five years.

Unless someone delivered consequences that didn't require victim testimony or prosecutorial discretion or juries deliberating reasonable doubt.

Unless someone worked entirely outside the legal framework that had failed so comprehensively and consistently.

And if Hale's suspicions about Alira Sinclair were correct, if she really was systematically eliminating predators who escaped legal accountability, then perhaps it was time for a different kind of conversation about justice and vengeance and what fathers did when the system failed to protect their daughters.

Chapter 6

A Father's Rage

Detective Marcus Hale spent the three weeks following the district attorney's decision in a state of barely controlled fury that his colleagues at the precinct recognized but carefully avoided acknowledging directly. He showed up for his shifts, performed his duties with mechanical efficiency, and maintained the professional competence that fifteen years of detective work had ingrained as second nature. But everyone who worked with him could see the rage simmering beneath the surface, the barely restrained violence of a man watching his daughter fight for survival while her attacker walked free.

Emily remained in her vegetative state, showing occasional signs of increased responsiveness but never achieving the kind of conscious awareness that would allow her to communicate or demonstrate purposeful interaction with her environment. Dr. Han continued providing cautiously optimistic updates about brain activity patterns and healing progression, but he was also careful to manage expectations about Emily's long-term prognosis.

"The brain is remarkably resilient," Dr. Han explained during one of his regular consultations with Hale and Patricia. "But it's also incredibly complex. Emily's injuries affected multiple regions responsible for different aspects of consciousness and cognition. Even if she emerges from the vegetative state—which I believe is likely given the improving patterns we're seeing—we can't predict what level of function she'll recover or how much of her previous cognitive capacity will be intact."

"What about her memories?" Hale asked, the question he'd been dreading but needed answered. "If Emily wakes up, will she remember what happened to her? Will she be able to tell us who assaulted her?"

Dr. Han's expression showed sympathetic honesty. "Almost certainly not. Trauma-induced amnesia is virtually inevitable with this severity of head injury. The brain erases memories formed immediately before and during traumatic events as a protective mechanism. Emily will likely have no recollection of the hours preceding her fall, possibly no memory of that entire day. The assault itself—assuming it occurred as investigators suspect—will be a complete blank in her consciousness."

Patricia made a small sound of distress, and Hale felt his own rage intensifying. The system required victim testimony to prosecute sexual assault cases effectively, but the assault itself had destroyed Emily's ability to provide that testimony. Sterling had created the perfect crime—one where the evidence of his violence had simultaneously eliminated the witness who could testify against him.

"Is there any possibility her memories could return?" Hale pressed, grasping at any thread of hope.

"In some traumatic brain injury cases, fragments of lost memories do resurface during recovery," Dr. Han acknowledged. "But they're typically incomplete, unreliable, and wouldn't meet the evidentiary standards required for criminal testimony. The memories that do return are often more like impressions or emotional responses rather than clear factual recollections."

After Dr. Han left, Hale and Patricia sat in heavy silence. Finally, Patricia spoke with quiet intensity.

"What are you going to do, Marcus?"

"What do you mean?" Hale asked, though he understood exactly what she was asking.

"I know you," Patricia said, meeting his eyes with an expression that mixed concern and something approaching permission. "I know how you think, how you operate, what you're capable of when someone threatens our family. The system has failed Emily. The district attorney won't prosecute. Sterling is going to continue running his gym and assaulting other women. So what are you going to do about it?"

Hale was quiet for a long moment, weighing how much to reveal about the thoughts that had been consuming him since the DA's decision. "I don't know yet," he said finally. "But I can't just accept this. I can't watch Sterling continue operating with impunity while our daughter lies in a hospital bed fighting for her life."

"Good," Patricia said simply. "Because if you were planning to just let this go, I was going to handle it myself. And I don't have your resources or your training, which would make things much messier for everyone involved."

The statement was delivered with such matter-of-fact certainty that Hale felt a flash of recognition—this was the woman he'd fallen in love with twenty-five years ago, the fierce protector who'd fought for Emily's wellbeing with the same intensity she now brought to demanding consequences for the man who'd destroyed their daughter's life.

"Let me handle it," Hale said. "I have options that you don't. And I can't afford to have you facing criminal charges if things go wrong."

Patricia studied him carefully. "What kind of options?"

"Better if you don't know the details," Hale replied. "Plausible deniability and all that. But I promise you that Marcus Sterling will face consequences for what he did to Emily. One way or another, he'll pay for destroying our daughter's life."

Over the following week, Hale began conducting his own unofficial investigation into Marcus Sterling—not building a case for prosecution, but identifying vulnerabilities that could be exploited to deliver consequences outside the legal framework. He used departmental resources carefully, running searches and accessing databases in ways that wouldn't trigger oversight or raise questions about his activities.

Sterling's background revealed exactly what Hale had expected—a pattern of predatory behavior dating back at least five years, possibly longer if earlier victims had never reported or settled without creating official records. Hale documented at least eight women who'd filed complaints or initiated legal action against Sterling, all cases resolved through confidential settlements that included substantial payments and comprehensive non-disclosure agreements.

The settlement amounts ranged from $75,000 to $200,000, suggesting that Sterling and his attorneys had developed a systematic approach to managing accusations—identify the victim's vulnerabilities, calculate how much money would ensure her silence, draft agreements that made violation economically catastrophic, and ensure the victim understood that speaking publicly would result in personal and professional destruction.

Hale also discovered that Sterling had connections within law enforcement—not direct corruption or conspiracy, but the kind of social relationships that created unconscious bias in investigations. Sterling played poker with two patrol officers and a district court judge. He'd trained the police chief's wife and daughter. He'd donated to political campaigns for the current district attorney and several city council members.

These connections weren't illegal or even particularly unusual in a city where social networks often overlapped between business, law enforcement, and politics. But they created subtle institutional protection—investigators who were less aggressive in pursuing leads, prosecutors who were more willing to accept reasonable doubt, judges who were more sympathetic to defense arguments.

Most importantly, Hale began researching Alira Sinclair more systematically, revisiting the pattern analysis he'd been conducting for months and approaching it from a different perspective. Instead of investigating Sinclair as a suspected serial killer who needed to be caught and prosecuted, Hale began studying her methods and operational security to understand how she'd successfully eliminated at least four predators without triggering serious investigation.

The more Hale studied Sinclair's suspected eliminations, the more impressed he became with her sophistication. Dr. Marcus Webb had died of apparent heart failure attributed to botanical poisoning that standard toxicology screening hadn't detected. Coach

Robert Daniels had died from anaphylactic reaction to contaminated supplements in ways that appeared to be manufacturing defect or accident. Senator William Hayes had died of stroke caused by gradual poisoning that mimicked natural medical decline. Richard Blackwood had died of cardiac arrest during an encounter that Sinclair had engineered to appear like justified self-defense.

Four different methods, four different circumstances, all appearing completely natural or justified. No physical evidence linking Sinclair to any of the deaths. No pattern obvious enough to trigger investigative recognition beyond Hale's own theoretical suspicions.

If Sinclair was responsible for these deaths—and Hale's certainty grew stronger with each passing day—then she represented something unprecedented in criminal behavior. Not a serial killer driven by compulsion, but a systematic hunter executing a carefully planned mission to eliminate predators who'd escaped legal accountability.

And if Hale's analysis was correct, Sinclair might already be hunting Marcus Sterling.

The connection between Sinclair and Sterling became apparent when Hale reviewed Apex Fitness membership records as part of his unofficial investigation. A woman named Lauren Mitchell had joined the gym six weeks ago and had been training with Sterling personally on a schedule that matched the typical grooming pattern Sterling used with potential victims.

Hale ran the name through various databases, finding financial records showing Lauren Mitchell as a hedge fund manager going through marital separation—exactly the kind of vulnerable, wealthy woman that Sterling targeted. But deeper investigation revealed inconsistencies that suggested the identity might be fabricated. The financial records were real but showed peculiar patterns. The social media presence was extensive but generic. References to Mitchell's workplace and colleagues were vague or unverifiable.

Most tellingly, surveillance footage from Apex Fitness showed Lauren Mitchell entering Sterling's private training room three weeks ago, followed by sounds of what appeared to be a violent confrontation. Jessica Rodriguez had mentioned the incident to Martinez during her interviews—she'd heard crashes and Sterling shouting, had considered intervening but decided against it when Sterling emerged looking angry but uninjured.

When Jessica had asked Sterling about the disturbance, he'd claimed it was nothing—just an equipment malfunction during an intense training session. But Jessica had noticed that Sterling seemed paranoid and agitated for days afterward, varying his routines and checking his car and office for surveillance devices.

The timeline was revealing. Lauren Mitchell had joined Apex Fitness shortly after Sterling's assault on Emily became public knowledge among Sterling's previous victims. The grooming pattern had proceeded normally for several weeks, then escalated to a violent confrontation that left Sterling frightened enough to change his security protocols.

And Lauren Mitchell bore strong physical resemblance to Alira Sinclair if one allowed for differences in hair color, makeup, and clothing style. Same approximate height and build, same facial structure beneath the alterations, same movement patterns that suggested extensive martial arts training.

Hale obtained security footage from Apex Fitness covering the past six weeks and studied Lauren Mitchell's appearances carefully. The more he watched, the more convinced he became that he was observing Alira Sinclair operating under false identity, infiltrating Sterling's operation with the same methodical precision she'd presumably applied to her previous targets.

Which meant Sterling was already being hunted. The question was whether Hale wanted to stop Sinclair or give her room to complete the elimination that the legal system refused to pursue.

The decision crystallized during a conversation with Detective Martinez three weeks after the DA had declined prosecution. Martinez had called to update Hale on a frustrating development—Sterling's attorney had filed a civil harassment complaint against one of his previous victims who'd been attempting to warn other women about Sterling's predatory behavior despite her NDA obligations.

"He's not just getting away with assaulting Emily," Martinez told Hale, her voice carrying the same frustrated rage that Hale felt. "He's actively using the legal system to silence the women trying to protect others from him. The victim who filed the harassment complaint is now facing potential financial ruin for violating her settlement agreement—Sterling's attorneys are pursuing damages that could bankrupt her."

"Who is she?" Hale asked.

"Name is Amanda Chen, assaulted by Sterling three years ago when she was a graduate student. She signed an NDA and took a $125,000 settlement because she couldn't afford to fight Sterling's legal team. But after hearing about Emily, she started reaching out to other women she knew had been victimized, trying to warn them and encourage them to come forward collectively."

"Let me guess—Sterling found out and is now destroying her financially and professionally," Hale said, the pattern depressingly familiar.

"Exactly. His attorneys sent her a cease and desist letter demanding she stop violating her NDA, followed immediately by a civil suit claiming breach of contract and demanding return of the settlement payment plus additional damages for harm to Sterling's business reputation. Amanda can't afford legal representation adequate to fight back, which means she'll likely have to declare bankruptcy and still face judgment that could follow her for decades."

"So Sterling assaults women, pays them to stay silent, then destroys them financially if they try to warn others or seek support from fellow victims," Hale summarized. "And the legal system not only allows this but actively facilitates it by enforcing the confidentiality agreements he uses to maintain his predatory operation."

"That's exactly what's happening," Martinez confirmed. "And there's nothing we can do about it within legal frameworks. Sterling's settlement agreements are valid contracts. His victims violated those contracts by speaking to each other about their experiences. The fact that the contracts exist specifically to enable ongoing predatory behavior is legally irrelevant—contract law doesn't care about the underlying moral purpose, only whether the terms were clearly stated and voluntarily agreed to."

After ending the call with Martinez, Hale sat at his desk and pulled out the file he'd been compiling on Alira Sinclair's suspected operations. He reviewed the timeline of deaths, the methods employed, the victims' characteristics, and the operational security that had allowed Sinclair to continue her work without serious investigation.

Then he made a decision that violated every principle he'd built his career on, that contradicted his oath to uphold the law, and that would haunt him regardless of how it ultimately played out.

He was going to let Alira Sinclair kill Marcus Sterling.

More than that—he was going to actively create conditions that would allow Sinclair to complete her operation without interference from law enforcement.

The decision wasn't impulsive or emotional despite the rage and grief that had driven his thinking. It was calculated and deliberate, based on cold assessment of several realities that Hale could no longer avoid acknowledging:

First, the legal system would never hold Sterling accountable for Emily's assault or for his pattern of predatory behavior over five years. The evidentiary standards and procedural requirements that protected defendants' rights also protected predators who understood how to exploit those safeguards.

Second, Sterling would continue assaulting women unless he was physically prevented from doing so. His pattern was established, his methods were refined, and his legal protections were comprehensive enough that he faced no meaningful deterrent to continuing his predatory operation indefinitely.

Third, Alira Sinclair—if she was what Hale believed her to be—represented a form of justice that operated outside failed institutional frameworks. She eliminated predators who'd escaped legal accountability, delivering consequences that courts consistently refused to impose.

Fourth, and most personally compelling, Hale's daughter was lying in a hospital bed with catastrophic brain injury because Marcus Sterling had drugged and assaulted her. Emily would likely never remember what happened to her, would potentially never fully recover her brilliant mind and promising future. And the man responsible would face no consequences unless someone delivered them outside the legal system that had failed so comprehensively.

Hale spent the next week carefully sabotaging his own investigation into Sterling. He didn't destroy evidence or engage in obvious obstruction—that would create liability and might trigger internal affairs scrutiny. Instead, he simply failed to pursue leads that might have built a stronger case, accepted Sterling's attorney's obstructions without pushing back aggressively, and allowed the investigation to languish in ways that were professionally defensible as workload management and resource allocation.

He also began creating conditions that would give Sinclair operational freedom to eliminate Sterling without triggering the kind of intensive investigation that might expose her involvement. He manipulated duty rosters to ensure that the officers who would respond to any incident at Apex Fitness were ones predisposed to accept straightforward narratives rather than digging for complex explanations. He influenced the medical examiner's office scheduling to ensure that Sterling's autopsy—when it occurred—would be conducted by an examiner known for accepting obvious conclusions rather than pursuing exotic possibilities.

Most importantly, Hale began subtle surveillance of both Sterling and the woman he believed was Alira Sinclair operating as Lauren Mitchell. He needed to understand Sinclair's operational planning, identify when the elimination would occur, and ensure he was positioned to manage the investigation in ways that would protect Sinclair from exposure.

The surveillance revealed that Sinclair's operation was entering its final phases. Lauren Mitchell had stopped attending training sessions at Apex Fitness after the violent confrontation three weeks ago—the encounter had apparently served its purpose of demonstrating to Sterling that she wasn't a vulnerable victim he could exploit. But Sinclair was conducting extensive reconnaissance of Sterling's routines and patterns, documenting his movements with the kind of systematic attention that suggested she was planning something imminent.

Sterling himself had become increasingly paranoid following his confrontation with Lauren Mitchell. He'd hired a private security consultant to evaluate Apex Fitness safety protocols, installed additional cameras in previously blind areas, and begun varying his daily routines in ways that suggested fear of targeted violence. But his security improvements were reactive rather than comprehensive—they addressed obvious vulnerabilities without accounting for the kind of sophisticated attack that someone with Sinclair's capabilities might employ.

Three weeks after making his decision to allow Sinclair to operate, Hale received a phone call from Patricia that temporarily derailed his operational planning.

"Marcus, you need to come to the hospital right away," Patricia said, her voice carrying an emotion Hale couldn't immediately identify—not fear or grief, but something closer to cautious hope. "Emily's awake. She's actually awake and responsive."

Hale arrived at the hospital within twenty minutes, finding Patricia and Dr. Han in Emily's ICU room. His daughter was sitting partially upright in bed, her eyes open and tracking movement, her expression showing genuine awareness rather than the vacant confusion that had characterized her vegetative state.

"Emmy?" Hale said, moving to her bedside with his heart pounding.

Emily's gaze shifted to his face, and her expression showed recognition. "Dad," she said, her voice weak and hoarse from weeks of intubation but unmistakably purposeful. "What... what happened? Why am I in the hospital?"

The question confirmed what Dr. Han had predicted— Emily had no memory of her assault or the circumstances that had brought her to the ICU. Her consciousness had returned, but the traumatic memories had been erased by the brain injury that Sterling's violence had caused.

"You had an accident," Hale said carefully, using the vague language that Dr. Han had recommended for initial conversations with emerging consciousness patients. "You fell and hit your head pretty badly. You've been in the hospital for almost a month while your brain healed."

Emily's expression showed confusion and frustration. "I don't remember falling. I don't remember... the last thing I remember is studying for my anatomy exam. That was..." She struggled to calculate time. "That was weeks ago, wasn't it? I've lost weeks of my life."

"The brain injury caused some memory loss," Dr. Han explained gently. "That's very common with the type of head trauma you experienced. Your memory should gradually improve, though you may never recover the memories from immediately before your accident."

Over the next hour, Dr. Han conducted neurological assessments that showed Emily's cognitive function was remarkably intact despite the severity of her injuries. She could answer questions appropriately, demonstrate reasoning and problem-solving, and maintain coherent conversation. Her motor function showed some deficits—weakness on her left side that would require physical therapy—but nothing that suggested permanent severe disability.

"This is actually a remarkably good outcome given the extent of Emily's injuries," Dr. Han told Hale and Patricia privately after completing his examination. "She's emerged from the coma with most of her cognitive capacity intact. The memory loss is significant but not unexpected. With rehabilitation and therapy, I'm cautiously optimistic she can make a substantial recovery."

"What about the lost memories?" Hale asked. "Will she ever remember what happened to her?"

"Almost certainly not," Dr. Han replied. "The trauma-induced amnesia appears to have erased everything from approximately twenty-four hours before her fall until she regained consciousness. Those memories are gone permanently—the brain injury prevented them from being consolidated into long-term storage."

After Dr. Han left, Hale sat with Emily while she slept—exhausted from the effort of staying conscious for over an hour. Patricia had gone to get coffee, leaving Hale alone with his thoughts and his daughter.

Emily's awakening was a miracle—she was alive, conscious, and apparently on track to recover substantial cognitive function. But she would never remember what Marcus Sterling had done to her, would never be able to testify about the assault that had nearly killed her, would never provide the evidence needed to hold Sterling accountable through legal channels.

Which meant Hale's decision to allow Alira Sinclair to operate was the right one. Emily deserved justice even if she couldn't remember what had been done to her. Sterling deserved consequences even if the legal system refused to deliver them.

And Hale would ensure those consequences were delivered, even if it meant becoming complicit in vigilante murder.

He pulled out his phone and sent a carefully worded text message to an untraceable number he'd set up for this purpose—a message that would reach Alira Sinclair if his operational analysis was correct:

"Target continues operating with impunity. Victim has awakened but remembers nothing. Legal system will not pursue. Proceed with your operation. I will ensure investigation does not interfere."

Hale didn't know if Sinclair would receive the message or understand its implications. But if she was as sophisticated as he believed, she would recognize it as permission and protection from a detective who'd chosen to prioritize his daughter's justice over his oath to uphold the law.

The message was sent. The decision was made. All that remained was waiting to see if Alira Sinclair would deliver the consequences that Marcus Sterling had earned and that the legal system had refused to impose.

VOX *Voice*

_____

"They stole her voice. She answered with action."

Chapter 7

Paths Cross

Alira received the encrypted message on a burner phone she'd been monitoring as part of her standard operational security protocols. The number was unknown, the routing deliberately obscured through multiple relay servers, but the message's content was immediately clear in its implications:

"Target continues operating with impunity. Victim has awakened but remembers nothing. Legal system will not pursue. Proceed with your operation. I will ensure investigation does not interfere."

Someone knew what she was planning. More concerning, someone knew she was planning Sterling's elimination specifically and had taken the extraordinary step of offering protection from investigative interference.

Alira's first instinct was operational caution—the message could be a trap, law enforcement attempting to bait her into revealing herself or proceeding with an operation they could document and prosecute. But the phrasing suggested something more complex than simple entrapment. "Victim has awakened but remembers nothing" indicated the sender had direct knowledge of Sterling's most recent assault and understood the evidentiary implications of the victim's memory loss.

More significantly, "I will ensure investigation does not interfere" represented an offer of active assistance rather than passive observation—someone in a position to influence law enforcement response was explicitly offering to protect Alira's operation.

The only person who fit that profile was Detective Marcus Hale, the investigator Alira had been monitoring peripherally since he'd begun showing interest in the pattern of deaths surrounding her previous eliminations. Hale had interviewed her multiple times—after Blackwood's death in January, after Hayes's death in May—his questions growing more pointed as he recognized connections that other investigators had missed.

During those interviews, Hale had been professional but increasingly suspicious, his detective's instincts clearly recognizing patterns that suggested Alira's involvement in deaths that appeared natural or justified. She'd maintained perfect composure during each encounter, providing plausible explanations and demonstrating the kind of controlled emotional responses that made her seem like an unfortunate victim of circumstance rather than a systematic hunter.

But apparently something had changed in Hale's calculations, something significant enough to transform him from potential adversary into active ally.

She spent several hours researching recent developments in Hale's life, using the same intelligence-gathering techniques she'd employed to study her targets. What she discovered explained everything: Hale's daughter Emily had been assaulted at Apex Fitness approximately one month ago, suffering traumatic brain injury that had left her comatose for weeks. Emily had apparently awakened recently but with no memory of her assault—exactly the evidentiary problem that would prevent prosecution.

The parallel to Sierra's situation was immediately obvious. Hale's daughter had been victimized by Marcus Sterling, left with brain injury that prevented her from testifying, while the legal system protected Sterling from accountability despite overwhelming circumstantial evidence of his guilt. Hale was experiencing the same comprehensive institutional failure that had driven Alira to become a hunter of predators seven years ago.

And Hale had apparently reached the same conclusion that Alira had reached after Sierra's assault and Cassie's murder—that some forms of justice required working entirely outside legal frameworks that consistently failed to protect vulnerable people from predatory violence.

The message represented an unprecedented opportunity but also significant risk. If Hale was genuinely offering protection, his assistance would dramatically reduce the operational hazards of eliminating Sterling. But if the message was some kind of elaborate entrapment or if Hale's motives were more complex than simple desire for his daughter's justice, proceeding could expose Alira to capture and prosecution.

She needed to meet with Hale directly, to assess his intentions and determine whether his offer was genuine or represented a threat to her continued operations.

Alira sent a reply to the encrypted number: "Meeting required before proceeding. Neutral location, public enough for safety but private enough for conversation. Tomorrow, 2 PM, Riverside Park, east bench near the boathouse."

The response came within minutes: "Agreed. I'll be alone and unarmed. This conversation is off any official record."

The following afternoon, Alira arrived at Riverside Park forty-five minutes early, conducting counter-surveillance to ensure Hale wasn't bringing backup or recording equipment. She positioned herself in locations that allowed observation of the designated meeting spot while remaining concealed, watching for any indication that law enforcement had established perimeter security or surveillance.

Detective Hale arrived precisely at 2 PM, walking alone toward the east bench near the boathouse. He wore civilian clothes rather than his usual professional attire, moved without the tactical awareness that would suggest he was coordinating with backup teams, and carried himself with the exhausted posture of someone operating under tremendous personal strain.

Alira watched him for ten minutes, confirming he'd come alone and that no obvious surveillance was monitoring the meeting. Then she approached from behind, her movement silent enough that Hale didn't notice her presence until she spoke.

"Detective Hale," she said quietly, positioning herself where she could observe both him and the surrounding park. "Our previous conversations were conducted in interview rooms with official documentation. This feels considerably different."

Hale turned slowly, his hands visible and empty, his expression showing no surprise at her appearance. "Ms. Sinclair. Yes, our prior meetings were under very different circumstances—me investigating deaths you'd been tangentially connected to, you providing plausible explanations that I couldn't refute despite increasingly strong suspicions about what you actually were."

"And what am I, in your assessment?" Alira asked, maintaining careful distance while assessing Hale's body language for signs of threat or deception.

"A systematic hunter of predators who escape legal accountability," Hale replied with such blunt honesty that it momentarily disarmed Alira's suspicions. "Someone who's eliminated at least four men—Dr. Marcus Webb, Coach Robert Daniels, Richard Blackwood, Senator William Hayes—through methods sophisticated enough to appear completely natural or justified. Someone who's dedicated her life to delivering consequences that courts consistently refuse to impose."

He paused, his expression showing no judgment or condemnation. "I've spent eight months documenting the pattern, recognizing the connections, understanding your operational methods. I interviewed you twice—after Blackwood's death when you claimed justified self-defense, and after Hayes's death when you had connections to his staff. Both times I knew you were lying, knew you'd orchestrated eliminations that appeared natural but which were actually carefully planned murders. But I had no proof, and honestly, I wasn't sure I wanted proof."

"What changed?" Alira asked, though she already knew the answer.

"Marcus Sterling assaulted my daughter Emily four weeks ago," Hale said, his voice carrying controlled rage. "He drugged her with scopolamine and raped her in his private training room at Apex Fitness. She escaped and fell down a stairwell, sustaining traumatic brain injury that left her comatose for nearly a month. She woke up two days ago with no memory of what he did to her, which means the legal system will never hold him accountable."

"So you've decided to work outside that system," Alira said, recognizing the psychological journey Hale had completed—the same transformation she'd experienced after Sierra's assault.

"I've decided that some predators deserve consequences regardless of whether legal frameworks can deliver them," Hale replied. "Sterling has assaulted at least eight women over five years, possibly more. He's protected by expensive attorneys, institutional connections, and settlement agreements that silence his victims. The system I've spent fifteen years defending has failed my daughter comprehensively, just like it apparently failed your sister Sierra and led to your sister Cassandra's death."

The explicit acknowledgment of Alira's family history confirmed that Hale had conducted extensive research into her background and motivations. But it also demonstrated that his offer of assistance came from genuine understanding rather than theoretical sympathy.

"During our previous interviews, you were investigating me," Alira said carefully. "You suspected I'd killed Blackwood and Hayes, suspected I was responsible for a pattern of deaths that appeared natural. Why didn't you pursue charges when you clearly had strong suspicions?"

"Because I had no proof," Hale admitted. "Every death was thoroughly investigated and conclusively attributed to natural causes or justified self-defense. All I had were patterns and circumstantial connections that wouldn't support criminal charges. And because even as I was investigating you, part of me was... impressed by what you'd accomplished. Four predators eliminated without triggering serious investigation, without creating obvious patterns, without making the mistakes that typically lead to serial criminals being caught."

He met Alira's eyes directly. "I'm a detective. I'm supposed to catch people who kill outside legal frameworks. But I'm also someone who's spent fifteen years watching the system fail victims repeatedly, watching powerful predators escape accountability through wealth and institutional protection. What you were doing—if my theory was correct—represented a form of justice that actually worked when legal approaches consistently failed."

"And now you want me to eliminate Sterling," Alira said, making the implicit explicit.

"I want Sterling to face consequences that the legal system refuses to deliver," Hale replied carefully. "How those consequences are delivered is entirely your operational decision. But I'm offering protection and assistance to ensure that whatever you do doesn't result in your exposure or prosecution."

"Why should I trust you?" Alira asked bluntly. "The last two times we spoke, you were investigating me as a suspected killer. You documented my connections to suspicious deaths, built a pattern analysis suggesting I was responsible for multiple eliminations. How do I know this isn't an elaborate entrapment scheme designed to get me to incriminate myself?"

"You don't," Hale acknowledged. "Trust has to be built through demonstrated commitment rather than simply claimed. But I can tell you this: Emily woke up two days ago with no memory of her assault. She doesn't remember Sterling, doesn't remember going to his gym, doesn't remember anything from the day she was attacked. The brain injury erased all of it permanently. Which means she'll never be able to testify, never be able to help build a case, never be able to contribute to holding Sterling accountable through legal channels."

His voice carried raw emotion that couldn't be faked. "My daughter is alive, which is more than I had any right to hope for three weeks ago when her neurologist was preparing me for the possibility she'd never wake up. But she's alive without justice, without closure, without even the memory of what was done to her. And the man responsible is going to continue destroying other women's lives unless someone stops him permanently."

He pulled out a folder and handed it to Alira. "This is everything I've compiled on Sterling over the past three weeks—his pattern of assaults, his victims' statements, the settlement agreements he's used to silence them, his security protocols at Apex Fitness, his daily routines and vulnerabilities. I was planning to use this to build a case, but the district attorney declined prosecution due to insufficient evidence. Now I'm giving it to you because I know you can deliver the justice that the legal system refused to provide."

Alira accepted the folder, noting that it contained exactly the kind of detailed intelligence she would have gathered herself through months of surveillance. Hale had done comprehensive research, documenting operational details that would significantly accelerate her planning timeline.

"During our interviews after Blackwood's death, you asked me very specific questions about my martial arts training," Alira observed. "You were testing whether I had the skills necessary to kill him during our confrontation. You knew then that I was more than just a lucky victim defending herself."

"I knew you were highly trained," Hale confirmed. "Your efficiency in neutralizing Blackwood, the minimal injuries you sustained despite his size advantage, the precision of your defensive responses—all of it suggested extensive combat training rather than desperate improvisation. Combined with your biochemistry background and your family's history with predators who'd escaped legal accountability, the pattern was clear to anyone paying attention."

"And yet you didn't arrest me."

"Because I couldn't prove anything that would survive legal challenge," Hale said. "And because even as I was building my theoretical case against you, I was wondering if maybe the world was better off with Blackwood dead. He'd assaulted at least fifteen women over a decade, escaped prosecution every time through wealth and legal intimidation. You ended his predatory career permanently in a way that appeared completely justified. That seemed like a net positive outcome despite the legal complications."

Alira studied Hale's expression, his body language, the genuineness of his emotional response. She'd spent years learning to read people with clinical precision, to identify deception and manipulation through micro-expressions and physiological tells. And everything she observed suggested Hale was being completely honest—he was a father who'd chosen his daughter's justice over his professional obligations, a detective who'd recognized that some situations required working outside the systems he'd spent his career defending.

"What kind of protection are you offering?" Alira asked, her tone shifting from suspicious to cautiously collaborative.

"I can manipulate duty rosters to ensure that officers predisposed to accept straightforward narratives respond to any incident at Apex Fitness," Hale explained. "I can influence medical examiner scheduling to ensure Sterling's autopsy is conducted by someone who accepts obvious conclusions rather than pursuing exotic possibilities. I can manage the investigation to avoid the kind of intensive scrutiny that might reveal your involvement."

"In exchange for what?"

"Justice for Emily," Hale said simply. "I need to know that the man who destroyed my daughter's life faced real consequences. I need to believe that even when the legal system fails comprehensively, some form of accountability still exists for predators who believe their power makes them untouchable."

Alira was quiet for a long moment, weighing the operational implications of accepting Hale's assistance against the risks of proceeding alone. The offer was unprecedented—a law enforcement officer who'd previously investigated her as a suspected killer was now actively facilitating her next elimination. But it was also strategically valuable, reducing many of the hazards that typically accompanied her operations.

"I need to understand your boundaries," Alira said finally. "How much are you willing to compromise? How far will you go to protect this operation?"

"As far as necessary," Hale replied without hesitation. "I won't participate directly in Sterling's death—that's a line I can't cross without losing whatever moral credibility I'm still clinging to. But I'll manage the investigation, manipulate evidence if needed, obstruct inquiries, and do whatever else is necessary to ensure you're not exposed. Emily deserves justice, and if that justice requires me to become complicit in murder, then that's a price I'm willing to pay."

"What if Sterling's death can't be made to look natural?" Alira asked, testing the limits of Hale's commitment. "What if operational requirements dictate something more obvious?"

"Then I'll work harder to manage the narrative," Hale said. "Ideally, Sterling's death appears accidental or natural. But if you determine that's not operationally feasible, I'll construct a story that protects you—maybe your Lauren Mitchell identity resurfaces to file a restraining order against Sterling for his previous assault attempt, establishing a pattern that makes his death look like retaliation by unknown parties rather than systematic elimination by someone with your capabilities."

The operational planning in Hale's response suggested he'd been thinking through contingencies with the same systematic attention Alira brought to her own planning. He wasn't just offering vague assistance—he'd developed specific strategies for protecting her under various scenarios.

"During our second interview—after Hayes's death—you asked me about my relationship with Sarah Chen, Hayes's former aide," Alira said, testing Hale's memory of their previous interactions. "You were establishing that I had access to Hayes's inner circle, that I could have influenced his supplement regimen. You knew even then that I was responsible for his death."

"I strongly suspected," Hale confirmed. "The timeline was too coincidental—Hayes dies of stroke shortly after you'd been in contact with his staff, after months of what appeared to be surveillance and planning on your part. The method was sophisticated enough to appear completely natural, but the circumstances suggested deliberate elimination rather than medical coincidence."

"And yet you closed the investigation without pursuing me as a suspect."

"Because I had no concrete evidence," Hale said. "And because by that point, I'd done enough research into

Hayes's pattern to understand what kind of predator he was—sixty-two documented victims over three decades, all silenced through political power and institutional protection. If you eliminated him, you did the world a service that the legal system was incapable of providing."

Alira made her decision. "Sterling dies within two weeks. The method will be drowning in the hydrotherapy pool at Apex Fitness, staged to look like accidental death during a late-night training session. I'll provide you with the timeline once it's finalized so you can ensure the right people respond to the scene."

"I'll be ready," Hale confirmed. "And Alira... thank you. For Emily, and for all the other victims who never got justice through legal channels."

"Don't thank me yet," Alira said. "We both know this makes you complicit in murder. You'll carry that for the rest of your career, maybe for the rest of your life. Make sure you're genuinely prepared for that before we proceed."

"I've been carrying the knowledge that my daughter was raped and nearly killed while I stood by helpless," Hale replied. "Complicity in Sterling's death will be easier to live with than watching him continue operating while Emily struggles to rebuild a life she doesn't even remember losing."

They parted without further conversation, both understanding that they'd crossed lines that couldn't be uncrossed. Detective Marcus Hale had become an active accomplice to vigilante murder, abandoning his oath to uphold the law in favor of ensuring his daughter's justice. And Alira Sinclair had gained an unprecedented ally—a law enforcement insider who could provide protection and resources that would dramatically enhance her operational security.

The alliance was fragile and morally complex, built on shared recognition that some situations required working outside systems that had failed comprehensively. But it was also strategically valuable, creating conditions that would allow Sterling's elimination to proceed with minimal risk of exposure or prosecution.

As Alira walked away from the meeting, she felt the weight of Hale's trust and the responsibility it created. She'd never operated with active law enforcement protection before—her previous eliminations had succeeded through careful planning and forensic sophistication rather than institutional assistance. But Hale's offer represented an opportunity to deliver justice for Emily while also advancing her broader mission of eliminating predators who believed their power made them immune to consequences.

Sterling's days were numbered. The hunter had her prey identified, the method selected, and now an unprecedented ally ensuring that the kill could be executed with protection from the very systems designed to prevent exactly this kind of extrajudicial action.

Within two weeks, Marcus Sterling would be dead, Emily Hale would have the justice the legal system refused to provide, and Detective Marcus Hale would learn whether he could live with the choice he'd made to prioritize his daughter's vengeance over his professional integrity.

The game had changed. The stakes had escalated. And the fragile alliance between hunter and detective was about to be tested in ways neither could fully anticipate.

PATIENTIA *Patience*

————

"Revenge is a dish that must be eaten cold." — Old
Sicilian Proverb

Chapter 8

The Uneasy Alliance

Over the following week, Alira and Detective Hale established communication protocols and operational frameworks that would allow them to coordinate Sterling's elimination while maintaining the security necessary to protect both parties from exposure. They used encrypted messaging systems, burner phones that were replaced every few days, and carefully scheduled meetings in locations that couldn't be monitored or recorded.

The alliance felt surreal to both participants. Hale had spent his entire career building cases against criminals who operated outside legal frameworks, training himself to recognize patterns and gather evidence that would support prosecution. Now he was actively assisting someone he was nearly certain had killed at least four men, providing intelligence and protection to facilitate a fifth elimination.

For Alira, the partnership represented both opportunity and vulnerability. Hale's assistance would dramatically reduce the operational risks that typically accompanied her work—he could manipulate investigations, control evidence flow, and ensure that the right people were positioned to accept narratives that protected her involvement. But Hale also knew more about her methods and identity than anyone else who remained alive, which created dependency that violated every operational security principle she'd developed over years of hunting predators.

During their second meeting—conducted in a secure location that Alira had verified wasn't under surveillance—Hale provided additional intelligence about Sterling's current activities and the broader investigative landscape.

"Sterling has become increasingly paranoid since his confrontation with your Lauren Mitchell identity," Hale reported, spreading photographs and documents across the table between them. "He's hired private security consultants to evaluate Apex Fitness protocols, installed additional cameras in areas that previously had blind spots, and begun varying his daily routines in ways that suggest genuine fear of targeted violence."

"Good," Alira said, studying the security modifications Sterling had implemented. "Paranoid targets make mistakes because they're operating outside their comfort zones. They become hypervigilant about obvious threats while overlooking vulnerabilities they don't recognize as dangerous."

"The additional cameras are a problem though," Hale observed, pointing to updated facility diagrams showing new surveillance coverage. "Your original plan involved accessing the hydrotherapy pool area during hours when the gym was closed. But Sterling's new security system includes motion-activated cameras that cover all entrances and the pool facility itself."

"Then I'll need to access the facility during operating hours when motion in those areas won't trigger suspicion," Alira replied, already adjusting her operational timeline. "Sterling typically conducts private training sessions between 8 PM and 10 PM several nights per week. The gym stays open until 11 PM, which means there are legitimate reasons for people to be in the building during the timeframe when I need to operate."

She pulled out her own documentation—detailed surveillance notes on Sterling's schedule and patterns over the past month. "Tuesday and Thursday evenings, Sterling has standing appointments with a client named Victoria Ashford from 8:00 to 9:30 PM. The sessions occur in one of the private training rooms on the second floor. After these intensive sessions, Sterling follows a consistent recovery routine—he goes directly to the hydrotherapy pool on the third floor around 9:30 PM for approximately thirty minutes of recovery therapy."

"So the pool area is empty during his session with Victoria, then Sterling arrives alone for his recovery routine," Hale said, understanding the tactical opportunity.

"Exactly," Alira confirmed. "And that's when I'll already be there, established as a legitimate gym member using the hydrotherapy pool as part of my own evening routine."

She laid out a revised operational plan with the kind of meticulous detail that demonstrated why she'd successfully eliminated four targets without triggering serious investigation. "Sterling dies on Thursday evening after his session with Victoria Ashford ends, when he arrives at the hydrotherapy pool for his post-training recovery. I'll be in the pool area legitimately as part of my established routine—I won't be hiding or sneaking in. I'll be visible on security cameras as just another member using the facilities."

"So you'll already be there when he arrives," Hale said, recognizing the tactical advantage.

"Exactly. I'll be using the pool legitimately, appearing as just another gym member engaged in her normal routine. Sterling won't recognize me because I'll look completely different from Lauren Mitchell—different hair, different makeup, different body language, different name and identity. When he enters the pool area around 9:30 PM, I'll engage him in casual conversation, establish that I'm harmless and unthreatening, then wait for the opportunity to incapacitate him."

"How?" Hale asked, his detective's instincts wanting to understand the complete operational sequence.

"Scopolamine, administered through skin contact," Alira replied. "I'll apply a transdermal preparation to my hands before Sterling arrives. When we shake hands or I touch him during conversation—ostensibly just friendly social contact—the drug will absorb through his skin. It takes approximately fifteen to twenty minutes to achieve full effect, which gives me time to maintain casual interaction while waiting for the cognitive impairment to set in."

"The same drug Sterling used on Emily," Hale observed, the irony not lost on either of them.

"Poetic justice," Alira confirmed. "Once Sterling is sufficiently impaired, I'll help him into the hydrotherapy pool—he'll be conscious but suggestible, unable to resist or question what's happening. Then I'll hold him underwater until he drowns. The scopolamine will prevent him from fighting effectively, and the hydrotherapy pool's temperature and jets will mask the exact timeline of death."

"What about physical evidence?" Hale asked. "Won't the autopsy reveal that he was drugged?"

"Only if the medical examiner specifically tests for scopolamine," Alira replied. "And that won't happen if you ensure the autopsy is conducted by someone who accepts the obvious narrative—middle-aged man drowns in hydrotherapy pool after falling asleep or losing consciousness due to heat exhaustion and physical exertion from his training session. It's a plausible accident that won't trigger exotic toxicology screening unless someone specifically suspects pharmaceutical involvement."

Hale made notes about which medical examiner to ensure was assigned to Sterling's autopsy—Dr. Robert Chang, who had a documented pattern of accepting straightforward conclusions and avoiding the kind of comprehensive testing that might reveal unusual substances in victims' systems.

"What about your presence at the scene?" Hale asked. "Even if Sterling's death appears accidental, won't investigators want to interview everyone who was at the gym that evening?"

"Absolutely," Alira confirmed. "Which is why my false identity will be completely documented and verifiable. I'll have membership records, credit card transactions, previous visits establishing a pattern of legitimate gym use. When investigators interview me, I'll describe discovering Sterling unconscious in the pool, attempting to help him, calling for assistance. I'll be a cooperative witness providing information that supports the accidental death narrative rather than a suspect to be investigated."

"And if they want to verify your identity?"

"Every aspect will check out," Alira assured him. "Driver's license, employment records, residential address, credit history—all completely legitimate as far as any investigation will be able to determine. The identity will exist long enough to survive cursory verification, then dissolve once the investigation concludes without leaving trails that could connect back to me."

Hale studied Alira's operational plan with the kind of professional assessment he'd bring to evaluating any complex criminal scheme. The sophistication was remarkable—multiple layers of misdirection, carefully constructed false identities, exploitation of institutional assumptions about what warranted investigation versus what could be accepted as accidental death.

"You've done this before," Hale said, not a question but an observation.

"Different variations," Alira confirmed. "Webb died from botanical poisoning that appeared to be heart failure. Daniels died from anaphylactic reaction to contaminated supplements. Hayes died from stroke caused by gradual poisoning. Blackwood died during a confrontation that appeared to be justified self-defense. Each elimination required different methods and different operational security, but the underlying principle is always the same—make the death appear natural or justified enough that investigators accept obvious narratives rather than pursuing complex alternatives."

"What's your success rate?" Hale asked, genuinely curious.

"One hundred percent so far," Alira replied without arrogance, just stating operational fact. "Four eliminations, four deaths classified as natural causes or justified homicide, zero serious investigations that came close to exposing my involvement. The pattern analysis you conducted was the closest anyone has come to recognizing connections between seemingly unrelated deaths."

"And you would have continued operating indefinitely if Emily's assault hadn't forced me to reassess my priorities," Hale observed.

"Probably," Alira agreed. "I've been careful about spacing eliminations, varying methods, avoiding geographic clustering that might trigger pattern recognition. My original plan was to continue hunting predators for years or decades, moving between jurisdictions if necessary, maintaining perfect operational security through discipline and careful planning."

"Now you're operating with active law enforcement assistance," Hale noted. "How does that change your approach?"

"It reduces some risks while creating others," Alira said honestly. "Your protection means I don't have to be quite as paranoid about forensic evidence or investigative scrutiny—you can manage those elements in ways I couldn't control when operating alone. But it also creates dependency on your continued cooperation, and it means I'm trusting someone who has extensive knowledge about my methods and identity."

"You're worried I might change my mind," Hale said, understanding the vulnerability Alira was acknowledging.

"I'm aware that you're making this decision during a period of extreme emotional stress," Alira replied carefully. "Your daughter was assaulted, nearly killed, left with brain damage that prevents her from remembering her own victimization. That's created a situation where working outside legal frameworks seems necessary and justified. But emotions change, circumstances evolve, and what seems morally clear during crisis can become more complicated once immediate pain fades."

"You think I might turn on you once Emily is further along in her recovery," Hale said.

"I think it's a possibility I need to consider," Alira confirmed. "You've spent fifteen years building a career on upholding the law. Becoming complicit in vigilante murder represents a fundamental violation of everything you've trained yourself to value professionally. Once Sterling is dead and Emily has the justice you're seeking for her, you might decide that protecting a serial killer—which is how the law would classify me—is a moral compromise you can't sustain."

Hale was quiet for a long moment, clearly wrestling with the question Alira had raised. When he finally spoke, his voice carried careful honesty.

"I can't promise I'll never have doubts or moral conflicts about what we're doing," he admitted. "You're right that I'm making this decision during emotional crisis, and it's possible my thinking will change as circumstances evolve. But I can tell you this: even if I eventually decide I can't continue actively assisting your operations, I won't betray what we've done together. Sterling's elimination will remain protected regardless of how my personal feelings develop afterward."

"Why?" Alira asked, testing the strength of Hale's commitment.

"Because Emily deserves justice even if the method makes me uncomfortable in retrospect," Hale replied. "And because exposing you would mean admitting my own complicity in Sterling's death. I'm not willing to destroy my career and face criminal prosecution just because I develop second thoughts about the moral calculus we're operating under."

It was pragmatic rather than idealistic, but Alira appreciated the honesty. Hale wasn't claiming eternal commitment to their alliance or pretending he'd never experience moral doubt. He was simply acknowledging that mutual self-interest would protect their partnership even if emotional foundations eventually shifted.

"Fair enough," Alira said. "Then let's finalize the operational details for Thursday evening."

Over the next several days, Alira executed the preliminary phases of her plan with methodical precision. She established a new identity—Rachel Morgan, a forty-two-year-old physical therapist going through divorce—and joined Apex Fitness using completely legitimate documentation that would survive any investigative verification.

She visited the gym during evening hours on three separate occasions, establishing a pattern of using the hydrotherapy pool between 8:30 and 9:30 PM as part of her recovery routine after long workdays. She made casual conversation with staff members and other gym members, creating witnesses who could confirm that Rachel Morgan was a regular, unremarkable presence in the facility.

Most importantly, she prepared the transdermal scopolamine formulation that would incapacitate Sterling without leaving obvious evidence. The preparation required careful pharmaceutical work—the drug needed to be concentrated enough to achieve rapid effect through skin contact, but formulated in ways that would prevent immediate absorption through Alira's own skin when she applied it to her hands.

She used a lipophilic carrier solution that would remain on the surface of her skin until physical contact with Sterling transferred it to his more porous tissue. The formulation would be invisible and odorless, appearing to Sterling as nothing more than the slight moisture of normal skin contact during handshake or casual touching.

Detective Hale handled the investigative preparations, manipulating duty rosters to ensure that officers Roberts and Martinez—both known for accepting straightforward narratives rather than pursuing complex theories—would be the responding units if emergency calls came from Apex Fitness on Thursday evening. He also coordinated with the medical examiner's office to ensure Dr. Chang would be on call for any deaths requiring autopsy that night.

On Wednesday evening, Hale and Alira met for final operational coordination in a secure location.

"Everything is in place," Hale reported. "Roberts and Martinez will respond to any emergency calls from Apex Fitness. Dr. Chang is on call for autopsies. I've reviewed the security footage protocols and confirmed that the cameras covering the hydrotherapy pool area run on a seven-day recording loop that gets overwritten unless specifically flagged for preservation. Once Sterling's death is ruled accidental, there will be no reason to preserve the footage beyond the standard retention period."

"What about Sterling's attorney?" Alira asked. "If he suspects foul play, he might push for more intensive investigation regardless of what responding officers conclude."

"Sterling's attorney is a civil litigation specialist, not a criminal defense lawyer," Hale replied. "He's excellent at drafting settlement agreements and handling harassment complaints, but he has no particular expertise or interest in death investigation. Unless there's obvious evidence of murder, he'll accept the medical examiner's conclusion and move on to handling Sterling's estate and any potential wrongful death claims against the gym."

"And Jessica Rodriguez?" Alira asked, referring to the Apex Fitness receptionist who'd been cooperative during Martinez's investigation into Emily's assault. "She knows more about Sterling's pattern than most staff members. Will she accept an accidental death explanation?"

"I've spoken with Martinez about Jessica," Hale said. "Jessica is terrified of losing her job and facing retaliation if she says anything that damages Apex Fitness's reputation. She'll be relieved that Sterling is dead rather than suspicious about how it happened. And even if she has doubts, she has strong financial incentives to keep them to herself rather than triggering investigation that might expose the gym to liability."

Alira nodded, satisfied that the major vulnerabilities had been addressed. "Then we proceed tomorrow evening. I'll be at the gym by 8:15 PM, establishing presence in the hydrotherapy pool area before Sterling finishes his session with Victoria Ashford. The elimination will occur between 9:30 and 10:00 PM, when Sterling arrives at the pool for his post-training recovery routine."

"And if something goes wrong?" Hale asked. "If Sterling recognizes you despite your disguise, if he becomes suspicious, if the scopolamine doesn't work as planned?"

"Then I abort and wait for another opportunity," Alira replied. "I don't take unnecessary risks or force operations that aren't proceeding according to plan. Sterling will die when conditions allow for clean execution, whether that's tomorrow or next week or next month."

"Emily's neurologist says she'll be released from the hospital on Friday," Hale said quietly. "She's made remarkable progress—cognitive function is nearly intact, physical therapy is addressing her motor deficits.

She'll need ongoing rehabilitation, but Dr. Han is optimistic about substantial recovery."

"I'm glad," Alira said, genuinely meaning it. "Emily surviving with her mind intact is the best outcome anyone could have hoped for given the severity of her injuries."

"She asked me yesterday why someone would want to hurt her," Hale continued, his voice heavy with the weight of explaining incomprehensible violence to his daughter. "She has no memory of Sterling, no recollection of anything from that day. All she knows is that she woke up in a hospital with a fractured skull and weeks of her life missing. I didn't know how to explain that a predator targeted her specifically because she was vulnerable and trusting."

"What did you tell her?"

"That sometimes bad people exist in the world, and that the best we can do is ensure they face consequences even when the system fails to deliver them," Hale replied. "She didn't understand what I meant, and I couldn't explain without revealing things I can't burden her with. But after tomorrow, I'll at least know that the man who destroyed her life faced real accountability."

They parted with a final review of communication protocols and contingency plans. Tomorrow evening, Marcus Sterling would die in the hydrotherapy pool at Apex Fitness, his death appearing to be a tragic accident—heat exhaustion and drowning during recovery routine following intensive training. The investigation would be cursory, the medical examination would confirm accidental death, and Sterling's pattern of predatory behavior would end permanently without anyone recognizing that he'd been systematically eliminated by a hunter who'd been studying his vulnerabilities for months.

And Detective Marcus Hale would learn whether he could live with the choice he'd made—prioritizing his daughter's justice over his professional integrity, becoming complicit in murder to ensure consequences that legal frameworks had refused to deliver.

The uneasy alliance was about to be tested in its first operational deployment. Within twenty-four hours, they would both know whether their partnership could survive the reality of deliberately orchestrated killing, or whether the moral weight would prove too heavy for a detective who'd spent his career on the other side of investigations like the one he was now actively sabotaging.

Chapter 9

The Kill

Thursday evening arrived with unseasonably warm weather that made the hydrotherapy pool at Apex Fitness particularly appealing to members seeking relief from the day's heat and physical exertion. Alira arrived at the gym at 8:12 PM as Rachel Morgan, dressed in conservative athletic wear with her hair styled differently from any of her previous identities, her makeup applied to subtly alter her facial structure in ways that security cameras wouldn't detect as deliberate disguise.

She signed in at the reception desk with the friendly professionalism that had characterized Rachel Morgan's previous visits, exchanging pleasantries with the evening staff member—a young man named David who'd worked the Thursday shift consistently enough that he recognized regular members by sight.

"Evening, Ms. Morgan," David said with practiced enthusiasm. "Pool again tonight?"

"Absolutely," Alira replied, her voice carrying the slight vocal strain that a physical therapist might develop from long days of patient consultations. "Long week, and the hydrotherapy does wonders for my back and shoulders."

"I hear you," David commiserated. "Enjoy your session."

Alira made her way to the women's locker room, where she changed into a one-piece swimsuit and prepared the final operational details. She applied the transdermal scopolamine preparation to her palms with careful precision, using a technique that ensured even distribution across the skin surface while preventing absorption through her own tissue. The carrier solution felt slightly oily but would appear to be nothing more than the natural moisture of skin during handshake or casual physical contact.

She wrapped her hands in a towel as she walked toward the third-floor hydrotherapy pool area, a natural gesture that prevented accidental contact with surfaces or people before she encountered Sterling. The towel also served to warm her hands slightly, which would enhance the drug's transfer efficiency during skin-to-skin contact with her target.

The hydrotherapy pool area was empty when Alira arrived at 8:24 PM, exactly as her reconnaissance had predicted. The space was designed for recovery and relaxation rather than intensive exercise—subdued lighting, comfortable ambient temperature, the gentle sound of water jets creating a therapeutic environment. Large windows overlooked the city, though the evening darkness reduced them to reflective surfaces that showed Alira's movement as she entered the pool.

She positioned her towel on a nearby bench, noting the security camera in the northeast corner that captured the entire pool area. The camera was functioning normally—a small LED indicator showing active recording—which meant Alira's presence would be documented as completely legitimate gym member activity rather than suspicious infiltration.

Alira entered the pool at 8:27 PM, allowing the warm water and therapeutic jets to work on her muscles while she waited for Sterling to arrive. She maintained the appearance of genuine relaxation, occasionally adjusting her position to access different jet configurations, demonstrating the behavior of someone actually using the facility for its intended purpose rather than lying in wait for a target.

At 8:52 PM, another gym member—a woman in her fifties—entered the pool area and exchanged friendly greetings with Alira before settling into the opposite side of the pool. The woman's presence was unexpected but not problematic; she would serve as an additional witness to Rachel Morgan's legitimate use of the facility, further establishing the narrative that Alira was simply another member enjoying the gym's amenities.

The two women made casual conversation about the heat, the benefits of hydrotherapy for various physical ailments, and the general pleasures of having access to such excellent facilities. Alira learned that the woman— Margaret—was recovering from knee surgery and found the pool's buoyancy helpful for gentle exercise that didn't stress her healing joint.

"Do you come here often?" Margaret asked, the question conversational rather than interrogative.

"Two or three times a week," Alira replied, establishing Rachel Morgan's pattern of regular attendance. "Usually between eight-thirty and nine-thirty in the evenings after work. The pool is rarely crowded during these hours, which I appreciate."

"Same," Margaret agreed. "I prefer the quieter times. Though I understand one of the trainers uses this pool regularly after his evening sessions. Marcus something?"

"Sterling," Alira supplied, keeping her tone neutral and uninformed. "I think I've seen him around the gym but haven't had any interactions with him personally."

Margaret's expression suggested she had opinions about Sterling but was too polite to share them with a relative stranger. "Well, he's certainly dedicated to his fitness regimen. Can't fault him for that, I suppose."

At 9:18 PM, Margaret decided she'd had enough pool time and left to shower and change, leaving Alira alone in the hydrotherapy area. The timing was fortuitous—Sterling typically arrived around 9:30 PM, which meant Alira would have a few minutes of solitude to prepare mentally for the elimination while maintaining her cover as a legitimate member who happened to be using the pool during his regular routine.

She adjusted her position to access a different set of jets, keeping her hands submerged to maintain the warmth that would enhance the scopolamine's transfer efficiency. The drug preparation would remain viable for approximately two hours after application, which gave her ample time to complete the operation regardless of small variations in Sterling's schedule.

At 9:33 PM, Marcus Sterling entered the hydrotherapy pool area, moving with the tired satisfaction of someone who'd completed intensive physical work and was looking forward to recovery therapy. He wore swim trunks and a towel around his shoulders, his muscular physique showing the definition that came from years of disciplined training and his professional focus on physical perfection.

Sterling paused when he noticed Alira in the pool, his expression showing mild surprise at finding the area occupied but no particular concern or recognition. His eyes assessed her with the practiced efficiency of someone who constantly evaluated bodies—noting her fitness level, her approximate age, her general attractiveness—but without the predatory intensity he reserved for potential victims.

"Evening," Sterling said with professional friendliness, setting his towel on a bench and preparing to enter the pool. "Don't see many people using this facility during late hours."

"I find it's the best time," Alira replied, keeping her voice pleasant and her body language relaxed. "Quieter than the peak hours, and the pool is usually available without waiting."

Sterling entered the water with the fluid movement of someone completely comfortable in aquatic environments, positioning himself in a section that accessed powerful jets designed for deep tissue massage. He settled into the water with an audible sigh of relief, the tension visibly draining from his shoulders as the heat and pressure began working on muscles stressed by his training session with Victoria Ashford.

"I'm Rachel, by the way," Alira said after a few moments of comfortable silence, using the introduction as an opportunity to move slightly closer to Sterling while maintaining appropriate social distance. "I've been a member here for about two weeks. Still learning my way around all the facilities."

"Marcus Sterling," he replied, his professional persona engaging automatically. "I'm one of the trainers here. If you're interested in personal training or have questions about optimizing your fitness routine, feel free to stop by my office."

The offer was delivered with the smooth practiced quality of someone who'd perfected the initial approach—friendly, professional, establishing himself as an authority figure while subtly suggesting that Alira might benefit from his expertise and guidance. Under different circumstances, with a genuinely vulnerable woman, this would be the first step in Sterling's grooming process.

"I might take you up on that," Alira said, allowing interest to color her voice while maintaining the slight hesitation of someone who was genuinely considering the offer rather than someone who'd already decided to exploit the opportunity. "I've been struggling with some lower back issues from my work as a physical therapist—long days spent treating patients takes a toll."

"Physical therapist," Sterling said, his interest increasing slightly. "That's excellent background for understanding how the body works. Makes training much more effective when clients understand the biomechanics we're working with."

He shifted position slightly, moving closer in ways that appeared casual but which Alira recognized as tactical—reducing the physical distance between them, establishing proximity that would make future boundary violations seem like natural progression rather than sudden escalation.

"The hydrotherapy helps with the back pain," Alira continued, "but I know I should probably be doing more targeted strength training to address the underlying issues."

"Absolutely," Sterling agreed with the enthusiasm of someone discussing his professional passion. "Core strength is essential for protecting the lower back, particularly in careers that involve repetitive movements or sustained postures. I specialize in rehabilitation-focused training that addresses exactly these kinds of chronic issues."

He extended his hand across the water for a handshake, the gesture appearing friendly and professional—a trainer introducing himself to a potential client, establishing rapport through conventional social contact.

Alira accepted the handshake, her scopolamine-treated palm making contact with Sterling's hand for approximately three seconds. The drug transfer was invisible and imperceptible, feeling to Sterling like nothing more than the slight moisture that would naturally occur during a handshake between two people in a warm pool.

"Nice to meet you, Marcus," Alira said, releasing the handshake at the socially appropriate moment. "I'll definitely consider setting up a consultation once I've settled into my routine here a bit more."

"Take your time," Sterling replied, settling back into his preferred jet position. "The offer stands whenever you're ready."

They continued casual conversation for the next fifteen minutes, discussing the gym's facilities, Sterling's training philosophy, Rachel Morgan's fictional work as a physical therapist, and various other topics that established comfortable social rapport without triggering any suspicion that their encounter was anything other than two gym members sharing pool space during evening hours.

Alira monitored Sterling carefully for the first signs of scopolamine effects, noting the subtle physiological changes that indicated the drug was beginning to impact his cognitive function. At approximately 9:51 PM—eighteen minutes after their handshake—Sterling's speech began showing slight irregularities, his words taking marginally longer to form and his sentence construction becoming less complex.

"You know what's interesting about hydrotherapy," Sterling said, his voice carrying the first hints of cognitive impairment, "is how the... the pressure and the heat work together to... to affect the muscle tissue differently than other recovery methods."

The slight hesitation and simplification of language structure indicated that scopolamine was beginning to disrupt Sterling's executive function, making complex thought processes more difficult while leaving him conscious and apparently functional. To a casual observer, Sterling might appear slightly tired or relaxed, but not obviously impaired in ways that would trigger concern.

"Are you feeling alright?" Alira asked with apparent concern, moving slightly closer while maintaining her friendly, helpful demeanor. "You look a bit flushed. The water temperature combined with your training session might be affecting you."

"I'm fine," Sterling replied automatically, though his expression showed confusion about why he was feeling disoriented. "Just... tired from the session with Victoria. She's been pushing harder in her training lately, which is good, but it takes more out of me than usual."

"Why don't you move to the shallower section," Alira suggested, positioning herself to appear helpful rather than threatening. "Sometimes the deeper water combined with the jets can make people feel lightheaded if they've been exerting themselves heavily."

Sterling accepted the suggestion with the kind of compliance that indicated the scopolamine was affecting his judgment and resistance to external guidance. He moved toward the shallower section of the pool, his movements slightly uncoordinated in ways that would be attributed to fatigue rather than pharmaceutical impairment.

Alira moved with him, maintaining her position as a concerned fellow gym member rather than revealing any predatory intent. She continued making casual conversation, asking about his training philosophy and his recommendations for core strengthening exercises, keeping Sterling engaged and distracted while the drug continued compromising his cognitive capacity.

By 9:58 PM, Sterling was showing clear signs of significant impairment—his eyes had difficulty focusing, his responses to questions were delayed and simplified, and his motor coordination had deteriorated noticeably. He gripped the edge of the pool for support, his expression confused and concerned but still not recognizing the danger he was in.

"I think... I think something's wrong," Sterling said, his voice slurred and uncertain. "I feel really strange. Maybe I should... should get out and..."

"Let me help you," Alira said, her voice carrying soothing authority as she positioned herself to appear supportive while actually controlling Sterling's movement options. "Just relax and take some deep breaths. You're probably experiencing heat exhaustion from the combination of your intensive training and the pool's temperature."

She guided Sterling toward the deeper section of the pool, her movements appearing helpful to any security camera reviewing the footage—a concerned gym member assisting someone who appeared to be experiencing medical distress. Sterling complied with her guidance, his scopolamine-impaired consciousness unable to recognize that he was being maneuvered toward deeper water by someone with lethal intent.

"Just lean back and relax," Alira continued in her soothing tone. "Let the water support you. I've got you, you're safe."

Sterling's resistance was minimal—the scopolamine had stolen his capacity for critical thinking and self-protective behavior, leaving him suggestible and compliant even as Alira positioned him in the deepest section of the pool where his feet couldn't touch the bottom.

At 10:02 PM, Alira executed the kill with clinical efficiency. She positioned herself behind Sterling, her arms appearing to support him in the water while actually controlling his position and preventing escape. Then, with movements that would appear ambiguous on security footage, she pushed Sterling's head beneath the water surface and held him there.

Sterling's scopolamine-impaired consciousness registered that something was wrong—that he was being held underwater rather than supported—but the drug prevented him from mounting effective resistance. His movements were weak and uncoordinated, his attempts to break free easily controlled by Alira's superior positioning and training.

She held him underwater for approximately ninety seconds, feeling his struggles gradually weaken as oxygen deprivation combined with drug-induced cognitive impairment to shut down his consciousness. The hydrotherapy jets created turbulence that disguised the exact nature of what was happening, making it appear on security footage like Alira was attempting to help someone who was thrashing in the water rather than deliberately drowning a man she'd incapacitated through pharmaceutical means.

At 10:04 PM, Sterling's movements stopped completely. His body went limp in Alira's arms, his consciousness extinguished by the combination of scopolamine impairment and prolonged submersion. She held him underwater for an additional thirty seconds to ensure complete drowning, then brought his head above the surface while beginning to call for help.

"Help! Someone help!" Alira shouted with convincing panic, her voice carrying the genuine stress of someone who'd just witnessed a medical emergency. "He's unconscious! I think he's drowning!"

She maneuvered Sterling's body toward the pool edge while continuing to call for assistance, her movements appearing to be desperate rescue attempts rather than calculated staging of a crime scene. By the time gym staff responded to her calls—approximately forty-five seconds after she'd begun shouting—Alira had positioned Sterling at the pool's edge and was attempting what appeared to be rescue breathing.

David, the reception desk attendant, arrived first, followed quickly by two other staff members who'd heard Alira's calls for help. They immediately took over attempting to rescue Sterling, pulling his body from the pool and beginning CPR while someone called 911.

Alira remained in the pool, appearing shaken and traumatized, providing information about what she'd witnessed to the staff members who were trying to save Sterling's life. She explained that Sterling had seemed fine during their casual conversation, that he'd mentioned feeling tired from his training session, that he'd suddenly appeared disoriented and begun having difficulty staying afloat.

"I tried to help him," Alira said, her voice carrying the trembling quality of someone in genuine shock. "I thought he was just dizzy from the heat, so I helped him move to the deeper water where the jets are stronger. But then he just... he couldn't keep his head up. I grabbed him and tried to keep him above water, but he was too heavy and I couldn't..."

The narrative was perfect—a concerned gym member who'd tried to help someone experiencing medical distress but who'd been unable to prevent the tragedy that unfolded. The staff members assured Alira that she'd done everything she could, that no one could have predicted Sterling would experience such a sudden medical emergency.

Paramedics arrived at 10:14 PM, continuing advanced resuscitation efforts while transporting Sterling to the university medical center. But Alira knew—as did any medical professional who might examine the timeline—that Sterling had been without oxygen for too long to survive with meaningful brain function intact even if his heart could be restarted.

Officers Roberts and Martinez arrived at 10:22 PM to conduct preliminary investigation into the incident, exactly as Detective Hale had arranged. They interviewed Alira with the sympathetic professionalism of officers who understood she was a traumatized witness rather than a suspect, documenting her account of events while expressing appreciation for her attempts to save Sterling's life.

"Can you describe exactly what happened?" Officer Roberts asked, his notebook open and his demeanor supportive.

Alira provided a detailed narrative that matched what security footage would show—she'd been using the pool for her regular evening hydrotherapy session, Sterling had arrived around 9:30 PM for his own recovery routine, they'd made casual conversation while sharing the pool space, Sterling had mentioned feeling tired from his training session, he'd begun showing signs of disorientation that she'd attributed to heat exhaustion, she'd tried to help him to a different section of the pool, and he'd suddenly lost consciousness and slipped beneath the water.

"I tried to hold him up," Alira said, her voice breaking with apparent emotion. "I grabbed him and tried to keep his head above water, but he's so much bigger than me and I couldn't support his weight properly. I got him to the edge and called for help as quickly as I could, but I don't know if it was fast enough."

"You did exactly the right thing," Officer Martinez assured her. "No one could have predicted he would experience this kind of medical emergency. You tried to help, you called for assistance immediately. That's all anyone could have done."

The officers asked for Alira's contact information, which she provided using Rachel Morgan's completely documented false identity. They asked if she'd be willing to provide a formal statement if needed for their report, and she agreed with the cooperative demeanor of a concerned citizen who wanted to help investigators understand what had happened.

"Do you need anything?" Roberts asked, noting that Alira appeared shaken and stressed. "Can we call someone for you, or would you like us to arrange transport home?"

"I'll be alright," Alira replied, maintaining her composure while appearing understandably upset. "I just need a few minutes to collect myself, then I'll drive home. Thank you for being so understanding."

After the officers concluded their preliminary interview, Alira remained at the gym long enough to provide her contact information to the facility manager and to speak briefly with other staff members who expressed sympathy for what she'd experienced. Then she changed, gathered her belongings, and left Apex Fitness at 11:04 PM, her departure documented by security cameras showing a visibly shaken woman who'd just witnessed a traumatic death.

She drove to a secure location where she could dispose of the scopolamine preparation that remained on her hands—washing thoroughly with industrial solvent that would eliminate any trace of the drug from her skin. Then she returned to her apartment, where she methodically eliminated all evidence of Rachel Morgan's existence—destroying the false identity documents, disposing of the clothing and personal items associated with the persona, and erasing digital trails that could connect Rachel Morgan to Alira Sinclair.

By midnight, Rachel Morgan had ceased to exist, leaving behind only official records showing her membership at Apex Fitness and her presence as a witness to Marcus Sterling's tragic accidental drowning during an evening hydrotherapy session.

At 1:47 AM, Detective Marcus Hale received the phone call he'd been expecting—Marcus Sterling had been pronounced dead at the university medical center after unsuccessful resuscitation attempts following his drowning at Apex Fitness. The medical examiner's preliminary assessment was that Sterling had experienced heat exhaustion and possible cardiac event during his post-training recovery session, losing consciousness and drowning before anyone could rescue him effectively.

Hale listened to the report with professional attention while feeling emotions he'd never experienced during his career—satisfaction that Sterling was dead, relief that Emily would have justice even if she'd never know it, and guilt about the role he'd played in facilitating a murder despite spending fifteen years upholding the law.

"I'll review the incident report in the morning," Hale told the officer who'd called with the notification. "Sounds like a straightforward accidental drowning, but we should document it thoroughly to protect the gym from potential liability claims."

After ending the call, Hale sat in the darkness of his living room, processing the reality that he'd become complicit in vigilante murder. Marcus Sterling— predator, rapist, destroyer of at least eight women's lives including Emily's—was dead, eliminated by someone Hale had actively protected and assisted despite knowing exactly what she was planning.

His phone buzzed with an encrypted message from an untraceable number: "Operation complete. No complications. Thank you for your assistance."

Hale deleted the message without responding, understanding that their communication needed to remain minimal to protect both parties from exposure. But he sat for a long time in the darkness, wondering whether he'd made the right choice and whether he could live with the consequences of prioritizing his daughter's justice over his professional integrity.

Emily was being released from the hospital in the morning, beginning her rehabilitation and recovery with no memory of what Marcus Sterling had done to her. But somewhere in the city, the man who'd destroyed her life had faced consequences that the legal system had refused to deliver, eliminated by a hunter who understood that some forms of justice required working entirely outside failed institutional frameworks.

Detective Marcus Hale had crossed a line he could never uncross. And only time would tell whether he could live with the choice he'd made, or whether the weight of complicity in murder would eventually destroy him just as comprehensively as Sterling had destroyed his victims.

FINIS *The End*

————

"Every predator believes himself the apex—until he meets his hunter."

The Weight of Compromise

Three weeks after Marcus Sterling's death, Detective Marcus Hale sat in his living room reviewing the closed case file one final time before submitting it to archives. The investigation had proceeded exactly as he and Alira had planned—Officer Roberts and Martinez had documented a straightforward accidental drowning, Dr. Chang had conducted an autopsy that confirmed death by drowning with contributing factors of heat exhaustion and physical exertion, and the case had been officially classified as accidental death with no indication of foul play.

The security footage from Apex Fitness showed exactly what Alira's operational plan had predicted it would show—Rachel Morgan using the hydrotherapy pool legitimately during evening hours, Marcus Sterling arriving for his regular post-training recovery session, casual conversation between two gym members sharing pool space, Sterling showing signs of distress that appeared to be heat-related medical emergency, Rachel Morgan attempting to help him before calling desperately for assistance.

No investigator reviewing that footage would see anything other than a tragic accident—a man who'd pushed himself too hard during intensive training, who'd used the hydrotherapy pool despite being physically exhausted, who'd experienced medical emergency that a concerned fellow gym member had tried unsuccessfully to prevent.

The toxicology screening had shown nothing unusual—standard tests didn't include scopolamine unless investigators had specific reason to suspect exotic drug involvement, and nothing about Sterling's death suggested pharmaceutical cause rather than simple drowning. Dr. Chang's report concluded that Sterling had likely experienced cardiac arrhythmia triggered by the combination of physical exertion, heat stress, and possibly underlying cardiovascular issues that hadn't been previously diagnosed.

Sterling's attorney had reviewed the findings and accepted the medical examiner's conclusion without pushing for additional investigation. Apex Fitness had conducted internal review of their safety protocols and made minor adjustments to prevent similar tragedies, but no one had suggested that Sterling's death was anything other than an unfortunate accident.

Rachel Morgan had been interviewed once more by Officers Roberts and Martinez as part of their final report documentation. She'd provided the same consistent account she'd given on the night of Sterling's death, expressing continued distress about witnessing the tragedy but also accepting that she'd done everything possible to help. The officers had thanked her for her cooperation and closed their witness interview without any indication that they suspected her involvement in anything other than being an unfortunate observer to accidental death.

Two weeks after providing her final statement, Rachel Morgan had quietly terminated her Apex Fitness membership, citing understandable reluctance to return to a facility where she'd witnessed such a traumatic event. The gym had processed her cancellation without question, and Rachel Morgan's brief existence in the city's records had begun its planned dissolution—apartment lease ending, employment records becoming inactive, financial accounts being closed.

Within another month, any investigator attempting to locate Rachel Morgan would find that she'd apparently relocated to another city for personal reasons related to her divorce proceedings. The trail would be plausible enough to satisfy cursory inquiry but would gradually become more difficult to follow until it dissolved completely into the background noise of people moving between jurisdictions for unremarkable personal reasons.

Hale closed the case file with finality, his signature on the closure documentation representing the last official action in an investigation that had been carefully managed to protect the person who'd actually killed Marcus Sterling. He felt the weight of that signature— the legal and moral implications of a detective deliberately sabotaging investigation into a murder he knew had occurred.

But he also felt something approaching peace. Sterling was dead, unable to assault any more women, unable to continue the pattern of predatory behavior that had destroyed at least eight lives over five years. Emily would never know that her father had become complicit in murder to ensure her attacker faced consequences, but she was alive and recovering and safe from the man who'd nearly killed her.

That had to count for something, even if it violated every principle Hale had built his career on.

Emily Hale sat in her father's living room three weeks after her hospital discharge, working through physical therapy exercises that were gradually restoring the motor function and coordination she'd lost during her traumatic brain injury. She'd made remarkable progress—Dr. Han had been cautiously optimistic about her prognosis, and Emily was proving his optimism justified through disciplined commitment to rehabilitation.

But the memory loss remained absolute and permanent. Emily had no recollection of joining Apex Fitness, no memory of Marcus Sterling, no awareness of what had been done to her beyond the clinical facts that doctors and police had shared during her recovery. The assault existed for her only as abstract knowledge—something terrible that had happened but which she couldn't actually remember experiencing.

"Dad, can I ask you something?" Emily said during a break from her exercises.

"Of course," Hale replied, setting aside the newspaper he'd been pretending to read while actually watching his daughter work through her rehabilitation routine.

"The detective who investigated my assault—Detective Martinez—she came by yesterday while you were at work," Emily said carefully. "She told me that the man who attacked me died a few weeks ago. An accident at the same gym where I was hurt."

Hale felt his pulse accelerate but maintained carefully neutral expression. "Yes, I heard about that. Marcus Sterling drowned in the hydrotherapy pool. Tragic accident."

"Martinez said it was just a coincidence," Emily continued, studying her father's face with the kind of analytical attention that suggested her cognitive capacity was indeed nearly fully recovered. "But she also said the timing was... she used the word 'fortuitous.' That Sterling's death meant I wouldn't have to worry about encountering him if I ever went back to that area of the city."

"That's true," Hale acknowledged. "You're safe from him now, regardless of what you remember or don't remember about what happened."

Emily was quiet for a moment, her expression thoughtful in ways that made Hale wonder exactly what Martinez had said during her visit. "She also mentioned that you'd been very involved in making sure the investigation into my assault was handled properly. That you'd been checking on case developments even though you couldn't be the official investigator due to family conflict of interest."

"I wanted to make sure you got justice," Hale said, the statement carrying more truth than Emily could possibly understand.

"Did I?" Emily asked directly. "Get justice, I mean? The district attorney told me they couldn't prosecute because I can't remember what happened and there wasn't enough physical evidence to proceed without my testimony. So legally, no one faced consequences for what was done to me. But Martinez seemed to think... I don't know. She seemed to think the outcome was still somehow satisfactory even without prosecution."

Hale chose his words carefully. "Justice doesn't always come through legal channels, Emily. Sometimes the world delivers consequences through other means. Sterling is dead. He can't hurt you or anyone else ever again. Maybe that has to be enough."

Emily studied her father with the kind of penetrating attention that made Hale uncomfortable—she was too smart, too analytical, too capable of recognizing when people were being evasive or hiding information. Even with traumatic brain injury, even with permanent memory loss, his daughter's brilliant mind was reasserting itself through her recovery.

"You're not telling me something," Emily observed. "I can tell when you're being careful about what you say— you get this particular tone of voice, this expression that means you're editing your thoughts before speaking. What aren't you telling me about Sterling's death?"

"That it was a convenient accident that eliminated a predator who would have escaped legal accountability for destroying your life," Hale replied, the statement technically true even if it omitted critical details about how that "accident" had actually been carefully orchestrated murder.

Emily absorbed this for several seconds, then asked the question that Hale had been dreading. "Do you think someone killed him? Made it look like an accident because the legal system wouldn't hold him accountable?"

"I think accidents happen," Hale said, deflecting rather than lying outright. "And I think sometimes the timing of those accidents serves justice better than courts ever could. Does it matter whether Sterling drowned accidentally or whether someone helped him drown? Either way, he faced permanent consequences for his actions."

"It matters if you were involved," Emily said quietly. "It matters if my father—a detective who spent his career upholding the law—compromised his principles to ensure some kind of justice for me. I don't want you destroying yourself morally because of what happened to me."

The concern in Emily's voice was genuine and devastating. Hale had spent three weeks telling himself that becoming complicit in Sterling's murder was justified by Emily's need for justice, that protecting his daughter outweighed his obligation to uphold legal frameworks. But hearing Emily express concern about his moral wellbeing forced him to confront the full weight of what he'd done.

"I didn't kill Sterling," Hale said, the statement technically true even if it obscured his active role in facilitating the murder. "But I also didn't cry when I heard he was dead. And I'm not going to pretend I wish the investigation had uncovered evidence that might have prevented his 'accident.' You deserved better than what the legal system could provide, Emily. If Sterling's death delivered consequences that courts refused to impose, then I'm at peace with that outcome."

Emily reached out and took her father's hand, her grip strong despite the motor deficits she was still working to overcome. "I love you, Dad. And I appreciate everything you've done to protect me and to ensure I got some kind of justice. But please don't compromise yourself in ways that will destroy you long-term. I'm alive, I'm recovering, and the man who hurt me is dead. That has to be enough—we can't let what happened to me corrupt everything you've built your life on."

"It's enough," Hale assured her, though he wasn't certain whether he was convincing Emily or trying to convince himself. "Sterling is dead, you're safe, and we can focus on your recovery without worrying about potential future encounters or ongoing legal proceedings. That's the best outcome we could have hoped for."

They sat together in silence, hands clasped, both processing the moral complexity of a situation where justice had been delivered through murder rather than legal accountability. Emily didn't push for additional details about her father's potential involvement, and Hale didn't offer information that would burden his daughter with knowledge she couldn't unhear.

But the conversation had clarified something important for Hale—Emily's recovery didn't require her father's moral compromise, and his complicity in Sterling's murder had been driven by his own rage and helplessness rather than Emily's actual needs. She was finding her own path toward healing and acceptance, processing her trauma in ways that didn't depend on her father becoming a vigilante accomplice.

Which meant Hale needed to decide whether his alliance with Alira Sinclair would continue beyond Sterling's elimination, or whether he would step back from active facilitation of vigilante justice even if he maintained his promise not to expose what they'd done together.

Detective Marcus Hale met Alira Sinclair one final time four weeks after Sterling's death, using the same secure communication protocols and anonymous meeting location they'd employed during operational planning. Both understood that the meeting carried risk—their alliance had achieved its immediate purpose with Sterling's elimination, and continuing contact created unnecessary exposure for both parties.

But Hale had questions that needed answering before he could determine how to move forward, and Alira had her own assessment to conduct about whether their partnership could continue or whether Hale's moral conflicts would make him a liability rather than an asset.

"Sterling's case is officially closed," Hale reported without preamble. "Accidental drowning, no indication of foul play, no ongoing investigation. Rachel Morgan provided cooperative witness testimony and then relocated to another city for personal reasons. The narrative is complete and accepted by everyone involved in the investigation."

"Thank you for your assistance," Alira said simply. "Your protection made the operation significantly safer than it would have been if I'd proceeded alone. Emily has justice, even if she'll never know how it was delivered."

"That's what I want to talk about," Hale said, his voice carrying the weight of weeks of moral wrestling. "Emily's recovering well—better than anyone expected given the severity of her injuries. She's regaining cognitive function, working through physical therapy, processing her trauma in healthy ways. And she's doing all of this without needing to know that her father became complicit in murder to ensure her attacker faced consequences."

"You're having second thoughts," Alira observed, recognizing the pattern.

"I'm having complicated thoughts," Hale corrected. "I don't regret Sterling's death. I don't wish I'd stopped you from eliminating him. I believe the world is objectively better without him operating as a predator. But I also recognize that I made the decision to assist you during a period of extreme emotional crisis, and that my thinking might not have been as clear as I believed it was."

"What are you saying?"

"I'm saying that I need to step back from active involvement in your operations," Hale said carefully. "I won't expose what we did with Sterling—that would destroy both of us and wouldn't serve any purpose. But I also can't continue being an accomplice to systematic vigilante murder, even when the targets deserve elimination. It's too far outside my moral framework, too contradictory to everything I've built my career on."

Alira nodded slowly, accepting Hale's decision without apparent surprise or disappointment. "I understand. And I appreciate your honesty about your limitations rather than pretending you can sustain commitment you're not actually capable of maintaining."

"Will you continue?" Hale asked, genuinely curious about Alira's plans.

"Yes," Alira confirmed without hesitation. "Sterling was my fifth elimination. I've identified dozens more predators who meet my criteria—powerful men with documented patterns of sexual violence who've escaped legal accountability through wealth, institutional protection, or procedural manipulation. The legal system will continue failing their victims comprehensively, which means someone needs to deliver consequences that courts refuse to impose."

"And you'll do it alone, without law enforcement protection," Hale observed.

"I operated successfully for years before you offered assistance," Alira reminded him. "Webb, Daniels, Hayes, Blackwood—all eliminated without active law enforcement facilitation. Sterling's death was easier with your help, but I'm fully capable of continuing my work without it."

Hale studied Alira's expression, recognizing the absolute conviction that drove her mission. She wasn't killing to satisfy psychological compulsion or to exercise power over victims—she was executing a carefully planned campaign to protect vulnerable people from predators that institutions consistently failed to hold accountable. The moral clarity was both impressive and troubling.

"What happens if I change my mind again?" Hale asked. "If I encounter another situation where the legal system fails comprehensively and I decide I need your capabilities?"

"Then we'll have this conversation again," Alira replied. "Our alliance doesn't have to be permanent or continuous. You can reach out when circumstances justify working outside legal frameworks, and I can decide whether to accept your assistance or protection on a case-by-case basis. We're not bound to each other—we're simply two people who understand that some situations require operating outside failed systems."

It was pragmatic rather than idealistic, but Hale appreciated the honesty. Alira wasn't demanding ongoing commitment or pretending their partnership was anything other than tactical collaboration based on shared recognition that legal frameworks sometimes failed so comprehensively that alternative approaches became necessary.

"Will you stay in the city?" Hale asked.

"For now," Alira confirmed. "I have targets here who require elimination, and Sterling's death didn't create patterns that would trigger investigation into my other operations. But I'm prepared to relocate if necessary—my mission isn't geographically limited, and there are predators operating with impunity in every jurisdiction."

They parted with mutual understanding that their alliance had served its immediate purpose but couldn't be sustained indefinitely. Hale had his boundaries—he could protect one operation driven by personal rage over his daughter's assault, but he couldn't become a systematic accomplice to ongoing vigilante murder. And Alira had her mission—she would continue hunting predators with or without law enforcement assistance, operating with the same discipline and sophistication that had allowed her to eliminate five men without triggering serious investigation.

As Hale drove home that evening, he felt the weight of his choices settling over him with permanent heaviness. He'd become complicit in murder, had deliberately sabotaged investigation into a killing he knew had been orchestrated rather than accidental. Those actions would define him for the rest of his career and his life, regardless of whether anyone else ever discovered what he'd done.

But Emily was alive and safe and recovering. Marcus Sterling was dead and unable to continue his pattern of predatory violence. And somewhere in the city, a systematic hunter of predators would continue delivering consequences that legal frameworks consistently refused to impose.

Detective Marcus Hale would live with the weight of compromise, carrying knowledge and complicity that violated everything his career had been built on. But he would also live with the satisfaction of knowing that when the system failed his daughter comprehensively, he'd found another way to ensure justice was delivered.

The moral calculus was complex and troubling. But it was also done, irreversible, permanent.

And Marcus Hale would spend the rest of his life determining whether he could live with the choices he'd made, or whether the weight of complicity would eventually destroy him just as comprehensively as predators like Sterling destroyed their victims.

Alira Sinclair stood at Sierra's bedside in the care facility, reading aloud from a children's book about animals preparing for winter. Her sister listened with the kind of rapt attention that her damaged mind brought to simple stories, her face showing contentment and peace.

When the story ended, Sierra looked up at Alira with sudden clarity, her expression losing its usual childlike vagueness and becoming focused and purposeful.

"You stopped another bad man," Sierra said, her voice steady and certain. "The bad man who hurt the detective's daughter. The bad man who hurt lots of women at the gym. You made him go away like you made the other bad men go away."

"Yes," Alira confirmed quietly, never surprised by Sierra's occasional moments of lucidity. "He's gone now. He can't hurt anyone anymore."

Sierra smiled with childlike satisfaction. "Good. That's important work. That's the work angels do—protecting people from monsters when nobody else will protect them. Keep doing the angel work, okay? Keep stopping the monsters."

"I will," Alira promised. "For you, and for Cassie, and for all the other people who need someone to deliver consequences when the system fails them."

Sierra squeezed her hand, the moment of clarity already beginning to fade back toward her usual cognitive confusion. "I'm proud of you. Cassie would be proud too. You're doing what we couldn't do—making the bad men face consequences even when everyone else protects them."

As Alira left the care facility that evening, she carried Sierra's blessing like armor against doubt and moral complexity. Her sisters' suffering had created her mission, their destroyed lives had given her purpose, and their implicit approval validated the path she'd chosen.

Dr. Marcus Webb, Coach Robert Daniels, Richard Blackwood, Senator William Hayes, and Marcus Sterling—five predators eliminated, five patterns of serial violence permanently ended, five situations where institutional protection had been overcome through methods that operated entirely outside failed legal frameworks.

And somewhere in the city, other predators continued operating with similar impunity, unaware that a systematic hunter was identifying their patterns, studying their vulnerabilities, and planning their elimination with the same methodical precision she'd brought to her first five operations.

The mission would continue. The hunt would expand. And Alira Sinclair would keep delivering consequences that powerful men believed their privilege would always prevent, proving that some forms of justice required working entirely outside the systems designed to protect predators rather than their victims.

Detective Hale had stepped back from active assistance, but he'd also learned that his oath to uphold the law was complicated by the reality that legal frameworks sometimes failed so comprehensively that alternative approaches became morally necessary. That knowledge would stay with him, shaping how he approached investigations and how he understood the relationship between law and justice.

And if circumstances arose where the system failed again as catastrophically as it had failed Emily, Hale would know exactly who to contact to ensure consequences were delivered even when courts refused to impose them.

The alliance was dormant but not dissolved. The understanding remained intact even if active collaboration had ceased. And both hunter and detective would carry the weight of their choices forward, determining through their continued actions whether complicity in vigilante murder was a moral compromise they could sustain or a corruption that would eventually destroy them.

The game continued. The stakes remained high. And the fragile balance between law and justice, between institutional accountability and vigilante consequences, would be tested again and again as long as powerful predators believed their privilege made them immune to the kind of justice that Alira Sinclair had dedicated her life to delivering.

www.ingramcontent.com/pod-product-compliance
Lightning Source LLC
Chambersburg PA
CBHW031149020726
47499CB00002B/301